REIGN OF A KING

KINGDOM DUET
BOOK ONE

RINA KENT

To Cassie,
For being Jonathan King's number one fan ever since
he was the villain.

AUTHOR NOTE

Hello reader friend,

If you haven't read my books before, you might not know this, but I write darker stories that can be upsetting and disturbing. My books and main characters aren't for the faint of heart.

To remain true to the characters, the vocabulary, grammar, and spelling of *Reign of a King* is written in British English.

Reign of a King is the first book of a duet and is NOT standalone.

Kingdom Duet:
#1 *Reign of a King*
#2 *Rise of a Queen*

Don't forget to Sign up to Rina Kent's Newsletter for news about future releases and an exclusive gift.

FOREWARD

Quick note,

These special edition covers are for all the lovers of spice who prefer "Safe for work" covers! Enjoy!

XOXO,
Rina

Nothing is fair in war.

Jonathan King is every bit his last name.
Powerful.
Untouchable.
Corrupted.
He's also my dead sister's husband and way older than me.
When I first met him as a clueless child, I thought he
was a god.
Now, I have to confront that god to protect my
business from his ruthless grip.
Little did I know that declaring a war on the king will
cost me everything.
When Jonathan covets something, he doesn't only win,
he conquers.
Now, he has his sights on me.
He wants to consume not only my body, but also my
heart and my soul.
I fight, but there's no escaping the king in his kingdom…

PLAYLIST

Elastic Heart (Rock Version)—Written by Wolves

In The End—Linkin Park

Broken Into Two—Scarlet City & Devin Barrus

Crutch (Piano Version)—Scarlet City & Sarah Aviano

Just—Ghostlight Orchestra

The Hardest Part—Coldplay

Graveyard—Halsey

Burn It Down—Linkin Park

The Catalyst—Linkin Park

Battle Symphony—Linkin Park

Until It's Gone—Linkin Park

Sharp Edges—Linkin Park

Lose Somebody—Kygo & OneRepublic

Close—Nick Jonas & Tove Lo

Hollow—Scarlet City & Stetson Whitworth

Drowning—Scarlet City & S.P.I.T

Saved My Life—Sia

Cold—James Blunt

Wish It Was Love—Cemetery Sun

You can find the complete playlist on Spotify.

REIGN OF A KING

ONE

Aurora

DRASTIC MEASURES.

They aren't something I want to take, but something I have to.

I'm only playing the cards I've been dealt. Well, I'm also paying for not being more careful, but it's pointless to ponder on the past.

I, of all people, know that so well.

The wedding isn't what I expected from grandiose families like the Kings and the Steels.

It's a simple ceremony with a few people present. They're probably the elite of the elite if they managed to get invited to this event.

I sure wasn't.

Instead, I spent an entire week trying to forge an invitation. I ended up going out with one of Steel Corporation's leaders, Agnus Hamilton. He's not just the CFO. He's also Ethan Steel's right-hand man.

In a way, I killed two birds with one stone. I got to learn more about the corporation—not that he talked a lot on that subject. I also got invited to the wedding as his plus-one. I didn't even have to try as hard as I predicted.

Agnus gave me a direct opening into Ethan Steel's entourage.

He only escorted me inside the reception area, then disappeared somewhere.

I'll have to find him so he can introduce me to Ethan, but first... I need to practice my pitch again.

That's why I'm standing in a secluded area by the buffet table, nibbling on a piece of lobster and taking note of my surroundings.

The wedding reception is set up around the pool of the Steel household. The bride's home.

The afternoon's dim sun glints on the surface of the water, illuminating the light blue colour. It's an elegant picture frame filled with distinguished men in expensive tuxedos and women in designer gowns.

My research paid off in recognising almost all of the big shots present here today. I learnt early on to never be blindsided, and for that very reason, I did as much research as possible.

For instance, the shorter man in a sharp tuxedo is Lewis Knight, secretary of state. He's smiling at something the two men with aristocratic features have said. They're actual nobles with titles. Duke Tristan Rhodes and Earl Edric Astor.

It doesn't end there, though. The Prime Minister, Sebastian Queens himself, and his wife are congratulating the bride and groom.

It shouldn't be a surprise.

They all belong to the same circle of influential figures. Power oozes from every corner of this 'familial' reception.

Corrupted.

Infinite.

Untouchable.

It's like being in the sun's immediate orbit. If a normal person wants to approach that type of power, they should be ready to be burn.

I guess I am.

Because I have no choice.

Desperation leads you to radical decisions you would've never considered before.

This is my only chance to save the livelihood of hundreds of workers, their families, their futures, and their debts—that they funnel for these rich people. They say you always have a choice, but distinguishing between those choices is never clear cut.

Making decisions is even more difficult. If it were up to me, I wouldn't have stepped a foot here. If it were up to me, I would've avoided this circle of people like the plague.

The groom lifts his head and I slowly retreat behind a young couple who are laughing. Xander Knight, the son of the secretary of state, and a green-haired girl, who, if I remember correctly, is the daughter of a famous artist and a diplomat.

They're university kids. Just like the happy couple who got married today.

When I first heard they were both nineteen going on twenty, I admit to being surprised. I didn't realise kids these days married so young. I'm twenty-seven and it's not even on my radar. Not that it ever will be.

I'm defective, and I won't inflict my atypical life on anyone.

But hey, I'm thankful they chose to get married now. It's given me a straight opening to this scene that I would've never dreamt of walking into.

Even if Agnus had helped beyond inviting me, he wouldn't have presented me the chance to have a meeting with the great Ethan Steel, even if I'd offered my body.

Not that I would.

This is my perfect opportunity.

Today is the union of two powerful families in the United Kingdom. Ethan Steel's daughter is marrying Jonathan King's son.

In other words, the long, ruthless rivalry between the two ex-friends, Ethan and Jonathan, is coming to an end.

King Enterprises and Steel Corporation are turning the page

with their children's union. They even joined forces for a partnership with the family business of Tristan Rhodes's—the duke I saw earlier.

Or that's what the magazines say. In reality, it could be something entirely different.

If there's one thing I've learnt in my life, it's that the truth isn't always what it seems. Especially with the powerful and the mighty.

The people who have money and influence pumped through their veins instead of blood think differently than the rest of us peasants. They act differently too, which is why I need to be careful.

I *can't* be caught.

Especially not now.

I do another discreet sweep of the guests, searching for Agnus. There's no trace of him or Ethan. Could they be in a private meeting?

No. The prime minister, the duke, the earl, and the Secretary of State are outside. Since Agnus and Ethan belong to their closest circle, they wouldn't leave them out. Did they perhaps go to the other side of the garden?

I need to get this over with and leave before I meet *him*.

Or worse, before he recognises me.

I can't stress enough that I can*not* be caught. It'll blow everything up in smoke.

That's the only downside of coming here instead of scheduling a meeting in Steel Corporation. I have better chances of striking a deal, but there's also the risk of confronting *him*.

Sucking deep breaths through my nose then mouth, I smooth down my black mermaid dress with a double deep V at the front and back. It shows a bit of skin, but not too much, and moulds against my curves perfectly. I've accentuated the look with the pearls my best friend got me for my birthday.

My hair is tied elegantly at my nape and my makeup is bold—red lipstick, heavy eyeliner, and too much mascara. It's nothing like I would normally wear on a day-to-day basis.

Living my whole life in the shadows has taught me to never stand out. If I do, it's game over.

Today, I've had to go against my core survival method for a different survival game.

My appearance suits being on Agnus Hamilton's arm. Not that the man knows how to compliment, but considering his position in the great scheme of things, I needed to look the part of his date.

And also, to pique Ethan's attention.

I'm about to head back to search for them when a presence suddenly materializes by my side.

My heel steps back involuntarily and a shudder shoots up my spine and engulfs me in a thick shroud of fog.

Run.

They found you.

Fucking run.

I swallow those thoughts and steady my breathing. I've lived here for five years. No one knows me.

No one.

Smothering the panic, I plaster on a smile and stare up at the person who's appeared out of nowhere—without even making a sound.

I know because I'm usually the best at hearing the smallest noises. It's how I've survived this long.

Glancing over my shoulder, in my closet, and under my bed isn't just a nasty habit. It's the only way I can exist.

My smile falters as I come face-to-face with none other than the groom himself.

Aiden King.

Jonathan King's only son and one of his two heirs, along with his nephew, Levi.

He has sharp features and an impressive height that allows him to look down at me. His metal grey eyes zero in on my face with awe, wonder, and what seems like...loss.

The small mole on the side of his right eye catches my attention first, causing my legs shake.

It's the same as in my memories.

His lips part, but it takes him a second to speak, "Mum?"

A tremor grips my fingers as I place the unfinished lobster back on the plate and pretend to fiddle with the food even though I'm seeing blurry shapes. I'm thankful my voice comes out calm, unaffected even. "I'm sorry. You've got the wrong person."

He says nothing, but he doesn't attempt to move. I feel his gaze digging holes into the top of my head like a hawk.

"Why aren't you looking at me?"

I lift my head and flash him the serene smile I can fake so well. The one that hides endless chaos underneath.

Aiden continues watching me with judgemental and calculative eyes. "You're not my mother."

Phew. "That's what I said."

"Then who the fuck are you?" His attention doesn't leave my face, almost as if he's searching for something.

Or, to be more specific, *someone.*

"Excuse me?" I feign innocence.

"If you're not Alicia, why do you look exactly like her and what the fuck are you doing at my wedding?"

I keep my cool. "I was invited by Agnus."

"Why?"

"I don't know how to answer that."

He steps closer, his face and voice losing their surprised element and morphing to a steel so cold, it matches the colour of his eyes. "Why are you here? Who the fuck are you? And don't tell me this is a coincidence, because I don't believe in that."

No wonder people call Aiden a replica of his father. If he weren't eight years my junior, I'd actually be scared of him.

Scratch that. The only reason I'm standing my ground in front of him is because I'm already acquainted with the devil.

People are nothing compared to the devil. So they don't frighten me.

"Aiden?"

The bride appears by his side, holding the hem of her ample white dress. Her blonde hair falls in elegant waves down her back, giving her an angelic appearance.

"What are you doing…" she trails off when her blue eyes meet mine. Her surprised expression is louder than her new husband's and she blinks a few times. "A-Alicia?"

"I was just telling Aiden you've got the wrong person." This time, I recover quickly.

He narrows his eyes. "How do you know my name?"

Shit. "It's all over the place. Congratulations on your wedding."

I turn around and leave before Aiden can catch me. I have no doubt he'd question me, and I can't allow that to happen. Besides, I have no answers for him.

I'm on a mission.

All I have to do is finish it and get it over with.

I slip through to the other side of the garden, quickening my pace as if I'm being chased. Which I might as well be.

A breath leaves me when I'm out of Aiden's visual range. I take a pause at the back corner and collect myself.

That was close.

Which means I'm pressed for time and need to get this over with as soon as possible.

As expected, I find Agnus and Ethan here. They stand around a table with Calvin Reed, a diplomat and the father of the green-haired girl I saw earlier.

I touch my wristwatch, the one I have on me at all times. My lucky watch that's saved me more than once. It's almost like the one who gave it to me is looking out for me.

Here we go.

Putting my smile in place, I take a champagne flute from a passing waiter, snap my spine into a straight line, and waltz towards them.

Just when I'm about to reach them, a child no older than ten crashes into Calvin's leg and demands his attention. The diplomat nods at the other two, takes the boy's hand, and leads him towards the house.

Ethan and Agnus continue talking amongst themselves.

My perfect chance.

Like the pictures on the internet, Ethan's appearance is striking with light chestnut hair, a sharp jawline, and a tall, fit figure. From afar, he doesn't really share many features with the bride, but as I approach them, the resemblance is there, subtle and creeping under the surface.

I touch Agnus's bicep. "There you are."

His bland eyes fall on me. It's like they have no colour; their pale blue is washed out, almost non-existent. He's broader than Ethan, but with a less sharp edge and a more silent demeanour. His physique is very well-built for someone in his mid-forties, and he gives untouchable vibes.

When I first made him my target and figured out where he takes his morning coffees, I thought I'd have the hardest time getting him to notice me, considering he never dates or even shows interest in women.

Colour me surprised when he offered to pay for my coffee that morning.

Maybe I'm majorly underestimating myself? Who knows? No matter how tough it got, I've never reduced myself to playing these types of games before, so I have no past experience to compare to.

"Right." He smiles. Or tries to, anyway. Agnus barely has any expression, like they were washed out at birth or something. When he speaks, there's a hint of a refined Birmingham accent to his words. "Aurora, let me introduce you. This is Ethan Steel. Ethan, Aurora Harper."

We exchange business cards and I try not to grin. Acquiring Ethan's with his personal phone number on it is like hitting the jackpot.

"I told you about her," Agnus adds.

He told him about me?

Yes!

My victory dance is halted when I perceive the pause in Ethan's features. He's the emperor of Steel Corporation, mid-forties, and has a presence so strong, you're tempted to stop and look at him. It's not the intrusive type, though. It's more like the welcoming type where you just have to get in his vicinity.

That's why he's the most fitting candidate to help me out. He was in a coma for nine years, and since he returned almost three years ago, he's been investing in small companies and building back his empire by using several investments in different fields.

The fact that he's pausing isn't good. *Please don't tell me he'll act as if he's seen a ghost like his daughter and Aiden did.*

"Ms Harper." He takes my hand a places a kiss at the back of it, never cutting eye contact. "It's nice to meet you."

Phew.

"The pleasure is all mine, and please, Aurora is fine. Congratulations on your daughter's wedding, Mr Steel."

"Ethan is fine. Agnus tells me you sell watches?"

Thank you, Agnus. I throw him a grateful glance and focus back on Ethan. "Yes. In fact, it's my passion."

"How so?"

I motion at his wristwatch. "That must've cost a fortune, but do you know why?"

"The brand."

"Yes, brand awareness. But also, the work the brand established to have said awareness. Your watch is custom-made to fit your wrist size and be comfortable, even if you spend twelve hours in the office and then a few more hours at dinners or parties. It's there to help you get through your day, but it remains unnoticed. Almost like background motivation."

"Impressive." He glimpses at his right-hand man.

"I told you," Agnus says with the same blank face.

"Let's make a toast." Ethan raises his glass. "To background motivation."

"To background motivation." I raise my flute in return, a wide grin on my face.

I did it.

I'm saving the company.

All I have to do is keep up with pleasantries, offer him another custom-made, and move on to business talk.

I have no time to waste. Countless people in H&H look up to me and I will not let them down.

"I'll go get another drink." Agnus nods at us before disappearing out of view.

That leaves only Ethan and me. I smile, even though I prefer having Agnus around. He's a great backup, considering he did most of the work for me. I may not click with him emotionally, considering he doesn't really have those types of connections with women—or any human being, but I'll be forever grateful for the help he offered.

Ethan leans closer, his features welcoming but concentrated. "Tell me more about the business side."

As I'm about to start, my mind rushes with all the pitches I've spent a long time preparing.

I lift my head slightly and my smile disappears when my gaze collides with sinister grey eyes.

Killer eyes.

His presence rips me from the now and slams me to eleven years in the past.

I'm back to that day, catching my breath at the side of the road. I broke to pieces and I'm still unable to pull myself together again.

He is one of the reasons I never will.

Jonathan King.

A ruler in this world.

An actual king who holds more power than the queen herself.

My worst enemy.

TWO

Jonathan

GHOSTS ARE SUPPOSED TO STAY WHERE THEY BELONG.

Dead.

So why the fuck is that ghost looking at me as if she's ready to drag me with her to the grave?

In my world, it's the other way around. I'm the one who drags things—and people—to wherever I please.

It's bad enough that I have to be in Ethan's house to celebrate my son's marriage to his daughter—which I still don't think is the brightest decision Aiden's made.

I don't need the situation made worse with this…ghost.

If I hadn't seen Alicia dead with my own eyes, I would believe she'd somehow resurrected.

Perhaps she's returned for vengeance. Perhaps it's time for her to serve justice.

Only, what's justice? If everyone's perception of that word is different, whose truth is the real truth?

For me, justice doesn't exist. It's a useless word the politically correct folk have picked up to put their little minds at ease.

Justice is a delusion in a world where the likes of me grip the reins of power with ruthless hands.

I don't believe in justice. My father did, and he died still searching for it. What did justice give him? Fucking condolences, that's what.

Since then, I've built my kingdom with merciless methods and brought justice to its knees right in front of me.

That's where everyone who defies me belongs. On their fucking knees.

Alicia—or her doppelgänger—stands around a table with Ethan, drinking from a flute of champagne. Her dainty fingers painted red surround the glass with infinite elegance.

She's the same. From her dress and uptight posture to the curve of her neck and the softness of her cheeks. Her inky black hair and her petite nose. Even the contours of her full mouth.

It's all a replica.

One thing is wrong, though. Or more accurately, two.

One, the red lipstick. Alicia would never put that on.

Two, the colour of her eyes. It's like dark blue skies right after a war.

Or right before a storm.

As it seems, wars and storms are my specialities. If there's a chance to disturb someone's peace and grab what's there for the taking, I don't hesitate.

Contrary to common belief, I'm not heartless. I'm relentless. I don't stop until both the war and the storm end in my favour.

If they don't, they might as well go on until they fall to their knees in front of me—like everyone else.

For the first time in a decade, I don't act first.

I stop.

I watch.

I savour the moment and the shock value of it.

She surprised me, I'll give her that.

I don't like surprises—unless I'm the one who issues them.

It takes me a moment to separate what's in front of me from what I already know.

The reality from the past.

The truth from the imagination.

And it is *her*.

Not Alicia.

But someone so close, she managed to slip from under my radar for years.

Fucking years.

I thought she died in a hole somewhere, or that she pissed off to another corner of the world.

Turns out, neither are the case. She's here in my empire. Right under my nose.

She appeared out of thin air like a fucking ghost.

Does she think she'll slip between my fingers this easily? Or that she can escape me in my own territory?

Now that I'm past the haze and thinking more rationally, I recall the first and last time I met her.

It was at my wedding to Alicia.

A little girl with barely brushed hair ran into me, lifted up her huge sparkling eyes and her mouth formed into an 'O'. Her first words to me were, "I'm sorry, sir."

She'll be more than sorry now.

She'll wish she'd stayed far away from my kingdom.

That lowlife Ethan must've played a part in this, but he'll also pay. And it'll be by using *her*.

The ghost.

The sneak.

My dead wife's little sister.

THREE

Aurora

O H, NO.

No, no, no.

He wasn't supposed to come now, of all times.

My gaze is held captive by his darker, grim one. He doesn't even blink or show any reaction.

Jonathan stands a small distance away, but he might as well be wrapping his hands around my throat in a tight noose.

A sharp tux flatters his broad frame and highlights his long legs. It's almost as if he's in his late thirties instead of his mid-forties. His appearance is taut, hard, and fierce—like everything about him.

His midnight-coloured hair is styled back, revealing a strong forehead and an angular jawline that could cut me in half if I get any nearer. A slight stubble covers his face, giving him an older, harsher, and untouchable feel.

The king.

Literally.

Figuratively.

It's more than his last name and all about his power that knows no limits.

The queen? Forget about her. She does nothing in the real world. It's the likes of Jonathan King who toys with the economy like it's his personal chessboard.

The prime minister? Forget about him, too. Jonathan was the main sponsor of his campaign and that should explain everything about how far his influence can reach. It's scary to think what else he could have under his control.

Or if there's anything that isn't.

Of all things, running into Jonathan King is the risk I took when I came to the wedding of his son—my *nephew*—who doesn't even know I exist.

Here's hoping Jonathan doesn't either. We only met that one time, during his wedding to Alicia. There was also that phone call, but it was so long ago. Surely he doesn't remember me.

I remember him, though. I don't think it's possible to erase the few memories I have of him.

Jonathan has a presence that creeps up on you out of the blue and soon enough, it takes over everything in your surroundings. It's the bombing from an aeroplane.

The sound of thunder.

The eruption of a volcano.

And that? That's not even close to forgettable. For so many people, meeting Jonathan is the highlight of their existence.

At his wedding, I was young. Seven. He was twenty-four. But I clearly recall how larger than life he looked.

Like a god.

I couldn't stop staring at him while hiding behind Alicia's wedding dress. I dug my little fingers into the cloth and peeked up at him, making her laugh in that radiant way that warmed my chest. She told me I didn't need to hide and that he was family now.

I did, though.

Because he was a god, and gods have wrath so brutal, it eradicates everyone in their path.

If Jonathan was larger than life then, he's now a force not to be reckoned with. He's the fury whose path I don't want to walk through, no matter how much I hate him for what he did to Alicia.

Maybe he's forgotten about me. It's possible, right? Alicia's been dead for eleven years and I last met him twenty years ago.

Stay calm.

Breathe in.

Breathe out.

Jonathan strides towards me with steps so strong, it's almost as if I can feel them in my bones.

He stands beside me. Not beside Ethan—*me*.

The itch to touch my wristwatch rises to the forefront of my psyche, but I shut it down as fast as I can possibly manage.

Jonathan's not close to the point of invading my personal space, but he's close enough that I can smell his strong, distinctive scent that for some foolish reason, I still recall.

Back then, I didn't know how to categorise that scent except for it being so addictive. Now, I recognise it as spicy and woodsy. Jonathan is all about power, even in the way he smells.

It shows in his entire appearance. The specially tailored suits with diamond cuffs. The custom-made Italian shoes. The luxury Swiss watch.

Everything about him says without words, 'I'm not a man to be crossed.'

If anyone tries, I have no doubt he'd crush them under the sole of his leather shoes.

"Jonathan," Ethan greets with a tone so dispassionate, I feel the subtle aggression behind it.

"Ethan." The deep tenor of his voice hits my skin like a whip.

I tighten my fingers around the champagne flute, and that's when I realise how my head has been bowed since he started standing here.

My sole attention is on the blue watch strapped on his wrist. Watches are my speciality, my passion, and they usually boost me with confidence.

Not today.

Today I feel like I bet myself and lost. I made a risk and it's now biting me in the arse.

If only I had just kept my accountant on a leash and checked everything he did, he wouldn't have stolen the company's funds and left us with bankruptcy flags in the distance.

I trusted him. We all did.

We're a family at H&H. We started so small and we grew in the span of a couple of years. We began to take bigger contracts and were given better exhibition opportunities. We were ready to take it to the next level until Jake ruined everything.

Then we had to beg for investors when we always thought we were above them. However, the moment they found out about the numbers and that our next product was a gamble, they pulled back.

The bank refused to give us any more loans, considering the amount we already owe them.

Ethan is my last resort before I have to cut back on employees and eventually announce bankruptcy and kill the dream I started with my own bare hands.

The thought alone makes me lose sleep.

"Who's your company?" Jonathan asks Ethan with an unreadable tone.

I release a breath. This means he doesn't recognise me, right?

Ethan smiles, but it's projecting the exact opposite of what a smile should. Instead of being welcoming, it's downright ominous. "I don't see why that should concern you."

"Is that so?" Jonathan's gaze falls back on me. I feel it without having to look up. And I won't look up. That's like signing my own death certificate.

He's studying me. Actually, no. It's more like he's sampling me before he pounces like a hungry predator.

Only, I'm not his prey.

It's been a long time since I swore to never be anyone's prey again.

I already brought down one predator in my life and I'll do it all over again if I have to. Consequences and nightmares be damned.

However, having Jonathan King as an opponent is the last thing I want. There's being brave and then there's being downright foolish.

Challenging the king in his kingdom is the latter.

It's how messengers sent by monarchs got their heads chopped off and hanged on the entry of the capital for everyone to see.

"If you'll excuse us," Ethan says, "Aurora was in the midst of telling me something."

"Aurora," Jonathan muses. "That's not the right name, though, is it?"

Shit.

Fuck.

Damn it!

I feel as if I'm about to vomit my guts out as I peek up at him. He's watching me with a cool, almost manic expression that betrays nothing of his thoughts. But I can feel it loud and clear.

He knows.

He *remembers*.

My fingers shake around the flute and it takes everything in me to place it on the table without spilling it and making a fool out of myself.

"Did you not hear the part where you should excuse us?" Ethan raises a brow.

"I did. Though, as it happens, I don't take orders." Jonathan is speaking to Ethan, but his entire attention falls on me.

Impenetrable.

Unemotional.

Unmoving.

With each passing second, his focus hones, turning harsher

and darker. If anything, it becomes lethal with the intention of destruction.

A god about to unleash his wrath.

I need out of here. *Now.*

Plastering on a smile, I face Ethan. "I'll go search for Agnus. I have your card, so is it okay if I call you?"

"I have yours. I'll be the one to call."

"Thank you." I barely acknowledge Jonathan with an unintelligible nod as I turn around and stride out of the scene.

It takes everything in me not to run and give away my discomfort or the sense of how royally I fucked up.

This is bad. No. It can be disastrous to everything I've spent years building while I carefully stayed in the shadows so I didn't get noticed.

I've ruined everything in one night.

As soon as I'm in the pool area, I avoid Aiden, which isn't super hard. He's slowly dancing with his bride, her head hidden by his shoulder as he rests his chin on top of her hair.

For a second, I stop and stare at the scene, at how serene and happy they both appear. It's similar to Alicia and Jonathan's wedding day twenty years ago. Although…Jonathan didn't dance. I suspect whether the tyrant even knows how.

I pull myself out of my stupor and sneak to the car park.

So I lied.

I wasn't going to find Agnus. That meant I would've had to linger around, and there's no way in hell I was spending a minute longer in Jonathan's vicinity.

As for my other side of the plan? Now that I broke the ice with Ethan, we can have a meeting at his company, and hopefully, I won't have to see Jonathan again in this lifetime.

He'll be on his throne and I'll go back to my small corner of London that he doesn't focus on. Being a ruler means he doesn't care to look at insignificant presences, and that's exactly where I plan to stay.

I don't ask any of the staff to bring my car and, instead, quicken my pace towards it, not sparing a glance behind me.

If you don't look behind, no one finds you.

Or so you think.

I shake my head at that sinister voice. *His* voice. The devil I'm acquainted with.

My fingers are unsteady as I pull out my keys from my bag. I push the button on my car keys, causing my Toyota to unlock with a beep.

The moment I open the door, a hand comes from beside my head and slams it shut. I flinch as the same strong woodsy scent I've never forgotten invades my nostrils.

Jonathan's hot breath leaves goosebumps on my face as he whispers in a low, almost threatening tone, "Long time no see, Aurora. Or should I call you *Clarissa?*"

FOUR

Aurora

I'M TRAPPED.

This sensation of being in a confined place with no way out was supposed to be over eleven years ago.

I'm supposed to be free.

But am I? Really?

I step away from Jonathan's clutches, and that leaves me with my back against the closed door of my car.

Jonathan towers over me like a large wall. I miscalculated his height. I'm not short by any means, yet in order to meet his gaze, I have to tilt my head up.

I have to step out of my comfort zone and pay the price for the risk I took.

Clarissa.

He remembers. Why does he remember a name he's only heard twice in his damn life?

Alicia wouldn't have talked about me. She came to see me in

secret and told me it was our private little world that no one needed to know about. We even did it behind my father's back as I grew up.

We only shared a mother who died soon after I was born, and then Alicia wanted to fulfil that role.

She tried to, anyway.

But I was already acquainted with the devil and I had no way out. Nothing Alicia could've done would've saved me. If anything, it might've accelerated her death.

Bottom line is, Jonathan shouldn't care about my existence, let alone remember my old name.

"Aurora. My name is just Aurora Harper now."

He remains motionless like a mountain. "I see you're killing your association with Maxim Griffin."

Black images assault my head. The cries. The shouts. The assault of the angry crowd.

My bottom lip trembles and I trap it under my teeth to put a halt to it.

"Don't." I wrap a hand around my waist and hug myself. The old scar is way underneath my clothes, but I feel the burn as if it's happening right now.

"Don't?" he repeats.

"Don't say his name."

"That doesn't erase him from existence."

"Just *don't*. Stop it."

"I might consider it if you tell me something."

"What?"

"Where have you been, Clarissa? I mean, *Aurora*."

"Why should I tell you?"

He tilts his head to the side, watching me for a few seconds without blinking. Being under Jonathan's brutal scrutiny is like kneeling in a king's court, waiting to be judged.

"You think you can show up out of nowhere, at my son's wedding, no less, and pretend like nothing happened?"

Yes.

But now that I hear it in that haughty, almost condescending voice, I feel like I was being childish for ever thinking that.

"Let's pretend we never met," I try in my soft tone.

"I don't pretend." He steps closer, purposefully invading my personal space as if it's his God-given right. "So how about you tell me what the fuck you were doing with Ethan?"

"Nothing."

"Try again, and this time, don't lie to me. If you do, I'll take it as in you're ready to bear the consequences."

I could lie to him and get myself out of this pinch, but that will only take me so far. I might not have seen Jonathan in person for twenty years, but his name can't be escaped in this country or even in the international business scene.

He's an investor. A commander. A *ruler*.

If he sets his sights on something, there's no stopping him until he either gets it or ruins it.

Black or white. There's no grey in his dictionary.

And for that reason, I need to tactfully slip out from under his radar as smoothly as I was trapped within it. I crossed the enemy's lines by mistake and now, I need to find the safest way out.

I suck in a deep breath. "Business."

"What type of business?"

"Just business."

"Did you not hear me ask what type of business it is? I do not like repeating myself, Aurora."

Damn him and the authoritative way he speaks. It's like he expects everyone to fall at his feet with a simple command.

I might not want to provoke Jonathan on purpose, but I will not get on my knees in front of him.

Not now. Not ever.

I'm done with kneeling for a lifetime.

"It's nothing that concerns you."

"Nothing that concerns me, but it concerns Ethan. Correct?"

"Yes."

"No."

"No?" I repeat with a confusion that must be written all over my face.

"You'll end whatever business venture you have with Ethan."

"Why would I do that?"

"Because I said so, wild one."

Is he fucking kidding me? He's not. I know Jonathan isn't the type who jokes around, but does he honestly believe I would follow simply because he ordered?

So what if he has power? It's not absolute. Nothing and no one is.

I lift my chin. "And if I say no?"

"Then we'll do it my way." A small smile lifts his lips. His sensual, well-proportioned lips.

And now, I'm staring at his lips.

Stop staring at his lips.

I lift my gaze to his and the whole image is clear. He's not even smiling, and it's downright menacing. This is the look of a man who's preparing for a battle.

A man who's so used to war that peace bores him.

And I'm another battlefield in his path of conquering.

So no, it's not a smile. It's a declaration of something sinister and potent.

"Why would you care who I do business with, Jonathan?" Last time I checked, he wasn't my guardian.

"You think you can skip me in my own territory and choose someone else to do business with? And not just anyone, but Ethan. What's your message there? Are you trying to challenge me?"

"No." That's the last thing I want.

"Then why didn't you come to me?"

"I don't like mixing familial affairs with business." And I hate him for the way Alicia died. If I didn't know he would overpower me, I'd punch him in the face and relieve the tension I've been carrying for eleven years.

"The only family I have has the King's last name. You're not my family, wild one. Never was. Never will be."

"Mutual."

"Glad we agree on that front. Now, you'll cut off any contact or communication with Ethan—including Agnus."

"That would be a no."

"Did you just tell me no?"

"Yes, Jonathan. I don't know what your deal is, but you don't get to tell me what to do."

Silence.

He watches me with that hollow expression that I'm now certain harbours a monster. "Is that so?"

I keep my chin held high, not cutting off eye contact.

Jonathan takes a step forward. My back flattens against the metal of the car door as his chest nearly touches mine. My bare skin tingles, goosebumps erupting at the surface and I have no idea why.

He places a hand near the side of my head, slowly resting it on the car's metal, and grabs my chin with his free one. My pulse roars in my ears as he cages me in.

There's no escaping him, even if I try.

Not that I will.

I'm trapped by his sheer presence and held prisoner by the darkened depths of his grey eyes.

It's like being caught in the eye of a hurricane and all I can do is fall.

Drown.

Down...

Eventually disappear.

That's what people like Jonathan do. If they wish, they can make you vanish as if you've never existed.

The feel of his skin on mine is like being burned from the inside out. No one is supposed to ooze so much control as he does.

It should be forbidden. Illegal.

"This is my first and final warning. Do not keep in contact with Ethan. Understood?"

I want to say no, to shout it, but it's like my tongue is knotted in itself. I'm too caught up in his close proximity, in his lethal presence and the intimidation he plays so well.

I'm not the type to be intimidated, but this is Jonathan.

He's in a special category all on his own.

He takes my silence for approval and releases my chin. Instead of leaving my space, he rummages through my bag and yanks out the card I accepted from Ethan.

Before I can stop him, he rips it in four and throws it behind him. The torn pieces fly in the wind.

Then he reaches into his jacket, retrieves his own card, and slips it in on behalf of Ethan's. "This is the only contact information you need. Call me, apologise for skipping me over, and depending on my mood, I might consider helping you."

Damn him. Who does the bastard think he is?

He steps back, all physical contact gone, and I finally breathe properly—or try to anyway. I don't think it's normal to remind myself to inhale and exhale on a regular basis. But if I don't, I might stop my oxygen intake altogether.

His eyes roam over me one more time with a suffocating intensity that robs me of breath all over again. I resist the urge to fidget as his gaze pauses at my face. "And then you'll tell me where you've been."

And with that, he turns and leaves.

I sag against my car, sucking air into my lungs as if I've just learnt how to breathe. The act is there, but the weight slamming into me makes it almost impossible to gather my bearings. It's the first time in ages that I've felt so trapped and with no way out.

Didn't I promise myself I would never be in this position again?

You know what?

Fuck Jonathan King.

No one tells me what to do.

FIVE

Jonathan

AURORA HARPER.

Previously Clarissa Griffin.

That's how I lost her—not that I've been actively searching for her. Alicia mentioned in her will that she wanted Clarissa taken care of. Then Clarissa disappeared off the face of the earth.

She couldn't have been more than sixteen when the whole shitstorm with Maxim Griffin went down. She was a minor, yet she disappeared. I went as far as asking around in the UK Protected Persons Service with underhanded methods and they also said she was a missing person.

It's like she vanished into thin air.

Granted, I didn't put my all into searching for her, because I didn't want a reminder of Alicia right after her death. I needed to move along, and Clarissa would've hindered that process.

Still, how dare she disappear then reappear without my permission?

Does she think this is a game? That she can do as she pleases and get away without paying the price?

And Ethan.

That's a bold move that she'll be punished for. Eventually.

I slip into the back of my car and find my assistant and right-hand man, Harris.

He's one of those nerds who's spent his entire life studying and is a genius, not only with numbers but also with information. He knows everything about everything.

Greeting me with a small nod of his head, he focuses back on his tablet, adjusting his frameless glasses.

"How's the draft?" I ask.

"Eighty per cent completed. It's with the legal team and will be ready in two hours."

"Make it one and tell them to start drafting the additional merger contract."

"On it." He types at a rapid-fire pace on his tablet.

"And, Harris?"

"Yes, sir?"

"I need you to look up someone."

He lifts his head from his affair with the tablet to give me a quizzical glance. The only people I look up are the ones I'll do business with or whose companies I'll take over.

Harris doesn't need a reminder to do that. He forwards me all the relevant information before I even ask for it.

The reason behind his reaction is my change of pattern. He, of all people, knows I follow habits. It's what maintains the order and control. It lets me rule with an iron fist and without mistakes.

The fact that I'm breaking my own rule is disturbing his usual work methods. But he won't ask about the reason. And that's what I like about Harris the most. He keeps the unnecessary rubbish to himself and talks solely in data.

"Name?"

"Aurora Harper. Previously Clarissa Griffin. The daughter of Maxim Griffin, the duct tape killer in Northern England. I need you to tell me everything you know about her."

REIGN OF A KING | 29

I have a premonition she'll defy me.

My lips twitch fighting a smile.

It's been a long time since someone dared to challenge me after being given a warning. They usually fall to their knees without as much as a verbal command.

Let's see how Aurora will react.

Whatever path she chooses will only lead back to me.

Where she was supposed to be eleven fucking years ago.

SIX

Aurora

T HE FOLLOWING DAY, I GO TO WORK WITH FRESH MOTIVATION. I spent the entire night tossing and turning in bed, mad at myself for letting Jonathan treat me as his property or a small child. No idea which pissed me off the most, but they both left me boiling in pent-up rage.

So I decided to completely ignore him.

Yes, he tore Ethan's card, but I have direct contact with Agnus, which is the next best thing.

Today, I'm going to continue concept designing and forget about the bank's axe that's hovering over our necks like a guillotine.

They're only holding off the auctioning of the stocks because we begged them. 'We,' as in me and my partner in crime.

Speaking of which, I swing by her office, juggling two caramel iced coffees. The reason we're friends, as she likes to remind me.

She's not there.

I greet my workers good morning, keeping my face devoid of

the anxiety I see radiating off them. The atmosphere here has been grim and tense for a few months now.

The factory has been working irregularly lately and the bank's workers have come to define its value.

Employees gossip, no matter how much we try to convince them that we'll get H&H out of this funk.

Some even started to request days off to search for another job. I don't blame them. After all, they need to earn a living, and if this situation we're in continues, we'll be forced to let some of them go.

The moment I open my office, I'm greeted by the sound of "Don't Look Back in Anger" by Oasis. Layla's taste in music is kind of stuck in the past and she still mourns the band's break up.

My partner and best friend stands in front of the transparent board, scribbling at supersonic speed.

She has a tiny frame, so when she wears baggy trousers and oversized hoodies, she appears like a street hip-hop singer—a fact she's proud of that since she considers herself street-made through and through.

Her hair is covered by a scarf, tucked elegantly at her neck. Layla is also a devoted Muslim and a third-generation British citizen. Her father is of Pakistani heritage and her mother is Tunisian.

As a result, her skin tone is a shade darker than her Caucasian mother's and lighter than her South Asian father's. She has the smoothest skin I've ever seen, outside of Photoshopped advertisements, and her huge brown eyes can show you the world if you stare at them hard enough.

"Oasis this early in the morning?"

She reaches out to me without lifting her head. "My iced coffee, mate."

"Here." I push it into her hand and we take a slurp at the same time, then sigh.

I stand beside her in front of the board. She's writing up her marketing plan—the one we'll need if we get investments.

When we first started this adventure straight after graduating from uni, we agreed that I'd take care of the designing side of the business and she'd do the marketing because she's a genius at that.

Five years later, we were killing it. Our company had gone from two people to more than one hundred. We made that happen. Just Layla and I. Until that bastard Jake ruined what we built in years in a matter of months.

"This is the best." She takes another slurp. "I feel more energised and ready to kick butt."

"You must've had some coffee already."

"I need two to fully wake up. Remember dorm days?"

"Ugh." I used to literally splash her with water so she'd wake up and not be late for class.

"Uh-huh. Exactly."

"Looks good." I motion at the board.

"Not good enough, but forget about that." She takes my hand and leads me to the sofa opposite my desk, then tells Alexa to stop playing the music. "How did it go yesterday?"

"I told you."

"A text in the middle of the night that says, 'I think we're good, talk to you tomorrow' explains rubbish. I need details."

"Lay…"

"All of them," she speaks like a stern mother and I sigh, then tell her the gist of what went down yesterday and the dreadful meeting with Jonathan. I'd previously told her that the mere thought of that particular encounter scared the shit out of me.

"Bollocks," she breathes out after I'm finished.

"Bollocks indeed."

"So your nephew really called you Mum?"

"Seriously, Lay?"

"What? I think that's cute."

"Aiden is anything but cute. He's the mini version of his father."

"So what's the problem here?"

"Jonathan threatened me. If I go through with this with Ethan, he'll come after me."

"Not if you have Ethan's protection."

My brow furrows. "What do you mean?"

She takes a generous gulp of her iced coffee and crosses one leg over the sofa, fully facing me. "Okay, listen up. So Jonathan is like this big bad wolf, right? Guess who can kill a wolf?"

"A hunter?"

"Yeah, but we don't have that. What's the next best thing?"

"I'm not even sure where you're going with this. Is this another one of your crazy ideas?"

"Focus, mate. What else but a hunter can kill a wolf?"

"Spare me the suspense."

"Another wolf."

"Another wolf?"

"The only way to bring Jonathan down is to use Ethan."

"Really?"

"Why do you think Jonathan is so against the idea of you going to Ethan? He knows that if you have Steel Corporation's support, he won't be able to touch you. In a way, we'll be under Ethan's protection, and he's known to take great care of small businesses and even their lawsuits."

"You think?"

"I'm kind of sure."

"Kind of?"

"The fact that he insists to know where you've been in the past keeps throwing me off." She takes another sip of her coffee. "Why don't you clear that up?"

"I don't owe him anything."

"You don't, but if it can clear a misunderstanding, do it. It's better not to be on his radar at all."

Problem is, I think I already am. I screwed it up yesterday and I've been flagged by Jonathan whether I like it or not.

Besides, what misunderstanding could there be? Jonathan and I always lived in different worlds. Hell, his nineteen-year-old son doesn't seem to know he has an aunt.

We have that much distance between us, yet he acted as if it never existed.

"So?" Layla urges.

"What?"

"What are you waiting for? Call Ethan."

"Shouldn't I give him more time to think about it?"

"More like forget about it. A man like him must receive a hundred company offers per day. Okay, that's an exaggeration, but you get the idea. Hit it while it's hot, mate."

I hide my laughter at the way she talks. Being brought up as the youngest girl after four older brothers turned Layla adorably tomboyish.

"What are you laughing at?"

"You sound like a street thug."

"Suck my D."

Layla is the type who always wants to curse, but she refrains out of respect for her religion, so she either uses initials or spells the words out.

"You don't have a dick, Layla."

She makes a face, then claps her hands. "Come on, no time to waste. Get your designing mojo."

"I'm nervous about this one."

"That's what you say every time and you knock socks off. Now, off to work."

My heart warms at her words. Layla believes in me, even when I don't believe in myself. She's the best friend and partner I could've wished for.

It's due to those facts that I protect her from my past. All she knows about me is that I'm an orphan—which is far from the truth.

I stand up and hug her. She awkwardly pats my back. Another thing about Lay? She doesn't like hugs or being touched in general, but she puts up with me.

"Thank you," I say, pulling away. "You're my ride or die."

"That was your hug for the week." She waves on her way to the door.

"Suck my dick, Lay."

"You don't have one." She throws over her shoulder, laughing.

As the door closes behind her, I pull my phone out and dial Agnus. He picks up after the first ring.

"Morning, Agnus."

"Morning."

"Listen. I'm sorry about leaving that way yesterday. I was wondering if I could get Ethan's card? I think I lost mine." *Because of the brute Jonathan.*

"There's no need."

My heart falls. Does this mean it's over? Were they offended that I left yesterday?

"I was going to call to schedule a meeting between you and Ethan in your company. He wants to visit and consider an investment. Let's say, tomorrow at ten?"

Oh. God. He's considering an investment. Jackpot.

I try not to sound so excited as I say, "That would be perfect. Thank you."

Screw Jonathan. I'll follow Layla's advice. If I have Ethan, he won't be able to hurt me, even if he tries.

Or so I think.

SEVEN

Aurora

TODAY IS THE DAY.

Ever since we found out about Jake's betrayal, Layla and I—and everyone else in the company—have been working so hard to reach a day like this one.

Investors. Legitimate ones—not the others who backed away after a walk in the factory or in the offices.

Whenever I take them on a tour, I feel so vulnerable. In a way, I'm opening my home for strangers who might not like it. And they don't. Most of the time.

Ethan is different.

He hasn't shown any sign of displeasure as Layla and I take him and Agnus to the factory and talk about our plans for the up-coming product's launch.

Agnus remains expressionless as usual, but Ethan questions us about certain parts he'd like to understand better.

Our offices aren't extravagant. We occupy a modest building in London's industrialised area, but it's enough for the administration and the factory. We were thinking about expanding before the whole shitshow with Jake went down. Now, we'll be lucky if we get to keep this building.

By the time we're back to my office, I'm about to explode with anticipation and nerves. I touch my watch, then drop my hand so it's not perceived as a nervous gesture.

When I woke up this morning, I took extra care of my appearance. I wore my black pencil skirt and pressed white shirt with a black ribbon. My hair falls on either side of my shoulders and I even put on the red lipstick again. There's something powerful about looking the best I can; it fills me with a much-needed burst of confidence.

Even Layla put on a dress, which she usually only reserves for special occasions, and that says something.

The two of us sit beside each other as Ethan and Agnus occupy the sofa across from us.

Ethan is reading through Layla's marketing plan for the new launch, taking his time between pages. Agnus scrolls through our online store on his tablet.

Layla squirms beside me. Although she's never been the nervous type, I can almost see the anxiety halo surrounding her head. Like me, she realises this might be our last chance.

If we don't get this, H&H will have to close down and we might have to hunt for a corporate job that we both hate so much.

And worse, we'll let our employees down.

We have Mr Vincent, our French silent investor with eleven per cent of the shares. We only met him a few times at the beginning but never after that. He's a private man and barely comes to England anymore. We could offer him more of our shares for investment, but Layla and I are leaving that as a last resort. She and I own forty-five per cent each and we already used twenty per cent each to cover our last loan.

Sweat covers my back, gluing my shirt to my skin, and there's nothing I can do to make it stop. It's like my body is being pushed back to that flight or fight mode.

No. This is different. I'll never go back to those times.

"I must say." Ethan neatly closes Layla's organised plan. "I'm impressed. And I'm rarely impressed."

Both Layla and I release a breath at the same time.

"Thank you." Layla smiles.

"I'm kind of surprised Agnus here didn't snatch you as soon as you were out of university. He gathered the best of the best in our marketing department, and they could use a tip or two from you."

Layla grins. "That's because I'd already started my own company."

"My miss." Agnus nods.

"Aurora." Ethan faces me.

"Yes?"

"I believe the two of you complement each other really well. The designs are unique and Layla needs to get out of the box to find your special customers."

"I believe so, yes." That's why Layla and I rarely have any disagreements. We're not rivals; we complete each other.

"Let me ask you something." Ethan stares between the two of us. "What made you start designing watches?"

I could give him the generic answer I always give. Like how it's my passion and my art, and while it is, that's not the entire truth.

Ethan is the type who can detect a lie and I don't want to seem dishonest in front of him at such a sensitive time. He might take it as disrespect and that's the last thing I want. So I go the vulnerable route.

Because the situation we're in requires we become vulnerable. "When I was a child, my sister bought me a present. My first watch. I loved it so much, and since I didn't have such pretty things, I hid it and studied it at night when I was about to go to sleep. Then I started thinking about how it was made and why it was made like that. It became my passion, and over time, I realised that was what I wanted to do.

"Whenever I sit down to design, I recall the awe I felt when I looked at my first watch. I recall my sister and the happiness she brought me, and I strive to recreate that sensation. I want people to feel happy when they receive one of my watches."

"The art of time," Agnus recites our slogan.

"Exactly."

Layla touches my arm and I smile, trying not to get caught up in the memories.

"Your sister is…" Ethan trails off. "Alicia, I suppose."

My eyes widen. He knows, too? "But…how?"

"It wasn't that hard. Except for the eye colour, you're a carbon copy of her, Aurora."

I knew Ethan and Jonathan shared a history, a bloody one at that, but I never thought Ethan was an acquaintance of Alicia's.

Everything starts to fall into place. My gaze trails to Agnus. "Is that why you approached me?"

"I'd say we approached each other." Agnus remains completely unaffected.

Layla and I exchange a worried glance before I focus back on Ethan. "Does this mean you never intended to invest?"

"I have thought about it. I believe that your company can have a bright future."

"Really?" Layla and I say at the same time.

"Absolutely. I'll pay the bank's debt and provide a budget to boost the new product's launch. Agnus will send you the contract and details about how we perceive our partnership." He stands. "Until then."

A wide grin curves my lips as I shake his hand. "Thank you so much."

"We won't disappoint you." Layla shakes his hand next.

"I have no doubt."

I clear my throat. "Would you have invested if you hadn't figured out I'm related to Alicia?"

Layla pokes me in a reprimanding kind of way. I know what she's thinking—that we already got the deal, so why bother ask that? However, I need to know. Call it my worth or pride or whatever.

"Probably, but it would've been too late by the time your file landed on my desk. Let's say your acquaintance with Alicia, and also with Jonathan, quickened the process."

"Jonathan?" I ask low. What does he have to do with this?

It's taken me everything not to think about him today. There's always that small voice in my mind telling me I poked the lion and he'll come after me.

I know it's paranoia, but I can't stop thinking about it.

Damn him. I was doing just fine before meeting him again. Which was my fault for barging into his son's wedding, but it's not like I had a choice.

"Yes, Jonathan." Ethan's lips move into a predatory smile. "He won't like it."

Layla raises her brows at me as if saying 'told you so'.

The rivalry between Jonathan and Ethan must run deep if they keep getting at each other's throats. No idea how they allowed their children, who are their only heirs, to get married. Surely they know they'll inherit their dads' companies someday and both will probably have a full merger.

Not that I should care. As long as I have my investment, I don't care what two kings do in their kingdoms.

The door barges open and Jessica runs in after several men. "Sir, you can't go inside…"

My breathing shortens at the men crowding my office.

Scratch that. It's not even about all of them. Just one man holds my attention prisoner and refuses to let go.

I can feel the blood draining from my face as I get trapped in the hurricane in Jonathan's grey eyes.

The anger and disapproval there is so tangible, he doesn't need words to express it. It's like a deep, hollow well that will suck you into the unknown.

He stands at the front of four men, all of them dressed in dark suits, looking like they're out of a corporation show.

Though Jonathan's also wearing a suit, he manages to stand out compared to them. His larger-than-life presence conquers the air and confiscates all the oxygen. Suddenly, my office feels so small and suffocating.

I poked the lion and now, he's come to devour me.

"Sir, please…leave," Jessica, my assistant, tries again, throwing me awkward glances.

Even in her tries to be stern, she can't ignore the intimidation factor Jonathan has brought with him. Like a warlord out for a battle, all peasants need to bow down upon his passing.

Jonathan's gaze strays between me and Ethan as if we're annoying rocks in his shoe. The complete disregard on his face shoots bolts of discomfort down my back.

This is why I hate him so much. He has the ability to rattle me after the endless years I've spent stabilising myself.

His next words paint my entire world black. "I'm the last one who should leave. This is my company now."

EIGHT

Aurora

"T HIS IS MY COMPANY NOW."

I must've heard something wrong, because I think Jonathan said this is now his company.

"What are you talking about?" I meant to snap, but my voice comes out small, fearful even.

Jonathan motions at the men with him. "My lawyers will give you the acquisition papers. I bought the stocks you used as collateral with the bank."

Layla and I take the papers with unsteady hands and study them. My eyes bulge as I stare at the bank director's signature beside Jonathan's.

"But he said…" Layla swallows. "He said he'd give us time."

"Your time is up," Jonathan continues in his haughty voice that I wish I could mute or, better yet, throw it and him out the window.

"Still," I compose myself, even though my heart is about to leap out of my throat. "Layla and I have ninety per cent of the stocks.

We only used twenty per cent each for the bank's collateral. If you acquired forty per cent of the shares, we still have fifty combined."

Jonathan smiles as if he expected me to say that. It's a weird one, his smile. It always feels like a declaration of war and a promise to crush. Like he wouldn't willingly smile for any other reason.

"Correction. You both combined had eighty-nine per cent of the shares. Now, it's forty-nine."

"It's still more than your forty."

"Who said I have forty? Harris." He motions at the man beside him who's holding a tablet and a black document on which 'King Enterprises' is engraved in bold golden letters with a crown on top.

Harris, a lean man who appears prim and detached, adjusts his glasses with his index and middle finger and offers me the folder. I open it the fastest I've ever done anything in my life.

The world starts to blacken as I see the signature beside Jonathan's.

Lucien Vincent. Our silent investor.

"I've gotten in touch with your third investor and he transferred the whole eleven per cent of his shares to me. I now have fifty-one per cent and own H&H."

"Mr Vincent can't do that," Layla whispers to me. "We signed a contract."

"We did." I jerk my spine, facing Jonathan. "The transfer of Mr Vincent's shares is null. We signed a contract that he can't sell his shares unless he speaks to one of us first."

"Or in case of bankruptcy." Jonathan's words feel like a whip to my back. "Which is the current situation. The transfer is completely legal. Certainly, you can fight a few years in court if you feel entitled to, but you won't win, so you might as well save your efforts and finances."

My mouth opens, then closes again. No words would come out, even if I tried to speak.

God.

Oh, no.

I can't believe I lost the company this way. How? Where did I go wrong?

Blaming it on Jake is useless. He might have stolen from us, but I'm the one who trusted him when I shouldn't have.

"You manipulated the bank director, didn't you?" Ethan speaks for the first time since Jonathan came in. His expression has lost the triumph it gained when we shook hands earlier. "You must've switched banks for one of your subsidiaries that has a significant net profit to said bank to make the director agree to sell the shares."

Jonathan smirks with pure sadism. "One step ahead of you, as usual."

"I wouldn't light fireworks yet, Jonathan."

"Always a pleasure to crush you, Ethan. Needless to say, your investment in H&H is declined, effective immediately."

Ethan steps in front of Jonathan, and a clash of gazes erupts between them. It's like two Titans gearing up for a fight.

"This isn't over."

"It is," Jonathan says in that high and mighty tone. "Now, if you'll excuse us, I need to have a meeting with my employees."

Did he just call us his freaking employees?

"We'll meet again, Layla. Aurora." Ethan returns to us and shakes Layla's hand, then offers his to me. I take it, even though I'm dazed and unable to keep up with what has just occurred.

Agnus nods as he and his CEO leave the office with the same confidence they walked in with. Jonathan follows them with a gaze so dark, it's like he could set them on fire by merely looking at them.

Layla and I are left in the presence of Jonathan and whomever he's selected to bring here with him.

It's a tactic to show the power he possesses and how easily he can turn people to his side if he chooses to do so.

It's not pretentiousness, it's a carefully laid plan. Jonathan is the type of man who showcases his battalion before a war to shoot fear into his enemies' hearts. That way, he can win with minimum effort.

His gaze falls back on me, and I instinctively gulp. It takes everything in me not to tuck Layla under my arm and run far away from his vicinity.

Part of my defence methods is my ability to recognise threats—or at least sense them. It's what saved me eleven years ago, and it's what's screaming at me to save myself now.

Jonathan is a dangerous man, if not the most fatal of all.

Only, his weapons aren't knives or guns. It's his ability to strip you bare with the sheer power he's spent years cultivating and magnifying to impossible heights.

The fact that I bluntly went against his order has turned me into a problem he needs to solve.

Or eradicate.

I now recognise that he held back the day of Aiden's wedding. Because the Jonathan standing in front of me has come prepared for an all-out war.

And I'm that war.

"Harris. Wait for me in the car." He's speaking to his employee, but his unblinking, unnerving attention never breaks off me.

Harris nods and motions at all the other men, who follow him out without a word.

"You may leave too, Ms Hussaini."

"I will not. Aurora and I are partners. If you have any business talk, we'll both be present to hear it." Layla interlaces her arm with mine. There's a slight tremble in it, and I know how rattled she must feel right now. Jonathan isn't the type of man to be taken lightly.

Still, her loyalty and how she refuses to leave me alone warms my heart to the point of explosion.

However, I don't want her to face Jonathan's wrath. I'm the one who went against his order, and if anyone needs to stand in front of a god while he issues his punishment, it'll just be me.

Layla has done nothing to deserve this. Besides, I have somewhat of a familial tie with him. She doesn't. He wouldn't hesitate before he smashes her under his shoe.

"You can go, Lay." I pat her hand.

"No." She shakes her head in that stubborn way.

"Listen to your partner, Ms Hussaini," Jonathan chimes in.

Layla ignores him and focuses on me. "Are you going to be okay?"

"I can take care of him."

"Text me if anything happens," she leans in to whisper so only I can hear her. "If he hurts you in any way, I'm going to kick him in that straight nose of his, maybe bring it down to earth a little. Remember how I sent that thug who tried to rob us to the A&E? Next up will be Jonathan King's nose."

I smile, nodding as she finally releases me. Before leaving, she stops in front of Jonathan. She's so tiny next to him, it would be comical under different circumstances.

"I have a black belt in karate and two of my brothers are captains in the British Army," she tells him ever so casually.

"Lay…" I shake my head. The last thing she wants to do is threaten him or put herself on his radar.

Jonathan raises a brow. "Is that a threat, Ms Hussaini?"

"It's a piece of information, freely provided." Behind his back, she motions at me to text her, then leaves.

As the door closes behind her with a loud click, I feel the gravity of the situation before Jonathan even says a word.

I gulp down all the emotions rising to the surface and hold eye contact. I've never found a problem doing that with anyone in the past.

Now is different.

Everything is. Starting with the man who's standing in the middle of my office like he owns it—which, in a way, he does.

Maintaining eye contact with Jonathan is like being ripped to pieces and not having the ability to do anything about it. He feeds off my energy in the most savage way, and he has no plans to return it.

"What do you want, Jonathan?"

"I told you what I want, and you purposefully went against it. Very bold."

I swallow as he rounds my desk and lowers himself onto my chair with utter confidence as if it's always been his.

My legs are barely keeping me standing, so I don't attempt to move from my position. "Are you going to leave me alone now?"

He laughs, the sound hollow and frightening. "I'll take that as a joke."

"You got what you wanted. Ethan is already out."

"True, but I did it, not you. Why should you be rewarded for it?"

"So, what? You'll just own my company?"

"*My* company, but I digress."

"You can't do that."

"It's already done." He places his elbows on the surface of the desk and leans over, forming a steeple at his chin. "Unless you're willing to offer payment."

I perk up, hope blossoming in my chest like fireworks. "I am. I'll pay anything."

"Anything? Careful, wild one. That's a strong word to use."

"I meant within reason, and only if you allow us to pay in instalments."

"Instalments. I like that idea."

"Right." I round the sofa to stand in front of my desk, the one he so bluntly made his. "You can even keep some of your shares as a form of investment if you like."

"Is that so?"

"Yes," I'm blurting things out now, but I don't care as long as it gets us our company back. "Layla and I might even be willing to offer you a bit more than what you paid for the shares. All we need is the option to pay in instalments and time until our next product is launched."

"Shares and money aren't the payment I was thinking of."

I frown. "Then what is?"

"You, Aurora."

NINE

Aurora

I STARE AT JONATHAN WITH WHAT MUST LOOK LIKE A BLANK expression.

For the second time in the span of a few minutes, he's put me completely out of my element. It's like I'm suddenly stripped to my most basic form and I can't begin to explain what's happening.

"What did you just say?" I murmur, resisting the urge to fall on the chair opposite my desk—the one he's sitting behind like it's always been his to snatch. This whole situation feels like it's always been his to start and own.

"You heard me." Jonathan's expression remains calm, bored even, as if he didn't suggest that he take…me.

"What do you mean exactly by taking me for payment?" My voice regains some of its edge.

"It's as simple as it sounds. In exchange for transferring full ownership of the stocks, I want you to pay for them by becoming mine."

My cheeks heat with the humiliation of the thought, but my voice comes out strong and clear. "I'm not a whore."

"You'll be mine, not my whore. There's a difference. I'm not interested in a slut. If I were, I could've gotten her off the streets or scooped one up at a party. They're not worth the hundreds of thousands I paid for H&H's stocks."

"Is that supposed to make me feel flattered or something?"

"It's not my purpose, but if you are, by all means."

The dick.

My blood boils with the need to hit him across the face and scream bloody murder. But even I recognise that with Jonathan, he'll make it seem like I'm the one who committed murder, not the other way around.

I try to bargain with myself to remain cool-headed, realising full well that the agitation will only push me to make mistakes. Yes, his suggestion and the nonchalant way he said it—as if it's a given—is like having tentacles wrapped around my chest, but I need to find a way to deal with it. "You're crazy if you thought I'd agree to this."

"Watch that mouth, Aurora. I don't appreciate being called crazy."

"And I don't appreciate being treated like a whore in my own company."

"*My* company. It is now *my* property. You'll get used to it with time."

I cross my arms over my chest. "I'll buy back the shares for double the price you paid."

"Not interested."

"Why the hell not? You're a businessman. You're supposed to consider profit before anything else."

He stands up and it takes all of my self-confidence not to step back and glue myself to the wall—or better yet, turn around and get the hell out of his lethal presence. I haven't been breathing properly since he barged into my office.

But the fact remains, it is *my* office. I won't allow Jonathan or anyone else to make me abandon it.

"Have you heard about suffering small losses for the greater good? This is one of those situations, wild one. You can offer me ten times what I paid, and I still won't sell." He stops in front of me, a hand in his pocket and his arrogant nose nearly hitting the roof. "Here's how it'll go. You offer yourself to me willingly. And by willingly, I mean you're completely into this; there will be no bowing out, changing your mind, or playing the victim card."

"And if I don't agree?" I ask, even though my tongue sticks to the roof of my dry mouth.

"You'll give up ownership of H&H and I'll have the liberty to sell it or merge it with another company. I haven't decided yet."

"You…you can't do that. The artistic value of H&H will disappear."

"I have no fucks to give about that."

"How about the employees? Will you at least keep them? Many of them have debts and loans to pay. They've been with us since the start, and some are too old to work for larger corporations."

"I don't see why any of that is my problem." His face remains stoic, unchanging.

Tears gather in my eyes at the injustice of the world. A world ruled by the likes of Jonathan King. Large corporations like King Enterprises don't give a fuck about smaller ones. They don't stop to look under their shoes after they crush multiple families with their capitalist bullshit.

Gulping in a deep breath, I try to ignore how close he is and that his scent is enveloping me whether I like it or not. It's another one of the intimidation factors that he uses relentlessly and unapologetically.

It's useless to fight him on a bigger scale or in a company versus company type of argument. He came here already knowing he has the upper hand, so he'll never cave in.

I take an entirely different route. "You're my sister's husband. We can't possibly do this."

"I get to decide that, and I say we will."

"How could you do this to Alicia after…" I trail off before I blurt out all the thoughts I want to scream at his face. This is the worst time to confront him about the past.

He eradicates the distance between us in one step and holds my chin captive like he did at the wedding. I try to take a step back, but he wraps his other hand around the back of my neck, imprisoning me.

My pulse heightens until it's the only thing I can hear in my ears. His callous touch, and the way he does it, as if he has every right to—as if I'm already his property—should make me rage. However, I'm unable to get past the ball lodged in my throat. It's like I'm back to being that little girl who peeked up at him, because actually looking at him? That's like peering at the sun and being roasted alive.

"After what? If you start something, finish it."

"After she died." I'm glad my voice doesn't crack or break. "I can't do that to her. She was my sister."

"The one whose funeral you didn't even attend?"

I bite my lower lip, caging in the feelings trying to bleed out of me.

"That's what I thought." He releases me with what almost seems like…distaste.

I see it then, the darkness in his grey eyes. At first, I thought it was anger and disapproval, and while those are indeed there, it's so much deeper than that. There's also another potent emotion that's lurking beneath the surface.

Grudge. Hard and poignant.

Jonathan doesn't seek to own me because he wants me. Far from it. He has a hidden agenda and he won't stop until he achieves it. Whether I survive or perish at the end is the least of his concerns.

"I'll give you time to think about it, and then I'll send a driver to your house."

"How do you know my address?"

He continues as if I didn't just ask him a question, "If you don't show up at my house tonight, Harris will start H&H acquisition procedures tomorrow morning."

"How...how is that a choice?"

"It is. You'll always have a choice with me, Aurora. Be smart. After what you did to Maxim, I expect that of you."

"I told you not to say his name," I snap.

He watches me peculiarly for a second. I expect him to invade my space again and confiscate my oxygen, but he turns around and leaves with the same savage power he walked in with.

Air whooshes back into my lungs and I fall on the chair, my heels scraping against the ground. It's like he stole my thought process, and I can now have it back.

Or not really.

Now the air is thick with his indecent proposal that's hanging over my head like a guillotine. I'm not an idiot. I know Jonathan wouldn't pay so much money for pussy. I mean, he's *the* Jonathan King. He can have whomever he wishes.

So why me? What the hell does he want from me?

The door opens and Layla rushes inside holding two cups of iced coffee. "That bastard had a smile on his face as he left. That's not good, is it?"

"We're screwed, Lay."

We sit across from each other as I tell her all about Jonathan's proposal and the price he demands I pay.

"That piece of S!" She jumps to her feet, pacing the length of the office and slurping from her coffee cup. "You can sue him for sexual harassment."

"He didn't force me. If anything, he wants me to be one hundred per cent willing."

"D. I. C. K," she spells out.

"There's something else, Lay."

"What? What is it?" She crouches in front of me, her mouth releasing the straw with a gentle pop and dread forming a crease on her forehead.

"I don't think I'm his endgame. There's something else I can't put my finger on."

"Like what?"

"I don't know."

"Hmm. I must say, it makes sense. He's Jonathan King, right? He wouldn't pay so much for a mistress."

My nose scrunches at that word. I can't believe the bastard actually suggested that he gets...me. Out of all things, it had to be that.

"Is it because of your sister?"

"What?"

"You're a carbon copy of her, even Ethan noticed that. Surely Jonathan noticed it, too. Maybe he wants you to be her replacement."

"That's...sick."

"I know, but this is Jonathan. He's kind of sick. You can tell that underneath all the silver fox appearance, there's a Satan's spawn. You can't eliminate any possibility."

"You know, I always hated him because Alicia had acute depression and he made it worse. I could feel it even when I was a little girl. And remember those articles that speculated she didn't die because of an accident but from committing suicide? I believe them, Lay. I believe he's the major reason my sister could've made that decision. And now, I have to relive her fate?"

"Oh, come here." Layla wraps an arm around my shoulder. "You won't, okay? We'll start from scratch. Just the two of us, like when we were fresh out of uni and clueless. Remember those times we stayed up all night? You have the talent and I have the brains. We can totally do this again, mate. Jonathan King can suck our Ds."

I laugh despite myself. "How about our employees?"

"We can keep some and help others search for work. Many small businesses do that." There's a sadness in her voice as she speaks.

I shake my head. I can't do that to her and to them. Layla and I spent too many sleepless nights to stop now or to allow Jonathan to bring us down.

Besides, I doubt he'd leave us alone. If we choose to walk away, there's nothing that would keep him from coming after me again. Knowing him and his ruthless ways, he might even let us prosper for a while just so he could swoop back in and announce ownership of our new company like he did today.

I won't spend the rest of my life looking over my shoulder because of Jonathan King.

I'm already doing that because of another devil. I'll never let it repeat.

Jonathan wants to have me?

Fine.

But he'll regret every second of it.

TEN

Jonathan

ONTRARY TO POPULAR BELIEF, THE KEY TO BEING A
mastermind isn't your ability to plot. It's, in fact, your ability
to predict your opponent's moves before they make them.

To win, you can't be taken by surprise or driven out of your
element. It should be the other way around.

That's how I conquer.

How I win.

How I drag everyone down so I'm the only one who rules over
them.

Aurora is nothing but the latest addition to my collection. I
have no doubt she'll come tonight. It's not speculation. It's a fact.

According to the information Harris gathered about her, she
started H&H with her black belt friend as soon as they were out
of university. They even began planning and submitting requests
before graduation. She poured more than six years of sweat and
sleepless nights into that company. And according to their numbers, they were doing well.

If it weren't for their accountant's embezzlement, I wouldn't have gotten in that easily. It still wouldn't have been impossible, even if they were stable. However, it would've taken more time than I had to spare.

Time is the crown no one can acquire, and if I'd missed this chance, Ethan would've won.

Which is out of the question.

I had to lose a few favours in order to win over the bank director and Lucien Vincent. The first was easy to appease with a subsidiary that brings in five times more net profit than H&H. It's Lucien that was a bit of a problem. Sebastian Queens, the prime minister and one of my biggest allies, doesn't like him due to some idiotic jealous episode over his wife.

Lucien's condition to let go of those shares was partnering up with King Enterprises for import and export between the United Kingdom and his main factories in France.

Since I needed to get my hands on his H&H shares, I agreed. Sebastian will probably complain if he finds out, but what he doesn't know won't hurt him.

His reason for hating Lucien is foolish in the first place, and absolute blasphemy in the business world. If he didn't want his wife to fall in Lucien's hands, he shouldn't have divorced her.

But I digress, slightly.

Now that the core pieces have fallen into place, all I have to do is sit and wait until Aurora shows up.

Harris is with me in my home office, going through data for the joint project Ethan and I have been working on for the Rhodes Conglomerate.

Sooner or later, I'll buy him out of it. Or, more accurately, kick him out.

The problem with Ethan is that he's too tenacious and doesn't give up.

We'll meet again.

His words to Aurora today play on a loop at the back of my head.

I tighten my grip around the glass of cognac, then place it on the table.

There will be no seeing her again. Ethan's fucking nerves know no limit. How dare he get close to Aurora after everything that happened with Alicia?

Sooner or later, he'll pay for driving her to her death, and no, the years he spent in coma don't count. But before that, he and Aurora will remain continents apart.

I'll make sure of it. That will be my new mission—aside from the usual one that includes squashing him.

There's a soft knock on the door before Margot appears, carrying a tray full of appetisers and a coffee.

She puts them on the table and steps back, placing both hands over her stomach. She's a plump woman in her mid-forties with soft features and a kind nature. Margot was never married and has no family so her entire focus is on work. "Dinner?"

"In an hour. We'll have a guest."

"For three?" she speaks with a slight Irish accent.

She's been with us since Alicia was alive and was Levi and Aiden's nanny. They certainly show her more affection than they would ever show me.

Which is fine.

Those two punks would never admit it, but it's because of their upbringing that they are who they are today. King blood runs in their veins and they're born to rule, not to be stomped on.

I ignore the coffee and take another sip of my cognac, letting the burn settle in. "For two."

Margot throws a peculiar glance at Harris. He shrugs and focuses back on his tablet as if he were born with it attached to his hand.

"Do you fancy beef?" she asks me.

"I have no preferences, Margot. Just make it perfect."

"Always." She nods and retreats.

Am I doing this to impress Aurora? Probably. She needs to be impressed in order to be intimidated. They're weaker and easier to handle when they're put out of their element.

She seems to be the type who's not easily threatened, which is fine by me. The process of subduing people is more thrilling than watching from the top. It's what happens after their fall that bores me.

Harris slides his tablet into his leather briefcase and stands up. "I'll be leaving as well."

"You can have dinner here." Since Levi moved out two years ago and Aiden followed a year after for university, Harris has most of his meals here. He also spends all-nighters sometimes. Needless to say, he has no life outside of work, which makes him efficient.

"I'll have to decline, considering you're having dinner for *two*. Last I checked, I'm not one of those two."

"You're being petty."

"*Me*, sir?" He raises a sarcastic brow. "Never."

"Leave."

He smiles a little, but then his expression goes back to normal. "Sir?"

"Yes?"

He readjusts his glasses. "There are some rumours."

"What type of rumours?" Harris does a lot of media play on my behalf, so he knows most rumours are lies. He even uses them for King Enterprises' favour when needed, but if he mentioned it, there must be something behind it.

"In the juridical circle, there's talk about granting Maxim Griffin a trial for parole."

"I thought he wasn't eligible for parole because of the nature of his crimes."

"He's not, but there's a new psychotherapist on the line. Apparently, his lawyer is playing the mental health card. Or it could be new evidence."

I plant my elbows on the table and lean forward. "Who knows about this?"

"The inner circle."

"Your source?"

"Dr Lenin. The new psychotherapist works in his facility."

That's close enough to be chalked up to false rumours. Dr Lenin has no reason to lie to Harris, considering he gives him the best investments—on my behalf.

Since Aurora disappeared right after Maxim's trial, I had to at least keep an eye on him in case she went to visit her father.

She didn't. Not once.

Considering how she ended things with him, I'm not surprised. That woman has so much stubbornness in her, it sparks in her stormy eyes like waves. However, there's a slightly broken quality to her, too. A vulnerability I've caught a glimpse of whenever Maxim's name is mentioned.

"Keep me updated on that. And, Harris?"

"Yes, sir?"

"I need eyes on her."

"Consider it done." He nods again and leaves.

I rub my forefinger against my chin, contemplating where Maxim's call for parole is coming from. Does it have to do with Aurora's reappearance?

The image of her murky blue eyes returns to memory. The way she trembled in fear but still held her ground when I gripped her chin.

I've had grown men shake in front of me, yet Aurora didn't shy away from giving me a piece of her mind. Even after she knew I had her and H&H by the throat.

Literally and figuratively.

If I choose to, I can blow her little company to irredeemable pieces.

I won't, though.

At least, not until I have what I want from her.

I sip my cognac, letting the strong liquid burn my throat as I recall the slight twitch in those red lips while she stared up at me.

She held my gaze, I'll give her that.

Now I'm tempted to see how far I can push her before she stops doing so.

I'm no saint. I've had my fair share of women after Alicia's death, but each and every one of them were gone within the night. Harris made them all sign NDAs that ensure they'll run the other way the moment they see me again.

This is the first time I'll keep someone close. Not because I want her close, but because I'll untangle her piece by each bloody piece.

Aurora Harper might be a carbon copy of my wife, but I'm beginning to see they're nothing alike.

Clarissa—Aurora—was a wild child. She sang off tune and danced sporadically when she thought no one was watching, then hid behind Alicia's wedding dress when people were around.

Something tells me she's still the same. She's hiding something, and as it happens, I'm good with riddles and wars.

Especially wars.

I stand up and stop by my glass chessboard on the coffee table. It has an unfinished game from when I played alone this morning.

Now that both Aiden and Levi are gone, I have no one to play with but myself. There's Harris, but he's too obsessed with his tablet to pay enough attention to chess.

Usually, I make one of my sides lose just so I can win afterwards. Let's say it's a vicious cycle.

My phone vibrates in my pocket and I retrieve it.

Aiden. Speak of the devil.

"Jonathan, finally."

"Hello to you, too, son."

"Forget about that. Why haven't you been answering my calls?"

"One, you're on your honeymoon on my island, and if I might add, you still didn't thank me for it. Two, some of us have work to do."

To say my relationship with my son is strained would probably be putting it lightly. He's hated me since his mother's death. Not that I mind. It's his hatred for me that's made him grow up into the man he is today.

While I do not approve of his taste in women, I have no doubt King Enterprises will be in good hands twenty or thirty years from now.

There's a pause on the other end of the line before he speaks quietly. "Who is she?"

"Who is who?"

"You know exactly who I'm talking about. Who the fuck was that woman who looked like Alicia's ghost? And don't even try to tell me you don't know everyone who appeared at the wedding."

This is long overdue. Aiden's been trying to reach me since the wedding, and I know it's not because he misses me. Avoiding his question is only delaying the inevitable.

"She's your aunt."

"My aunt? Since when do I have an *aunt*?"

"You always did. Aurora is Alicia's half-sister. She was born after an affair between your grandmother and a commoner from the North. That's why no one likes to talk about her existence."

"Why didn't I know?"

"Because neither Alicia nor Aurora wanted you to."

"As if that explains everything. Why is she back now?"

That's what I would like to find out, and I will. She'll also tell me all about the shitstorm that went down after Maxim Griffin's arrest.

'I saw the devil today, darling. I think he's coming after me.'

At first, I thought Alicia said that as a result of her hallucinations. She often woke up in the middle of the night and roamed the house, scribbling words everywhere. However, more recently, I'm starting to think that maybe there was something different going on. Maybe she did *see* the devil.

The look on Aurora's face whenever I mention Maxim's name

is too similar to Alicia's horrified expression to write it off as a co-incidence. Not that I ever believe in those.

A knock sounds on the door. I check my watch. Ten minutes early. Impressive.

"I have company," I tell Aiden and hang up before he says any-thing. After slipping the phone back in my pocket, I say, "Come in."

But instead of being faced with the stormy blue eyes that look ready for trouble, my driver appears at my doorstep. His white-gloved hands lie inert at his sides and his bald head shines under the light.

"Sir."

"What is it, Moses? Why are you here?"

"The lady sent me back."

My fingers strangle the glass until I nearly break it. I was so sure she'd accept. She should have. All the facts point in that direc-tion, yet she went straight against that possibility.

Well played, Aurora.

She's taken me by surprise for the second time since her reappearance.

There will not be a third.

ELEVEN

Aurora

T HE FACT THAT I'M CORNERED DOESN'T MEAN I'LL BOW DOWN or drop to my knees.

It also doesn't mean that I will needlessly provoke a much stronger opponent than me. My survival instinct has taught me to pick my battles and learn my worth.

Just because I collapsed once doesn't mean I will allow myself to be broken again.

So tonight, I sent away Jonathan's driver. I also didn't give him a reason. I have no doubt his tyrant boss will not be pleased. I just hope he doesn't take it out on him or something.

It's not a vain provocation. It's my way to tell Jonathan with no words that he doesn't get to order me around.

I might be willing to do this, but it will be on my terms and my terms alone.

I step out of my flat and lock the door. The cold air from the corridor creeps into my bones, despite the beige coat that I'm wearing over my black knee-length dress. The one I reserve for funerals.

My face is makeup-free and I spent no effort in being presentable.

Screw Jonathan. I'll never get done up for him.

Not only did that tyrant push me into a hole, but he's also burying me alive.

Layla still insists on starting anew; however, my decision has been made. I'll play Jonathan's game, but unlike what he plans, I won't be the one coming out of this in pieces.

He broke my sister beyond repair and if he thinks he can do the same to me, he has a surprise waiting.

I'm the wrong sister to come after.

Where Alicia was soft and caring, I'm hard and unfeeling.

Since I was a kid, I've learnt to build stone around my heart because that thing will only lead me to doom. It will only push me into a path filled with wires and vacant eyes and…duct tape.

So much fucking duct tape.

I shake my head as I take the lift down.

I promised myself not to think about that time again. I'm not Clarissa anymore.

Clarissa is buried with those vacant eyes.

"Ms Harper," our building's concierge calls my name.

He's a short bald man with bushy brows and a beer belly. His cockney accent is noticeable when he speaks. He also always watches the Premier League games on the hall's TV with Shelby, the old man who resides next door to me.

When Layla and I first started out, I used to rent a room in a dangerous town in Eastern London. As soon as I could afford to, I moved into this building. The security is brilliant and most of the tenants are businessmen, lawyers, and doctors. The location is safer as well.

"Good evening, Paul. Shelby."

The concierge nods and stands up, his attention temporarily away from the game. Shelby doesn't even acknowledge my presence, deeply focused on the TV screen. Not that he ever returns my greetings. Since we moved in almost at the same time, I always try to be friendly, but it's rarely reciprocated.

Paul reaches behind the counter and retrieves a packet. "This came for you."

"Thank you, Paul." I take the small wooden box. I wonder what it could be. It's not large enough to be the new notebooks I ordered online.

As soon as I'm in my car, I check the box. Weird. My name and address is on there, but the sender's isn't.

I shake it and hear a faint sound coming from inside. When I open it, I find a flash drive.

That's all.

A flash drive.

Along with a note printed in a computer-generated font.

PLAY ME.

Curiosity gets the better of me, so I plug it into my car and hit Play.

At first, there's no sound and I'm about to chalk this up to a prank or something. Then I hear someone breathing and I freeze as a soft voice follows.

Alicia.

Oh my God.

It's Alicia!

"Hey, Claire. If you get this, it means I'm no longer with you. I debated about whether to leave you this, but I decided that I need to warn you. I need to protect you like I wasn't able to when I was alive. Claire, baby sis, someone is trying to kill me and I probably will die. I —"

The recording is cut off.

I hit Play and Forward, but it cuts off at the same point every time. I press the player again and again, my fingers shaking.

Damn it. A whole body shudder grips me, and tingles erupt all over my skin at the words I heard straight out of my sister's mouth.

Someone was trying to kill Alicia.

I knew it. I knew that her death was suspicious.

Now, I have to bring my sister justice.

Just like I did with those vacant eyes.

The moment I'm in front of the King mansion, the metal gate automatically opens like in some horror film.

I drive inside, watching my surroundings as if something or someone will jump me.

The silence of the night is deafening as I slowly go down the road that's faintly lit by tall street lamps.

A fountain sits in the middle of the garden with imposing grandiose. There's a statue of an angel pouring water from a jar as the virgin Mary holds him at a tilted angle.

I hit the brakes, staring with wild eyes of the statues. Both the woman and the angel are crying, their expressions wrenched.

I touch my watch, the one Alicia gave me as a present. That same image is engraved on the back of it.

This can't be a coincidence. There must've been something she wanted to tell me. Something that has to do with crying angels and the person who was after her life.

A shiver creeps down my spine as I hit the gas. I don't stop until I'm parked outside Jonathan's house.

Inhaling deeply, I step out of my car and stand in front of a large wooden door that appears ancient but elegant with an ornamental design that looks handmade. Not that it should be a surprise, considering this is the tyrant's residence.

The mansion stretches across a vast piece of land, accentuated by towers on the eastern and western sides. It's like a glasshouse from the amount of glass visible. Tall windows occupy the three floors and none of them have lights on.

That's not creepy at all.

This will be the first time I've stepped foot into Jonathan's house. After all, Alicia was the one who came to find me when I used to live in Leeds, not the other way around. The only two times she brought me to London was after Mum's funeral and during her wedding, and that didn't happen here. I think it was at her father's house.

The door opens on its own. Again.

I nearly jump when a petite woman appears at the entrance in utter silence. She's wearing a black skirt, a white shirt, and matching apron. Her brown hair is held in a stiff bun at the back of her head.

"Good evening, Miss," she speaks with an Irish lilt. "Mr King is expecting you in the dining room."

Of course he is.

She motions at my coat and I shrug it off, then awkwardly give it to her. I'm not used to people serving me, considering I was forced to fend for myself since I was sixteen.

Draping it over her arm, she starts down the corridor with moderate footsteps and I follow after her, trying not to gawk at the place.

Or more accurately, the palace.

Everything here is built to impress. From the high glass windows to the marble flooring and the golden vaulted ceiling. It's like he receives royalty here. Hell, maybe he does.

This is just another drop in the ocean for how far apart Jonathan and I are.

He was born a king—literally. I was born to become invisible.

And I succeeded at it for eleven years. Until he ruined everything.

The woman stops in front of a set of double doors, nods, then leaves.

I suck in a deep, shaky breath and touch my watch.

You can do this, Aurora. You've gotten through worse.

I push the doors open and close them behind me before I finally raise my head.

Jonathan sits at the head of a grand table fit for all of H&H's employees. No kidding. Does he receive the British Army in here, or something?

He's wearing a white shirt, his sleeves rolled to his elbows, revealing strong, veiny arms. He could snap me in half with those arms without even blinking.

The fact that he's all alone reduces nothing of his majesty. He doesn't appear lonely or even the least bit miserable. If anything, he looks every bit the tyrant king on his throne. If it were medieval times, Jonathan would be the type of monarch who orders the burning of an entire city so the others would learn a lesson and bend the knee for him.

"Well, well." He places his elbows on the table and meets my gaze with his unreadable one. "Have you changed your mind, wild one?"

"I agree."

"To what?"

"To the deal you offered."

"Smart. Now sit down."

He cuts a piece of whatever is in front of him, sure I'll comply with his order. Jonathan pauses with the fork halfway to his mouth when I reach a hand to the zip at the side of my dress and yank it down.

The cloth pools around my feet and I stand almost naked in front of him. "Get it over with."

TWELVE

Jonathan

EVER SINCE I SAT DOWN FOR DINNER, ALL I'VE BEEN THINKING about is how to bring Aurora to her knees.

It doesn't matter what methods I have to use. She's challenging me again and I'm not the type to be challenged.

Sending my driver back is a clear sign of her loathsome stubbornness. And I need to crush that stubbornness to smithereens.

So when she showed up on time on her own, I took a pause.

I don't take pauses.

Still, here I am. Taking another pause as I stare at her pale bare skin. My gaze trails from the defiant expression on her face—no red lipstick today—to the jutting of her nose and the slight crease in her chin.

Her long, delicate neck is taut—with tension, no doubt. Both her arms are inert by her sides, not trying to hide her half-nakedness. She's in an unflattering purple cotton bra and underwear, clearly highlighting that she didn't put any effort into how she looks before she came here.

It's her way of showing defiance. She's telling me this means nothing and she'll wake up in the morning and completely erase me.

Doesn't she know there's no erasing a king? At least, not when you reside in his kingdom.

I take my time sliding my gaze down her full, high tits that push against the bra with each harsh intake of breath. The pale skin contrasts against the purple like the type of art you only see in exhibitions.

Her body shape is slim, tall, and fit. Judging from her toned legs, either she jogs or hikes. There's no line of tan on her shoulders or around her hips, even though we're just out of the summer, which means Aurora doesn't do sunbathing.

Aurora doesn't wear swimsuits, but she runs or hikes.

I tuck that information away for later as I continue watching her rigid posture and the rebellion in her dark blues. They sparkle like a hurricane about to conquer an ocean.

My cock twitches and it's not just because of her half-naked state. It's that look in her eyes. The spirit, the fight. The damn stubbornness.

My blood rushes with a powerful heat at the idea of exploiting that fight, of digging my fingers into her armour and ripping it apart from the inside out.

How long has it been since I've had a worthy opponent? Aside from Ethan and his dog, Agnus, no one dares to look me in the eyes, let alone stand half-naked, in a vulnerable position, and still defy me.

My gaze slides to a medium length scar beneath her left breast. It's horizontal, a bit messy, and appears old.

How old, though? And what happened to give her that scar?

There's also what seems like a tattoo above it. It's too small to make out its details, but I'll have plenty of time to study that later.

Aurora wraps an arm around her midsection to hide her scar. She's either ashamed of it or she doesn't like to be exposed.

Fascinating.

"What do you think you're doing?" I ask in my firm tone that people usually bolt at hearing. I don't show that she took me by surprise. *Again.*

I thought I would have to fight her tooth and nail before she removed any piece of clothing. The fact that she's willingly offering her body is the last thing I expected. And well, fuck me if that isn't a turn on.

My dick thickens against my trousers, but I don't bother adjusting it.

"I'm doing what we agreed on. Isn't this what you want? I'm only giving you what you bargained for, Jonathan."

"You're not a whore, so don't act like one. Put your dress back on and sit the fuck down."

I'll have my hands full with this one.

My lips pull in a small smile.

I'm looking forward to it.

THIRTEEN

Aurora

DAMN IT.

Damn. It.

How does he always make me feel as if I've overstepped a line or that I'm doing something wrong? *He* is in the wrong.

He's the one who came up with this sordid deal. He's the one who's screwing up everything.

Jonathan watches me from across the table, his gaze going back and forth between my face and the arm I'm using to cover my scar and tattoo.

It's like he's intimidating me with his eyes alone to make me drop my hand and bare myself for him. Like it's his right and I've been depriving him from it all along.

Damn the tyrant and how much he can communicate with a mere glance.

Crouching, I retrieve my dress and turn away from him to slide it back on. Despite my brave façade, my fingers tremble.

Jonathan King is a frightening man. I might not be willing to let him stomp all over me, but he has the ability to make you feel non-existent by a mere look from his piercing metal eyes.

By the time I zip up my dress and turn around, he's still watching me with that unnerving focus. I could cut through the tension in the air with a knife if I had one.

He tips his stubborn chin at the chair beside him, repeating his order without having to say a word.

I snap my spine into a line as I walk in the most moderate manner I'm capable of before flopping on the seat at his left. There's a plate of steak and salad and two types of clear soup. The entire setting is straight out of an elegant restaurant.

"Eat." Jonathan's voice disturbs the silence of the room. "It's gotten cold, but since you're the one who's ten minutes late, you'll bear the consequences. You'll also pay for those ten minutes of tardiness."

"I don't want to eat." I bunch my fists on my lap. "I want to get this over with."

"You thought this would be a one-time thing?"

"No."

He wraps his lips around a piece of meat. I gulp at the sensual way his mouth slides over the fork before he chews leisurely, like this is some eating porn show.

I internally shake my head. Did I just see Jonathan in an erotic way? What in the ever-loving hell?

"Why don't you tell me what you think this will be, Aurora?"

"I don't know."

"That's not an answer."

"All I know is that I want to get on with it instead of wasting time on food and nonsense."

"If you don't watch that mouth, I'll fuck it right here, right now."

My breathing shortens and I stare at him with wild eyes, my attention involuntarily slipping down…

Down…

I jerk my head back up, refusing to entertain that idea. Problem is, he's painted that crude image in my head and now I can't purge it out.

Not that I didn't suspect Jonathan to be crude. His voice was created to command and say dirty things. However, I hadn't thought it would be to this extent, and the sudden attack isn't helping my bemused head.

"Now eat." He fixes me with a blank stare as if he didn't just spout those earlier words. "Or would you rather I fill your mouth with something else?"

My unsteady hand reaches for the fork and I inhale deeply to collect my bearings. I take the first bite of salad, trying to forget that a larger-than-life presence is watching my every move. It's like he's a scientist and I'm the rat in his lab.

I lift my head. "Now what?"

"Now, you eat."

"And then what?"

"And then I decide. After all, you're mine now and I get to do whatever I please."

I grit my teeth. "I'm *not* your toy."

"Oh, but you are, wild one."

A million profanities form in my head, but I don't say them. My being agitated will only give him the upper hand, and I can't give him more than he's already confiscated.

I hate that I have to consider my every word when dealing with Jonathan. If I don't, he'll twist them up and either use them against me or throw them back in my face.

That's why I need to be cool-headed about this.

"No other people," I say my first condition in the calmest tone I can manage under the circumstances. I won't be a side dish, and I sure as hell won't be compared to anyone else.

He takes a moment to focus on cutting his food, and I'm ready to bet a limb that he's doing it on purpose. It's like he uses everything as a weapon—silence included. It takes long, infuriating beats before he nods.

"I also want a time limit."

"Time limit?"

"Yes. If I'm going to agree to this, I need a time limit, after which you'll let me go and give me the stocks back."

He smiles, and this time, it's neither sadistic nor genuine. It's something different, almost like…pride? No, why would Jonathan ever be proud of me?

He chews slowly on his meat, intentionally keeping me on edge again, before he speaks, "I was wondering when you'd ask that. What did you have in mind?"

"A month. I'll be yours for a month to do whatever you please, and then you'll let me go and revert H&H's ownership back to Layla and me."

"A year."

I meet his impenetrable gaze with mine. "Three months."

"Six. My final offer."

"Fine."

It's better than what I would've hoped for. At least it's not a year in the company of this tyrant. This time will give me ample space to investigate Alicia's life here and try to solve the mystery of who threatened to kill her.

"You'll stay here."

"I have a flat."

"And I'm telling you that you won't live in it anymore. At least for the next six months. I expect you to move in tomorrow."

The arsehole. It's like a dictator's regime around here.

"Anything else, your majesty?"

"Yes. Lose the attitude. I don't appreciate it."

"You should've included that in the clauses. You want to keep me? This is me, Jonathan, attitude and all. I'm not the little girl who hid behind Alicia's dress."

He's silent for a bit, watching me closely as if he's meeting me for the first time. "I can see that."

I stand up. "Can I go now?"

"Not so fast." He motions at me to come to him.

I hesitate before I approach him until his woodsy scent is all I breathe in. He has the power to own everyone and everything in his immediate vicinity. It's less about his last name and more about his presence.

"Lift your dress."

"W-what?"

"Do it."

"Didn't you tell me to put it back on not two minutes ago?"

"And now I'm telling you to lift it." His vicious gaze slides up to mine. "Do you have an objection, Aurora?"

I stare directly into his harsh eyes, refusing to cower down.

"If you do, the door is right there."

"I don't."

"Then don't make me repeat myself."

My hands tremble as my fingers latch onto the cloth and I lift it up to my stomach. My bare thighs and cotton knickers are in his full, unnerving view. Unlike earlier, my sense of confidence is withering away. At least then, it was according to my plan. Now, it's his playground.

The fact that I have no clue about his plots is messing with my head more than the state of my half-nakedness.

"Up."

A shudder grips me at the authority in his tone. I slide the dress up one more inch, revealing my belly. Jonathan grabs my hand and yanks it up to my breasts.

The feel of his skin on mine sends electricity through my stomach, almost like he's trying to shock me to death.

"Hold it there. Don't move."

I don't know what he means by that until his fingers trace alongside my scar. A different type of bolt rushes through my skin and memories zap to my mind like lightning strikes.

Vacant eyes. Duct tape. Dirt. The crunching of a metal against bones.

There's nothing I can do to stop the memories. They suddenly attack and ravish my conscience as if it's an act of vengeance. The only way I know to deal with it is by hiding it and pretending, for the most part, that it doesn't exist.

I'm about to cover the scar or push him away, but Jonathan pins me in place with a glare. "Do not move or I'll lay you on my lap and spank your arse."

A shudder snaps my spine upright and it's different from the usual memories that assault me with no prior warning.

The promise in his words freeze me in place, my feet curling in my shoes as he continues his meticulous observation of my scar.

His fingers run across it with a softness that turns me breathless. His skin is not harsh, but not soft either—it's firm and as hard as him. The more his hand glides over the skin, the more impossible standing becomes. For some reason, I'd imagined a man like Jonathan wasn't capable of such tenderness.

My core pulses and I breathe harshly, almost like an animal who can't keep its instinct down.

His finger runs up and down above my scar. "What does this tattoo mean?"

"Nothing."

"You want to tell me you got a tattoo of a closed eye right above a knife scar for nothing?"

"What makes you think it's a knife scar?"

"It looks like a scar caused by a sharp object, but since you're stiffening at the knife part, then my guess was correct. What happened? How did you get stabbed?"

My hands quiver, but I manage to speak in a levelled tone. "That's none of your business."

"What did I say about that mouth? Maybe you do want me to fuck it."

"I don't care what you do to my body, Jonathan. This thing has been dead for eleven years."

I don't know why I freely offer that information. Maybe I

wanted to figuratively flip Jonathan the finger by letting him know I'm useless in the sex department. That no matter what he does, he won't be able to break me.

He can't break what's already broken.

His fingers trail down from my ribs to my stomach, leaving goosebumps in their wake. Then he cups me through my underwear.

I don't stiffen. I don't even try to wiggle free. It doesn't matter, because he can't get to me.

The few sexual encounters I've had were complete disasters. One of them even said, "You're dry as a desert." Then he soaked me in lube so he could get inside.

There's nothing Jonathan could do to change that. Sexual pleasure was purged out of me when I saw those vacant eyes.

So, in a way, Jonathan got defective goods.

Good luck with all the lube.

"You're telling me you're dead here?" His grip tightens. "Maybe I should find out."

"Show me your worst."

FOURTEEN

Aurora

ONATHAN WRAPS A STRONG, MERCILESS HAND AROUND MY wrist and tugs.

I follow his lead and stumble, ending up flush against his side. Even though he's sitting, it's almost as if he's towering over me.

"Lie on my lap. Face down."

I swallow at the command in his tone. The man was born to lead armies and control people.

"W-why?"

"Quit the habit of asking questions when around me. I don't answer them and they just make your situation worse."

"I have the right to know." Besides, the position he's suggestion isn't normal. Right?

"You already agreed to this, remember? The only right you have is to follow orders."

Ugh. The infuriating tyrant.

He presses his thumb against my clit, which I assume is a

warning. "Now, are you going to lie on my lap or should I make you? Disclaimer: the second option won't be pretty."

I swallow at the bleak promise in his tone. If I'm going to spend six months with him, I really need to pay more attention to picking my battles. "Fine. Let me go."

He tightens his grip on my sex for good measure. It's not meant to please, but as a stern non-verbal warning.

Inhaling deeply, I lean forward and lie on his lap. I don't miss how my arse is now in the air like that of a disobedient, naughty child. My movements are awkward as my breasts and stomach lie flush against his hard thighs.

It doesn't matter which position he has me in, Jonathan King won't be able to get to me.

A peaceful aura envelops me at that reminder, even when he slides my dress up to the small of my back. Cool air hits my thighs, and goosebumps break out on my flesh.

It's only because of the air.

Just the air.

His long, lean fingers glide my underwear down my thighs so I'm completely naked from the waist down.

I try not to think about the view he's seeing. The vulnerability of the situation grates on my nerves. This is the last position I want to be in with anyone, let alone Jonathan. Which was probably his plan all along.

He won't get to me. He won't get to me.

I may not have any confidence in this whole thing, but I have confidence in my dysfunctional body.

"You're telling me you're dead. Is that it, Aurora?"

"Yes."

"You think you can waste my time?"

"You made the deal before making sure of all the facts. That's your fault, not mine."

"That mouth will land you in trouble." Jonathan reaches a hand between my thighs and I open them, not presenting any protest whatsoever.

He drags a finger down my dry folds. The contact is neither pleasurable nor painful. It's just…nothing.

Numb.

That's what my therapist told me. Apparently, I've numbed myself to sex since I was a teen, which, in his words, could've been a knee-jerk reaction to sexual assault or rape.

Neither of those happened to me.

Since I never told my therapist about my past, he probably wrote it off as either of those reasons and categorised me in his neat folders as another statistic.

It's far from that. People like me need a special category dedicated to them.

Jonathan drags his finger up and down, and when he doesn't get the reaction he's looking for, he circles my clit. Nothing. Nada.

It doesn't matter if I do it or if anyone else does. Being wet is a myth I only read about.

Still stroking my clit, he thrusts a finger into my entrance. The resistance is real and I wince in discomfort.

He pulls his finger out but keeps it at my opening like a looming threat. "You *are* dead. Fascinating."

Fascinating, seriously? No idea which reaction I expected, but that's not it.

In the past, as in literally years ago, whenever any of my previous sexual partners touched me and found out that what I told them is actually true, it scratched their male ego.

Some went on with it and just used my body. Others tried everything to be crowned as the one who finally made me wet or susceptible to sexual pleasure. When it didn't work, they left and never returned. Not that I was ever looking for a relationship.

The way Jonathan finds this fascinating is throwing me off, like everything else about him. I can't even tell if 'fascinating' is his usual sarcastic reaction or if he's being genuine.

"What happened, wild one?"

"You might want to consider lube. You'll be able to get inside and—"

Slap.

My heart lunges in my throat as the sound reverberates in the air and soon after, my arse cheek catches fire.

Did he just...*spank* me?

"When I ask a question, I expect a direct answer, Aurora."

"W-why did you do that?" I breathe out, my voice jittery and all wrong.

His palm comes on my arse again and I jolt against his lap. My limp hands clench, needing to grab something. *Anything.*

My only option is his thigh, but I refuse to hold on to him.

"Do what?" He lands another slap on my heated skin. "This?"

"J-Jonathan..." Oh my God. What the hell is wrong with my voice? Why is it so breathy and almost like a moan?

"Do you have an objection, Aurora?" When I remain silent, he strokes my skin, and my eyes flutter closed at the soothing circles. "According to your terms, I can do, and I quote, 'whatever I please'. Which was a very reckless thing to say to me, I might add. Are you having second thoughts? Do you want to leave?"

I trap my lower lip against my teeth. "N-no."

Whatever foreign sensation is building inside me will go away. It's just a phase. I went to a sex club once, and none of what my partner at the time did turned me on. So Jonathan's methods won't affect me either.

It's just a phase. A mere phase.

He massages my heated arse cheek with slightly calloused, masculine fingers. "Good girl."

My muscles relax and I feel like I'm about to purr like a kitten or something. His palm comes down on my arse again and the sting jerks my spine upright. A squeal rips through the air as my eyes snap open.

I realise with horror that the sound came from me.

What is happening to me?

"Mmm." Jonathan slides his finger up my folds and I freeze as he meets slippery skin. "You're wet for me."

No. This can't be true.

"It is, wild one." His amused, smug tone engulfs me in its savage clutch.

Did I speak aloud?

"You know what I think, Aurora? I think you're not dead, you just needed something more with your pleasure. Something I'm happy to provide."

Jonathan thrusts two fingers inside me in one go and slaps my arse cheek at the same time. *Slap. Slap. Slap.*

He goes on and on until a sob tears from my throat and I'm submerged in a strange sense of arousal mixed with pain. "Ten, for every minute you were late. No one wastes my time."

Before I can speak, he pounds his fingers inside me over and over, and my cheeks burn at the sound of his skin slapping against my arousal. Heat bubbles in my veins, and my stomach contracts as if it's about to be smashed into.

Then, I'm hit out of nowhere.

I scream as a bolt of electricity shoots through my limbs and shocks my entire body. My nails dig into Jonathan's trousers, holding on to him so I don't fall.

It's useless, though.

My eyes roll to the back of my head as I keep falling and rolling down a cliff so steep, there's no landing in sight.

The rush of pleasure grips me in its vice until there's no way out. Until all I can do is feel my body's armour crack to pieces with no chance of putting it back together again.

I'm breathing heavily, my chest rising and falling like I'm coming down from an adrenaline wave.

When I finally return to the land of the living, Jonathan still has his fingers deep inside my slick core and his other hand covers my stinging, burning arse.

It's pulsing, but to my utter horror, it's not out of embarrassment or repulsion. It's pulsing with the need for *more*.

The other dooming realisation hits me straight in the face. Jonathan just brought me to my first orgasm.

My first ever in my twenty-seven-year life. And I didn't even last a minute under his fierce, firm hand.

He wrenched it out of me in one ruthless, unapologetic manner. As if it was his God-given right.

As if he was always meant to do it.

"Pain." His strong voice echoes around my dizzy head like a sinister, dark promise. "That's what you need, Aurora. Lucky for you, I have plenty to give."

FIFTEEN

Aurora

SECOND THOUGHTS.

A vile way in which your brain plants the seed so you'll suspect everything you do.

Last night, I was so sure I could take on Jonathan's offer and unveil the truth behind Alicia's death.

Then he lay me on his lap, spanked me, and thrust his fingers into me.

I orgasmed.

I fucking orgasmed.

Not being able to feel for such a long time has made me sure and even smug about my defectiveness. And yet, it happened. I *felt*. And it was in the most brutal way possible.

Leaning back against my chair, I close my eyes and try not to think about his hand, his fingers and how, when I finally got off his lap, I stumbled and nearly fell to my face.

Jonathan's lips set in a line as he watched me with those steel eyes that I'm now sure know no emotions whatsoever. The man is a blank board. He's a tyrant, and like any tyrant, only his benefit matters.

'I expect you here when I return from work.'

His parting words kept playing on repeat at the back of my mind during the entire drive home, then when I climbed under the covers and absentmindedly looked at the occasional memes Layla sent me.

I wasn't able to sleep.

I couldn't.

It's more than the soreness in my arse or the dark foreboding that comes every time I recall the ferocity of his slaps or how disastrously I reacted to them.

The moment I close my eyes, all I think about is the feel of his strong hand on my arse, or the sound my arousal made when he savagely pounded into me. To my horror, it's not feelings of humiliation or vulnerability, it's the acute lust, the flooding pleasure, the —

"Mate!"

I startle, and when my eyes open, I find Layla perching over me and waving her hands in front of my face. "There you are. Were you napping? And why do your cheeks look as red as a football player after playing the championship game?"

Standing up, I take her hand in mine.

Layla's eyes turn as wide as saucers. "No, nope. You already used your hug for the week."

"I need to talk to you." I lead her to the sofa and sit her so we're facing each other.

"Damn straight you do. I need deets. Did you throw Johnny's offer back at his face? What did it look like? Did his arrogant nose commit suicide? Ugh. I wish you'd caught it on camera."

"I accepted it, Lay."

"Wait—and I mean this in the most buggered off way—*what?*"

Yesterday, when I remained silent, Layla assumed we'd go with her plan and flip Jonathan the bird.

"I want to do it. It's the only peaceful and uncomplicated way to get the ownership back."

"Mate…" Aurora's eyes fill with tears. My best friend doesn't cry. She thinks it's beneath her 'street-made' status. "I don't want you to sacrifice yourself like that."

"I'm not." I tell her my suspicions about Alicia's death and how I plan to find out the truth behind it.

After I returned to my building, I asked Paul about the sender of that box in which I found the flash drive, and he said he found it in front of the building during his morning check-ups.

"I get that, I do. And I'm all for bringing your sister justice, but you have to be careful, Aurora. It's Jonathan King."

"I know."

"I don't think you do. Sometimes, it seems like you underestimate him because you knew him when you were a kid, but in this world, men like Jonathan King crush and move on. They start wars and end them without being hurt. It's *his* world, his territory, and his subjects. Just because he's playing this game doesn't mean he'll take it easy on you. He might choose to destroy you any time he wishes to do so."

I swallow, her words hitting me at my core. Despite my apprehension about Jonathan, the fact that I was immune to him—and every other man—gave me a false sense of power that crumbled to pieces last night.

"I know you're taking this risk because of your sister, but I don't want you to let your guard down in front of a man like Jonathan."

"What if it's too late, Lay?"

A line forms between her brows. "What do you mean?"

"He…he brought me to orgasm."

"What the F?" She holds up a hand like she needs to catch her breath. "He took your first O?"

More like wrenched it out of me, unapologetically and without a sliver of doubt.

"What happened to 'I never get wet'?" she whispers as if someone is eavesdropping. "Did he use lube?"

I shake my head, shame gnawing at my chest. "But that's not the worst part, Lay. He brought me to orgasm and I felt empty when he let me go. I need help, don't I?"

"No, you don't. Granted, I don't know what it feels like for someone else to give you an orgasm, but orgasms, in general, are a darn good feeling. You probably just wanted more of that."

Why do I feel like that's not the case? But I don't say that out loud in case Layla starts to think I'm sick in the head or something.

"And, mate, if that man gives you anything to enjoy, don't hesitate to take it. At least he has that whole hot daddy look going on for him. Just…"

"What?"

"Don't lose yourself to him. Men like Jonathan King have enough intensity to make you forget about who you are when in their company."

She's right.

But it's not like I'll ever let Jonathan consume me. I might have had second thoughts, but I've never strayed away from my initial goal.

"Are you sure you shouldn't have majored in psychology?" I poke Layla.

"I kind of did. They teach us a lot of psychology in marketing. We have to understand people in order to sell to them."

I rub her arm. "Thank you for being here for me, Lay. I would've gone crazy without you."

"Anytime. Remember, I don't care how much Johnny is daddy material. If he bothers you, I'll kick his arrogant nose."

We both laugh at the mental image, and for a moment, I pretend everything will be fine.

Six months.

I can survive six months.

After all, I survived sixteen years in the company of a monster.

Problem is, Jonathan is an entirely different monster altogether.

SIXTEEN

Aurora

I ARRIVE EARLY TO THE KING'S MANSION.

On purpose.

If I'm going to be stuck here for the next six months, then I might as well rip off the Band-Aid.

However, there's something else.

With the exception of the clusterfuck that happened around the dining table last night and how I embarrassingly came all over Jonathan's fingers, there's another issue that hasn't left my brain.

The recording of Alicia's voice. Her death message to me.

Considering Jonathan was her husband, he ought to inherit all that she left.

If he's had that recording for eleven years, why would he send me that message now? Why in this way?

Granted, he's lost track of me since Alicia's death, but could this be another game of his?

The only other people who could have Alicia's message for me is her lawyer or her son, Aiden.

The lawyer wouldn't play games, I don't think. As for Aiden...
Well, I don't know him enough to form any theories yet. What I'm
sure of is that he wasn't even aware I existed or he wouldn't have
called me Mum during our first meeting.

Besides, he's on his honeymoon right now. There's no way in
hell he has time to plot this.

The prime suspect is inside these walls. Jonathan fucking King.

Once again, the front gate automatically opens. And again, I
stare at the angel statue. My wrist, where my watch lies, itches as a
sense of foreboding trickles down my spine.

I'm sorry I couldn't protect you, but I'll bring you justice, Alicia.

When I was young and clueless, she used to hold me on her
lap and tell me stories about fairies and castles. She used to read
me fantasy novels like *Harry Potter*. I loved how her voice changed
every time there was danger in a scene. My eyes would bug out and
I'd wait with bated breath for the following chapters to unfold.

Even though we lived worlds apart, she never made me feel
like I was worthless.

We did have so many differences to count. I grew up in Leeds
while she lived in London. She was an aristocrat from both parents' sides while I was an illegitimate commoner. Her noble origins
showed in her tiniest gestures. From her smile to her delicate frown.

She was warm and softly spoken. Dying at only thirty was
too harsh.

And that's why she needs justice.

And that's why I can't let whatever happened with Jonathan
yesterday repeat again. He's my sister's husband for fuck's sake.

As soon as I stop in front of the mansion, I unload my suitcase. I brought necessities and my laptop, and since I kept my flat,
most of my stuff is still there.

The door opens and the woman from yesterday greets me. A
younger man dressed in an elegant butler suit stands beside her.
His skin is so pale that his green veins show through the surface
of his hand.

"Tom will get your suitcase." She motions at him and he silently springs into action. "Please follow me."

I do, and even though it's my second time here, the place's majesty doesn't lessen. If anything, it appears more grandiose in daylight.

"What's your name?" I ask the woman, who's walking one step ahead of me.

"Margot," she says without sparing me a glance.

"I'm Aurora."

"I know."

Okay. I suppose Jonathan's staff are as stand-offish as he is. They're not talkative either.

Margot leads me to the second floor and Tom follows behind us like a shadow, silent and a bit creepy.

The entire mansion is.

Despite the elegant wallpaper that's fit for a royal palace and the golden ornaments attached to the ceilings, something is off about this place.

Your sister got depressed and died here.

That's probably it.

Besides, the King mansion doesn't have Alicia's touch. At all.

Her only visible interference here is the angel statues outside. The inside, while it hints at a refined taste, is all Jonathan—rugged edges and authoritative masculinity.

This place isn't just meant to impress, it's also meant to intimidate. When you walk these halls, you sign an imaginary pact to do whatever the tyrant of the house demands.

Margot stops in front of a room and motions for Tom to go inside. He places the suitcase at the entrance, nods, and leaves.

The room is so large, it almost takes up an entire floor. An elegant queen-sized bed sits on a high platform in a classic way with a modern touch. The balcony is open, which allows the light-coloured curtains to flap inside.

There's also a desk and a small sitting area.

"This will be your room. Breakfasts are at seven-thirty. No lunches on workdays and dinners are at eight."

"I don't eat breakfast."

She throws me a weird glance like I murdered a puppy or something. What's so hard about not eating breakfast? All I need is coffee and I get that on my way to work.

Seeming to let it go, Margot resumes speaking in her impersonal tone. "You're not allowed on the third floor."

"Why not?"

"Mr King's orders."

"If he has orders, he needs to tell me himself."

She pins me with a stare for a long time, as if not believing I've just said that. Then she says in the same tone, "If you need anything, you can hit 'one' on any phone in the house. Dinner will be served in an hour." She nods, turning to leave.

"Wait."

She glimpses at me without saying anything.

"Where was Alicia's room? Her and Jonathan's, I mean." I realise I'm implying that Margot has been here since Alicia's times. She appears as old as Jonathan, if not older, so I assume she's been working for him all this time.

"On the third floor. The one you're forbidden to go to, Miss." She pauses. "And Mrs King didn't share a room with Mr King."

With that, she's out the door.

Her words float in the air like an invisible halo.

Did she just say Alicia and Jonathan didn't share a room? But why? They had Aiden, so naturally, they must have had sex. And they weren't that old to opt for separate bedrooms.

What the hell was going on in your life, Alicia?

The more I learn about her, the more shame I feel for not taking the time to get to know her as much as she knew me.

True, I was too young and focused on something more sinister, but that doesn't give me the right to believe Alicia was all that she showed to be on the outside.

Ignoring Margot's warning, I leave the room and head to the staircase we took earlier. There's another set of marble stairs that lead to the third floor.

At first, I keep glancing behind my back, expecting Margot to show up and drag me down by the hair.

I shake my head at that image. Not everyone is the devil from my past.

No idea why Jonathan didn't give me a room here, considering the floor is similar to the second one. Why do I feel like he likes to feel superior, even when it comes to the bedroom I'll be staying in?

I try the first door, but it's locked. Who the hell locks a door in his own house? Or did he do this because I'll be here from now on?

The fact that it's locked bugs me.

When I was young, I loved riddles, puzzles, and figuring out solutions. I used to love staking out, holding my breath, and waiting for prey to come out of their hiding places.

He taught me those things. The devil.

I followed him without knowing what he was capable of. I followed him because I trusted him, and that was the biggest mistake of my existence.

After he disappeared from my life, it took me so long to rid myself of habits associated with him, such as my love for puzzles and riddles. I erased every habit he'd brainwashed into me, I stopped believing in things I'd thought were a given, like love, care, and even puzzles.

Eleven years later, I still feel out of sorts when there's a puzzle that I can't solve. Like right now.

The locked door is a puzzle I have to walk away from.

Again.

With a deep breath, I go to the next door. It's a conference room. Bloody hell. Does the tyrant bring his entire office here?

The next is a reception area with high back chesterfield sofas and a massive golden chandelier hanging from the ceiling.

The moment I open the following room, it hits me.

Her scent. It's like summer breeze and marshmallow. Vanilla, lemon, and brightness.

It's crazy how I remember Alicia's smell eleven years later, and how I can smell it here, even though she's been gone for a long time.

Sweat trickles down my back and my hands shake as I release the doorknob and stroll inside. The room is clean, but all the furniture is covered with white sheets.

Like a coffin.

I never got the chance to say goodbye to her at her funeral. I never got to say goodbye at all.

My legs barely carry me as I run my fingers over the angel statues on her console. I open the first drawer, the sound echoing in the silence. Her elegant jewellery and makeup are tucked neatly in there.

I go to her wardrobe and it's full of her clothes. The fashion is eleven years outdated, but it's posh and refined, like everything about Alicia. I hug a dress to my face and inhale it. It doesn't have her scent.

It's faded away, vanished. Just like her.

A tear slides from my cheek and wets the cloth. I hang it back where I found it and close the wardrobe.

I move to her bed, where a few books sit on her bedside table.

There's no dust on them. Like the entire room, they're cleaned and taken care of. The pages have turned yellowish though.

The three books are black with a bold white font for the title.

Six Minutes.

Seven Bodies.

Eight Funerals.

The author is someone named Allen B. Thomas.

I don't really read thrillers, so I have no idea who that is.

Opening the first book, I'm struck by the dedication page.

To my muse,

May every muse be like you.

It's circled over and over with a red pen.

Was this Alicia?

The word 'muse' causes a premonition to hit me. Someone else used to call me that, and I still can't figure out the meaning behind it.

I check the other two books. Both of their dedications are also circled in red.

The second book's dedication is:

To my muse,
My reason for living.

The third book's:

To my muse,
See you in hell.

Sitting cross-legged on the floor, I open the three books and stare at them splayed out in front of me.

The way they were circled is aggressive, forceful even, to the point it's left a mark at the back of each page.

There must be a reason why Alicia did this. What was she trying to communicate?

I start reading the first book.

The language is chilling, horror-film like. The prologue is about someone digging holes into the earth.

I pause reading, my fingers shaking, and trickles of cold perspiration glues my blouse to my back. Taking a deep breath, I continue.

The digging goes on and on. The thoughts of the person who's doing the digging tighten my stomach and brings acute nausea to the back of my throat.

The memories I've spent so long burying rush to the surface like a demon snapping out of its chains. My head fills with dark, sinister images. The black dirt. The vacant eyes. The —

"What are you doing here?"

I startle, a yelp falling from my lips as I slam the book shut.

Fuck.

Jonathan towers over my sitting position, a hand tucked in the pocket of his trousers and his metallic gaze pinning me with utter disapproval.

Jonathan. It's just Jonathan.

I don't know why I felt like the character from the book would jump out from the pages and strangle me.

Or drag me to one of those holes he was digging up.

"You scared me," I breathe out.

"So you realise you're doing something wrong. Otherwise, you wouldn't be scared." The disregard in his tone throws me off.

It's almost like a completely different man from the one who pushed my buttons until I unravelled all over his lap.

The man who made me *feel* after I'd come to the acceptance that I never would in this lifetime.

I hate him for it, and I'll never forgive him for resurrecting that part back to life without my approval.

"Do you have trouble following instructions, wild one?"

"What?"

"Margot must've told you not to come up here."

I stand, steady my breathing, and grab the books from the floor and place them back on the bedside table. "I don't see what the big deal is."

"I do not care for being defied, Aurora. Is that understood?"

"Then you shouldn't have gotten me."

He grabs me by the arm and spins me around so fast, I gasp as I crash into his chest, my hand landing on his shoulder for balance.

Jonathan stares down at me with darkness so tangible, I can feel the smoke emanating from him and surrounding me in a halo.

That's what Jonathan is—smoke. You can't grasp him or escape him. The moment you think you're safe, he comes out of nowhere and thickens with the intent of suffocating you.

"I have already said this and it's the final time I'll repeat it. If I ask a question, I expect a direct answer."

"And if I have none?" My voice is breathy, small, *wrong*.

Damn you, voice.

"Then —" he reaches his other hand and grabs my arse cheek "— I'll spank this arse."

98 | RINA KENT

I instinctively push against him. Memories from last night flash
before my eyes and it takes all my will to hold in the foreign sound
fighting to get free.

"Now, is that fucking understood?"

"Yes," I mutter so he'll let me go.

It's not about being spanked, it's about the damn pulsing between my legs since he touched me or the promise that he'll repeat
what happened last night.

It's about how I can't stop thinking about the same fingers that
are now clutching my wrist being inside me. Or that veiny, strong
hand coming down on my soft flesh.

"Good girl." Jonathan lets my arm fall and I step back on damn
wobbly feet.

Why the hell did he have to say those two words using that
raspy tone? He's toying with parts of me I didn't even think could
be toyed with.

"I'm *not* a girl."

His lips twitch, almost as if he's about to smile, but Jonathan
doesn't do those. Not really. "Yes, you are."

"I'm twenty-seven." I don't know why I need that information
out there.

Maybe it's my brain's way to remind me that he's seventeen
years older than me.

Or that my sister, the only person I still consider family, had
him first.

Or that we're in her room.

The fact that Jonathan kept her room as it was without at-
tempting to get rid of anything means one thing: he's not over her
death.

That's why he wants me. I'm his sick way of bringing Alicia
back to life.

I hate him for putting me in this position.

I hate him for barging through doors even I didn't have the
keys to.

Most of all, I hate *him*. The man. The tyrant. The unfeeling bastard who couldn't protect Alicia.

"I know your age." He slips his hand back in his pocket. "I also know you've been a ghost since you were sixteen."

I thin my lips even when my scar tingles underneath my clothes.

"How does it feel to be a ghost, Aurora?"

"Peaceful."

"Is that how you spell fake?"

"I'm not fake."

"Is that why you invented a whole new persona, new name, new background, and even new habits?"

"Do you have a point here?"

"Does your black belt friend know about Clarissa?"

"Don't you dare, Jonathan."

"I do not care for being threatened, so for that alone, I might drop in unannounced and tell her."

"Jonathan...d-don't..." I'm ready to beg him, but I know that won't work. Layla and her family need to stay the fuck away from my past. I can't counter their kindness with malice.

"She's a Muslim, no? Do you know their take on murderers and accomplices?"

"I'm *not* an accomplice."

"Then what are you?" His voice drops in range. "Why did you disappear?"

"Because I needed a rebirth."

SEVENTEEN

Jonathan

A REBIRTH.

Fascinating.

I stare down at Aurora's defiant gaze, but I don't see the façade she's spent so long perfecting.

I don't see her stand-offish reaction to me or how she challenges me like it's her favourite sport.

Now, I see the girl who hid behind her sister's dress. The girl who was innocent and then was tarnished so badly that she wished for a rebirth.

But she didn't only wish for it. She made it happen.

Or so she thinks.

Even as a grown-up, there's still a spark in Aurora's eyes. Granted, it's not the same as the brightness of that little girl's. It's almost like an update—a second version of sorts.

She thinks she's had a rebirth, though.

That is fascinating.

People's misconceptions about themselves or the world surrounding them is a form of weakness I latch onto without mercy.

But this one?

This one will be more interesting to explore. I'm going to dig my fingers into Aurora and unravel her thread by each tangled thread.

It started with my hand on her soft skin last night, and what soft skin it was. My cock twitches at the remembrance of my red handprint on her pale flesh and how she held on to me as her body proved to be the opposite of dead.

This will end with her falling at her knees in front of me.

Willingly. Without a fight.

"Have you paid your debts, Aurora?"

She straightens, her long, delicate throat turning rigid with the motion. A throat that will have my hand wrapped around it soon. "Debts?"

"Surely you know that even with rebirths, the current life carries the legacy of previous lives. It's called karma. If you screwed someone over, you'll pay in full during the following life."

"You...you believe in rebirths?" Her full lips part. They're still not red, but the pink colour coupled with the hitching of her breath sends energy straight to my groin.

My dick strains against the confines of my trousers, demanding to thrust inside that mouth and fuck those lips. Since he didn't get his turn last night, it's making him even more riled up.

Soon, though.

I'll keep reviving that dead body and watch it fall apart by my own hands.

That's my form of rebirth.

"*You* do," I say. "I'm explaining it from your perspective."

She lifts her chin, but it trembles as she speaks, "I've done nothing to pay for."

Guilt. Fascinating again.

She feels guilty. But for what? For taking a stand? Does she regret being the reason she had to disappear?

Aurora Harper is nothing as she seems, and I'll take my sweet time breaking her apart and peering inside that well-strapped armour.

"Dinner time." I turn around and leave.

I need out of this room.

It should've been destroyed a long time ago, but I kept it as a reminder of what it feels like to lose.

Since then, all I've ever done is win.

Aurora follows soon after. From my peripheral vision, I catch a glance of her gazing at the door of Alicia's room with a nostalgic, almost tearful expression.

After rebirth, people tend to never look back. To pretend like they're newly born.

Not Aurora.

Her past has grown roots so deep, she couldn't get rid of them even if she tried.

And for that reason, I'll dig them up one by one.

Sure, I could've come with more underhanded methods. Threatening her company and her best friend could be only the beginning.

If I choose to, I could crush her and watch her wither to nothing at my feet.

But where's the fun in that?

Besides, I've grown to like the slight spark in her ocean eyes when she decides to challenge me, or the grumpiness whenever she begrudgingly agrees to my demands.

Falling under my influence will come naturally to her. Eventually.

In the dining room, I sit at the head of the table and she takes what's usually Levi's seat on my left.

That punk will throw a fit if he sees someone else in his place, but it's not like he ever shows up anymore.

For long seconds, Aurora and I eat our *spaghetti à la carbonara* in silence. Or, more accurately, *I* eat. She picks at her food, twirling the pasta around her fork, but barely brings anything to her mouth.

She did the same last night. I thought it was because she was nervous or out of sorts. Turns out, it's a habit.

"Are all dinners going to be like this?" she finally asks, boredom clear in her tone.

"Like what?"

"Like a funeral home. I'm used to chatter and people. I usually have dinners at Layla's family restaurant, where everyone is speaking and discussing the latest news or just…talking."

"Talking without a reason is idiotic."

"Are you calling my friends idiotic?"

"You're the one who just did."

She narrows her eyes, that spark rushing to the surface with a vengeance, but she quickly smothers her expression. It's fast, almost imperceptible if I hadn't been focused on her face.

She might share Alicia's physical appearance, but she's nothing like her sister.

Aurora is a fire where Alicia was earth. Deep and silent and everyone could step on her.

Aurora would burn anyone before they even attempted to.

"Surely you usually talk about something. How about if Aiden were here?" I don't miss the way her voice lowers when she says his name.

Guilt. Again.

This time, I can guess why. The fact she didn't make an effort to meet her nephew before now is eating at her.

And because she was careless enough to show me that bit, all I can do is use it.

"Aiden and I don't talk during meals. Due to the absence of a motherly presence in his life, he grew up to be emotionally abnormal."

She slowly sets the fork down but doesn't release it, her pupils dilating. "Abnormal how?"

"Ask him."

She won't. Ever.

If anything, I suspect she'll do everything in her might to avoid him. That's what she did at his wedding. She didn't dare mention that she was his aunt.

Her grip tightens around her fork as if accumulating strength before she completely releases it. "Do you enjoy it?"

"Enjoy what?"

"Making people feel small."

"People tend to commit mistakes when they feel small."

But it's not like that with her.

Aurora is closed off in a way that makes it almost impossible to get to the centre of her. In order to do that, I have to exploit her weaknesses, one by each bloody one.

"You're a sociopath."

"And you're not eating."

"I'm not hungry. A certain presence has made me lose my appetite."

"Watch that attitude, Aurora."

She lifts her chin, even though I can see the fear in her gaze. "I'm just saying, food tastes better when I'm with many people."

"False. You spend most of the time talking, so you don't eat then either, but since many people are there, it goes unnoticed."

She glares at me, and this time, she doesn't attempt to hide her contempt. The fact that I can read her is throwing her off, and she has no way to express it but through glares.

"You will eat."

"And if I don't?"

"Do you prefer I make you?"

"I prefer you leave me alone."

"Either you eat or you bear the consequences. Be smart and choose your battles, wild one."

Aurora stares at me, her gaze calculating my words before her brain chooses to take the intelligent route. She's well aware that she can't win against me on this, so she might as well cut her losses now.

"Fine." She picks up her fork again.

"Not there."

Aurora lifts her head, brows creasing.

I tap my lap. "Over here."

EIGHTEEN

Aurora

"OVER THERE?" I MEAN TO SNAP, BUT MY VOICE COMES OUT low.

Why the hell do I sound turned on?

I'm *not*.

It doesn't matter that his suit jacket moulds to his body with the sitting position or that the slow way he eats with those veiny hands is like watching a food porn show or that—

"Do you have a problem following simple instructions, Aurora?"

"Don't you dare question my worth, Jonathan."

"Then come here. *Now*." The edge in his authoritative tone leaves no room for negotiation.

Now I know why people fall at his feet—willingly or unwillingly. He's the type of person you can't say no to.

Especially in my case when he has a metaphorical gun pointed at my chest.

Or that's what I tell myself as I throw the napkin on the table and walk to him with angry steps.

I ignore how my legs slightly shake or how, with every movement, friction builds at my core. The idea that he'll repeat yesterday wraps around my neck like a tight noose, only it's not strangling me. Or maybe it is, but it's not the hurtful type.

Far from it.

Goosebumps break on my skin as a sudden thought assaults me out of the blue. Will my arse be so sore that I'll feel it for the rest of the night? Or when I sit the next day?

My nipples tighten against my bra. I'm so glad it's padded enough that the evidence of my arousal isn't visible through my thin white shirt.

Snap out of it, Aurora.

Stopping a small distance away from him, I try to ignore his sensual scent and cross my arms over my chest. "I can't eat if I'm face down, genius."

"If you don't lose the attitude, you'll get that arse spanked so hard, you'll be able to feel my touch on your skin for fucking days."

My spine jerks at the dark promise in his words. Instead of repulsion, a rush of heat invades me from head to toe. My scalp tingles and my feet wobble as if the world is about to drop me off. My hand wraps around my watch on my wrist to root myself in place.

His lips twitch as he tilts his head to the side. "You want that."

"I do *not*."

"Do you crave that sting of pain, wild one? Did your first taste turn you into an addict?"

"I said I don't."

"The reddening of your cheeks, the parting of your lips, and the way you keep touching your watch say otherwise. If you don't want to be so readable, school your reactions. Your tells are a sure way to have your weaknesses exploited."

Damn him. How come no one's attempted to kill this man before? It's been less than a week since I've been caught in his orbit and I already have the urge to strangle the life out of him.

"Because of your attitude, I won't give you what you want." He taps his lap. "Now, sit down."

I ignore the pang of disappointment settling at the bottom of my stomach as I lower myself to his lap. Despite the hardness of his thighs, the position isn't as uncomfortable as I originally thought it would be.

The only thing I can't get out of my head is the way his woodsy scent envelops me. It's like smoke, thick and impenetrable. In this position, he's engulfing me with his massive build. We're so close that his warm breaths trickle on the sensitive skin of my nape, eliciting a shudder down my spine.

Damn.

I didn't sign up for this intimacy. Sure, I knew he'd eventually fuck me, but the games and the push and pull are beyond anything I've experienced before.

How could he get me into a puddle of foreign emotions by just making me sit on his damn lap?

"Now, eat," he orders, his ferocious gaze never leaving my face.

There's something about the way Jonathan speaks that gets to me. All the way to my bones. His voice is that of a ruler, a warlord, or anyone who's out for destruction.

But at the same time, his authoritative tone causes my thighs to clench. The strength in it creeps under my skin and grips me by the throat.

Not making eye contact, I motion at the plate. When I speak, my voice is still in that foreign breathy range. "I don't have my utensils."

"Use mine."

"But —"

"Don't make me repeat myself. I do not like it and neither would you." The rumble of his voice so close to my ear tempts me to close my eyes so that I can get lost in it for a moment.

Instead, I grab the fork, thankful my hand doesn't shake as I twirl spaghetti around it and take a bite. Although I'm chewing, I barely taste anything.

It's impossible to.

All my senses are homed in on the warmth radiating off Jonathan's chest at my back and his thighs underneath my arse. The burn from last night revives, pulsing with the need for...what? More? What the hell is wrong with me?

"Eat," he enunciates. "And don't stop."

I take another forkful, trying to ignore him by focusing on the food.

Jonathan's fingers latch on the buttons of my blouse and he undoes them until he reveals the skin below my bra. He runs his long fingers across my pale skin with cruel gentleness.

"Lace today," he muses. "No ugly purple this time?"

"What are you doing?" I hate the neediness and the confusion in my tone.

"Keep eating."

"I-I'm already eating."

"You're not doing it enough."

"How about you? Aren't you going to eat?"

"Who said I'm not? I'm having you for dinner."

The chilling tone sends zaps of a foreign sensation down my back. Before I can focus on that, Jonathan wraps his hand around my throat, his long index finger pressing on the hollow skin. It's not hard, but it's firm enough to confiscate my attention.

My pulse skyrockets under his touch and something utterly strange happens as he glides his thumb on my pulse point, threatening to choke me, but not exactly going that far.

My underwear.

It feels slick.

Holy. Shit.

He didn't even inflict pain, right? And yet here I am, already delirious with a pleasure I can't wrap my mind around.

"Every time you make me repeat myself, you'll be punished.

Every time you show attitude, you'll also be punished. I have no tolerance for disobedience." His free hand reaches to my bra and yanks it down, exposing my breasts. He pinches my already taut nipple. "But I already told you that, didn't I?"

I gasp, nearly dropping my fork.

As if my reaction falls on deaf ears, he runs his finger over the assaulted nipple before twisting it again.

"Jonathan..." My moan echoes in the silence of the room like a mantra.

"You're not eating." His voice drops in range as his thumb squeezes on the pulse point in my throat. "If you don't, I'll stop."

I lift my next forkful, not even sure if I got food on it or not, and shove it in my mouth.

My hands are flat out shaking as he continues his assault on my nipple. No idea how Jonathan does it. All I know is that I've never felt this before.

I've never craved something as much as I'm burning for the foreign sensations he's injecting into my body.

I've never craved someone I hate so much.

Jonathan angles my body using my throat so my back meets the hard ridges of his chest. My breasts thrust in his face and he wraps his lips around a nipple. His slight stubble creates throbbing friction as he sucks and bites down on the tender flesh. His fingers continue torturing my other nipple while his other hand holds my throat hostage.

I shudder, the fork clinking on the plate as a thousand sparks hit me in the womb.

His movements come to a halt as he speaks in a raspy voice against my skin, "What did I say?"

I quickly pick up the fork, feeling like a kid learning how to eat as I roll the spaghetti on the tines.

The assault on my nipple turns me delirious. My core is slick and pulsing, close to the detonation point I reached last night, but not exactly.

"These are quite sensitive, aren't they?" He slides his tongue back and forth on the rosy peak. "Does it hurt?"

I'm munching slowly so I don't choke on the food, but I manage a nod.

"It does, doesn't it?"

I nod again, not even sure why I'm doing it.

"But it's not enough. You want more."

I stare at him with a wildness that beats under my skin like an animal's. Does he have telepathic powers?

Jonathan releases my nipple and slides his hand down my stomach over my dishevelled, barely buttoned blouse.

I suck in a fractured breath, but I make sure to take another bite of food. This is so fucked up, but I have no will to stop it.

I'm caught, hook, line and sinker. Instead of fighting and dying soon, I opt to enjoy one last swim.

Jonathan reaches into my skirt and underneath my underwear. His long, masculine fingers leave scorching hot trails on my bare skin as he circles my clit.

"Mmm. You're wet." His appreciative tone makes me close my eyes in pure bliss.

I've never, *ever*, tried to be wet for someone before. I recognised my numbness and rolled with it. If anything, I thrived in it. This is the first time I'm glad I am.

Am I a masochist or something?

Jonathan pinches my nipple and swollen clit at the same time.

There's no warning this time. No danger alarm or even the contracting of my stomach. Heat drags me into its burning clutches. I scream and explode all over his hand as if it was always meant to be.

This fall is like bungee jumping without a rope, yet it feels like the jump of a lifetime. One I'll never return from.

Oh, God.

I'm still catching my breath, trying and failing to regulate it when Jonathan releases my throat and motions at the plate. It's empty. Just like my insides.

The bastard manipulated me into eating it all.

"Good girl." He smirks, then pushes me off him so I'm sitting on the chair, stands, and leaves.

I remain there, my clothes rumpled, my core pulsing, and my nipples aching.

And yet, all I want is more.

I'm so screwed.

NINETEEN

Aurora

DID I SAY I COULD SURVIVE SIX MONTHS IN JONATHAN'S COMPANY?
It's only been two weeks and I'm already at my wits' end.

Every day, I've gone back to the house, shaking in anticipation of what he'll do next. What buttons he'll push. What ludicrous demands he'll make.

Every dinner and breakfast, Jonathan sits me on his lap and makes me eat my entire plate.

It's not even about the food anymore.

The way he touches me so unapologetically, or spanks my arse when I defy him, has become a habit. Worse, it's become something I look forward to.

I shouldn't.

Jonathan isn't the type of man I can get lost in or even allow close.

However, the moment he yanks me down on his lap, I don't even protest anymore.

It's become the most natural place to be.

After every session of fingering, torturing my nipples, and

holding my throat hostage, Jonathan leaves me in the dining room alone with my scattered thoughts and my shaking limbs.

Sometimes, he'll fetch me from my room when I'm late for breakfast, or lay me on the bed and spank me for giving him the attitude he hates so much.

Other times, he'll send me emails—no texts, because in his words, those are juvenile. The last exchanges were between last night and this morning.

From: Jonathan King
To: Aurora Harper
Subject: I'll be Late but Don't You Dare Sleep
Lie on your bed, face down, and don't put any clothes on.

From: Jonathan King
To: Aurora Harper
Subject: Second Reminder to Not Fall Asleep
You better be on your fucking stomach when I walk in, or that arse will pay the price.

I did fall asleep, more out of defiance than actually being tired, and my arse did pay the price before he wrenched a dizzying orgasm out of me that knocked me out for real.

Today, I woke up late because of how exhausted I felt.

From: Jonathan King
To: Aurora Harper
Subject: Your Morning Will Take a Turn for The Worse in Exactly Sixty Seconds.
Every minute you're late for breakfast is extra punishment. In case you want to sit at all today, come down. Now.

I went down, ten minutes late, and true to his word, I'm sitting sideways to not put pressure on my arse.

In no time, I've grown attached to his emails and the orders in them. The way he demands my attention and confiscates it as if it's always been his for the taking.

It doesn't help that I hear his commanding voice when reading them. Jonathan's authority is one of the few things I'll freely admit is attractive.

There's something about a man who takes what he wants with powerful self-assurance. I've always known I had a tendency to connect with dangerous men, but this is the worst possible scenario to practise that.

Other than the email exchanges and the power games, it's almost like we're living completely separate lives. Jonathan never invites me to his room or spends the night in mine.

And I'm thankful for that. After all the sexual stimulation and the explosive orgasms he coerces out of me, I need some time alone to come down from the high and the guilt trip I always find myself drowning in.

The shame of enjoying his touch when I shouldn't, and the reality of what Jonathan actually is always slams into me afterwards.

So to make myself forget about that, I've been sneaking into Alicia's room whenever he's not here—and behind Margot's back. She's as stand-offish as her tyrant master. The butler, Tom, doesn't speak either. Seriously. If I hadn't heard him ask Margot about something once, I would've suspected he was a mute.

There's also Harris, who joins Jonathan in his office or sometimes interrupts our breakfasts with a snobbish expression smearing on his face. He's the man in smart glasses who came with Jonathan to our office that first day. His bland eyes have the same disregard for humans as his CEO.

I swear the tyrant handpicks those who orbit his haughty arse so that they're an extension of him.

Anyway, my snooping in Alicia's room hasn't been useful. I can't bring myself to continue reading those books either. I just…can't.

The moment I open them, I get dark flashbacks filled with

vacant eyes and duct tape. There's a reason I don't read thrillers and keep to chick lit. I spent a long time slamming Pandora's box shut, and I can't willingly open it again.

Not that Jonathan would leave evidence behind. Next up, I need to go into that locked room, which I assume is his office.

I haven't mustered the courage to go up there when he's home. I might enjoy the spanking and how my arse feels afterwards, even now, but I'm not stupid enough to purposefully bring out his wrath.

Self-preservation has always been my strength.

Besides, the more time I spend in his company, the more anxious I get about why he's not taking the next step.

Jonathan has never tried to fuck me. Not even once. He seems content with owning my body, then turning it against me in the most brutal way possible.

Whenever I sit on his lap, I feel his hard-on, but he's never acted on it.

Not that I want him to.

I *don't*.

It's just that the unknown is keeping me on my toes.

"Earth to Aurora!"

I startle, biting my lower lip and the pen. *Ouch!*

I'm on the sofa, looking at proofs of the designs. Or *was*. Until I got lost in my head.

Layla slides an iced coffee in front of me and takes a long slurp of hers. Her baggy trousers fall all around her as she sits opposite me, knees splayed wide apart, and leans her elbows on her thighs.

That's the same position her army brothers sit in when they're in town. She's such a tomboy, and the most adorable thing is that she doesn't even notice it. When I call her out on it, she thinks I've lost my mind.

"Okay, shoot."

I take a sip of my coffee. "What?"

"Talk to me, mate. I'm all ears."

"About what?"

"About what you've been daydreaming about lately."

"Me?"

"Yes, you. Since you moved in with Johnny, you've been distant and often get lost in that pretty little head of yours."

"I have not."

"You have, too. He's consuming you, isn't he?"

"No. Maybe. I don't know." I sigh and push the proofs away. I'm not focused enough to do a good job at it anyway, so I might as well stop pretending. "Hey, Lay, can I ask you something?"

"I'm your man. Shoot."

"I know you're saving your virginity for marriage, but you know stuff about stuff. Being nosy and all." Layla's mum, her aunts, cousins and extended family—which is *huge*—are really forthcoming about sex, but only with their female friends and family.

I might have had sex before, but Layla knows more about it than I ever will. She's an encyclopaedia in practically everything.

"First of all, suck my D. Second of all, I'm not nosy. I like to know things so I'm prepared."

"Okay, fine. So my question is…" I trail off, wetting my lips.

"Any day now."

"What does it mean if a man only likes oral?"

"He needs Viagra. Wait a second, Johnny needs Viagra? Way to ruin my daddy fantasy. Hey, what do you think his reaction will be if I mail him a pack?"

I burst out laughing. "Don't do that."

"Why not? I'm giving the man a boost. If anything, he should thank me."

"It's not like that. He does get…you know…hard."

"Then his performance must be rubbish."

"I don't think so."

"I actually don't think so either."

"What do you mean?"

"He seems like the type of man who commands everything, even in the bedroom. Control is his kink."

She can say that again.

Layla drinks her coffee, seeming deep in thought. "How about you ruin it?"

I pause with the straw halfway to my mouth. "Ruin what?"

"His control. People like Jonathan get off on knowing the result before they even go in, so when you destroy that pattern, they act out, either by showing their ugly side or their hidden side. Both are their true selves."

"I do defy him. It's not always 'yes, sir' or 'whatever you wish, sir.'"

"That's probably not enough to warrant him acting out."

"How do I know I've pushed him enough? He's so unemotional, it drives me insane."

"Remember that day when he barged in here to announce that this company was now his property in front of Ethan Steel? That was his reaction to the way you pushed him."

It was. Jonathan said he'd put me in my place, and he did, ever so savagely.

"So you're saying Ethan is a key to Jonathan's ugly or hidden side."

"Could be. Do you know their history?"

"If I recall correctly, they were best friends who turned into rivals as their respective companies grew simultaneously. Then a few years ago, they fell from each other's graces. Ethan went into a coma and recently returned to the scene. The entire time, Jonathan has been ruling on his own."

"That's common knowledge, but I have the inside scoop." She grins like a Cheshire cat.

"Inside scoop?"

"My friend's cousin used to work in the Steel mansion in Birmingham—you know, his main residence aside from the one in London. Anyway, while you were targeting Ethan, I asked around about his history, and apparently, Jonathan caused the death of Ethan's wife. Some even say it was an affair, but no one confirms that."

"Oh my God."

"I know, right? Why would she want Jonathan when she has Ethan? Sister didn't know what she had."

"Lay, be serious."

"I am. Ethan is better looking than Jonathan, and he doesn't have *Bastard* written in bold letters on his forehead."

Ethan is handsome, but he doesn't have the lethal edge Jonathan does. His eyes aren't a storm brewing in the distance, threatening to take everyone hostage.

I shake my head. Did I just defend Jonathan? That's not allowed, even in my mind.

"Anyway, Ethan is Daddy in another universe."

"Lay!"

"What? You get your daddy. Why can't I fantasise about mine?"

"Bugger off, you twat."

"Fine, fine. Live the daddy fantasy for both of us."

"I'm not!"

She stands up, but before leaving, she cups her mouth with both hands and whispers, "*Daddy.*"

I throw a pen after her and her throaty laughter echoes down the hall.

Shaking my head, I focus back on the design I was working on. Something about it is bugging me, but I can't put my finger on it.

My hand finds my watch and a sense of calm engulfs me. Alicia's memory has always calmed me down and filled me with so much inspiration.

There's a knock on the door, and I expect Layla to be back for more taunts, but then I recall she doesn't knock. And neither do I.

We haven't had any boundaries since we met at uni—aside from the past that I'm shielding her away from.

Jessica, my assistant, appears at the threshold. She's petite with dark brown skin and huge, striking eyes. "Ms Harper, there's someone here to see you."

"I thought I didn't have any appointments until this afternoon."

"Yes, but he said it's urgent. He's a solicitor."

"Let him in." Could this be another one of Jonathan's games?

Jessica disappears. Soon after, a middle-aged man with dark brown hair and pale hazel eyes appears at my door. I stand and take his hand as he offers a handshake.

"Aurora Harper. How may I help you?"

"Stephan Wayne. I'm Maxim Griffin's solicitor."

I retrieve my hand from his at supersonic speed, as if I've been hit by lightning. My breathing catches; it takes everything in me not to collapse or run and hide.

"How...how did you find me?"

"It wasn't an easy thing to do, but blood speaks, Ms Griffin."

"My name is Aurora Harper."

"Why, yes." His expression remains unchanged as he motions at the sofa. "Aren't you going to offer me a seat?"

"Get out of my office. *Now.*"

"That's very unfortunate, Ms Harper. I was hoping to get you on the witness stand for Mr Griffin's parole hearing."

This time, I stumble backwards. I nearly fall on the sofa but manage to hold myself up at the last minute. My legs shake so prominently, I can't contain my stance or my emotions.

My worst nightmare rushes to the forefront of my mind, as if it's been lurking right beneath the surface all along.

Vacant Eyes.

Blood.

Duct tape.

The look of absolute desolation.

No. Not again. No.

"He's not eligible for parole." My voice is barely audible.

"The judge changed his mind for exemplary behaviour."

This can't be true.

This is a nightmare.

My heart beats loud and fast. I'm that girl running in the forest, my breathing constricted, my lungs suffocating, my head about to snap from the pain.

He's coming.

He's there.

They are also there.

"Ms Harper."

My head snaps up to meet the solicitor's gaze.

"Are you sure you won't change your mind? If you tell the judge you were young and confused —"

"I wasn't young and confused. I saw a monster for who he is and acted on it. Now, leave my office and never return again." My throat hurts from the force of my words. "You should be ashamed for defending a man like him. Those women could've been your daughter, your wife, your sister."

Stephan's expression doesn't change as he reaches into his jacket and retrieves an envelope and a business card. When I don't take them, he places them on the table. "Call me if you change your mind."

As soon as he leaves, I drop onto the sofa, my hands and legs trembling, sweat running down my back and temples.

My heart aches and I feel like I'm about to combust.

I pull my knees to my chest as memories start trickling back in. The attacks. The slurs.

The assault.

No. Please no.

The envelope stares at me. I know who it's from. I contemplate burning it, throwing it away, but the need to solve the puzzle strikes me again.

And this time, I can't ignore it.

I open it with unsteady fingers. Plain white paper with his messy handwriting taunts me.

Remember Muse,

Next time we see each other, either I kill you or you kill me.

TWENTY

Aurora

I LEAVE WORK EARLY.

But I don't go to Jonathan's house.

In fact, for a second, I contemplate driving my car to some-place else.

I could go to Wales. Or Scotland.

If that's still too close, I can go to another country. Pick a place on the map and fly over there.

I can start anew. If I've already had one rebirth, I can have an-other, right?

Only, I can't leave H&H and Layla and everyone else behind.

I can't abandon the dream I started with my own hands. I can't keep running for the rest of my life.

When I walked out of the court hearing that day, I promised he'd never be the master of my life again.

He won't control my every breath as if he has a right to. As if he owns my life just because he gave it to me.

Every time someone looks at me, I breathe wrong. I watch my surroundings as if expecting the eggs, the slurs, the *assault*.

"*The devil's spawn.*"

"*Her father's daughter.*"

"*Murderer! Murderer! MURDERER!*"

I hit the brakes and place both hands on my ears as if that will stop the voices from screaming louder in my head.

My breathing is non-existent. My heartbeat escalates like a heavy weight is perched on my chest.

No.

No one will find me. They *can't*.

Just because the solicitor did, doesn't mean my past will come rushing back in.

It takes me several minutes to compose myself and drive to my flat. All the way there, I watch the rear-view mirror and over my shoulder, imagining a hand coming out of nowhere.

By the time I reach the reception area, I'm a hot mess of screwed up nerves. My head is crowded with the screams and the cries of the victims' families, and the way they asked me *why*.

I didn't even know myself. How could I answer them?

"Ms Harper." Paul in reception intercepts me, lowering the volume of the TV.

I come to a halt and plaster on a smile. "Hey, Paul. How are you?"

"Good. Have you moved out?"

"Yes, temporarily. I'm keeping the lease, though."

"I…see." He tips his lips up, but I don't miss the pause. "There's a new package for you."

My heartbeat skyrockets with something a lot different than the reason behind the solicitor's visit.

Alicia's voice message.

"Where is it?"

Paul retrieves a small box from under the counter like the other time.

I take it with a slight smile. "I'll drop by to check my mail, but can you call me whenever I get any others?"

"Definitely, Miss."

"Thank you so much, Paul." I motion at the empty sofa in an awkward attempt to make conversation. "No Shelby today?"

"He's not feeling well." His cockney accent is thicker than usual as he slides his gaze back to the Premier League football game on TV.

I thank him again and count the minutes until I'm in my flat. As soon as I'm inside, I shrug off my jacket, kick my shoes away, and run to my TV. I plug the flash drive in and press Play.

Like the other time, there's silence at the beginning before Alicia's voice trickles in.

"I lied to you, Claire, and I'm sorry. I know I shouldn't have, but I thought I was protecting you. I thought the only way to protect you was to keep you in the dark. Maybe that wasn't my brightest decision, but I want you to know how much it pains me to have one hair on your head hurt. I hope you forgive me for what I'm about to confess."

Her voice goes dead.

I skip ahead, but just like the other time, the recording is over. Damn it.

It's like whoever sent this is playing a distasteful joke on me.

I slump in front of my TV, the screen blank, and pull my knees to my chest.

What could she have meant about keeping me in the dark? Was it about the devil we both knew? Though Alicia hardly met him. She usually came to me at school, not at home.

Or is this about something else?

I honestly don't know anymore. I'm too emotionally drained and exhausted to gather any logical thought.

My limbs shake as I recall the solicitor's visit. Parole. He said fucking parole.

Surely *he* can't get paroled after only eleven years.

The dark cloud hovers over me and my fingers quiver as I pull my knees to my chest, grip my trousers, and remain in place like a statue.

That's what I did that day.

I wasn't sitting, but I was a statue.

You see, my love for puzzles was my damnation. I shouldn't have gone to the forest that day. I shouldn't have tried to figure out Dad's puzzle.

But I did.

I wore my hoodie, took my bike, and followed close behind, a bit like a detective. I felt so smug at the time, thinking I was Sherlock Holmes or something.

Thinking Dad wouldn't win this time.

He always said I was an extension of him, and because of that, he could read me better than anyone else.

I was going to prove that I could read him, too.

Or so I thought.

Past

Dad's truck slows to a halt behind a small cottage. Hmph. He thought he could come here without me right after the business trip he took this morning. Well, he has a surprise waiting for him.

It isn't the first time I've come here. This is where he keeps his tools.

Dad's a hunter and a mechanic. He likes tools.

Tomorrow, we'll go hunt again. I don't really like it when the rabbits and deer die, but I like the stalking, the chase, and the rush of adrenaline.

Daddy says I need to perfect my hunting methods so that I can hit the target like he does.

After all, Daddy is the best hunter alive.

The door of his truck opens and he gets out. I smile with mischief as I hide with my bike behind a tree.

Daddy is a big man with broad shoulders and long legs. He

has blond hair and a beard and blue eyes so deep, they're mesmer-
ising. All the women in town gush after my daddy.

But he's never wanted to bring me a mum. He decided early
on it was only going to be the two of us.

We do everything together. We run and hunt and solve puzzles. We cook together and even go to the local festivals side by side.

I never knew my mother, and Alicia doesn't visit often. Daddy
is my world, and as he always says, I'll grow up to make him proud.

Dad puts on his baseball cap and rounds the truck, then goes
inside the cottage.

Maybe he's having fun without me. How dare he? I don't have
fun without him. Well, except when Alicia is in town. She doesn't
like to come home with me. I think she still hates Daddy from when
he followed us to London on her wedding day and yanked me away.
She never comes home with me and tells me not to mention I visited.

I hate keeping things from Daddy, but I'm cool if it's for Alicia.

I leave my bike behind the tree and inch closer to the cottage
by using the trees as camouflage. By the time I'm a few metres away,
Dad re-emerges.

But he's not alone.

A limp woman lies at his feet as he drags her out. At first, I
don't understand what I'm seeing. Dad and a woman.

I mean, I know Daddy is popular with women and goes on
some dates, but he never introduces them to me. Why would he
bring them to the cottage that's supposed to be our basecamp?

It's when he drags her across the harsh ground and her head
lolls that I catch a glimpse of the woman's side view. Her head is all
strapped with silver duct tape except for the eyes, which are bulg-
ing, bloodshot, and vacant. They're looking at me, but they're seeing
straight through me. Her arms are limp and a trail of blood trickles
down her body, soaking the hem of her dirty pink dress.

I gasp and quickly cover my mouth with both hands. Dad stops
and spins around, planting his shovel in the ground.

For a moment, I think he sees me. I think he'll come over and catch me.

I remain frozen in place, not making a sound. I don't even breathe, but I can't control the tears that slide down my cheeks and moisten my fingers.

The face of the man I call Daddy every day is the same. His features are the same, those deep blue eyes and that blond beard. Everything I see is Dad.

And yet…he isn't.

And yet…he's dragging the body of a dead woman. I want to go there and scream, ask why, demand he explain, but I can't move, let alone go to him.

I remain planted behind the tree as I stare at the man I call Daddy. My father. My only family.

Instead, there's a devil in his place.

Dad whirls around, and the woman's head hits the ground, her hand lifelessly sliding behind her.

I think I'm going to throw up.

As soon as he's out of view, I run back towards my bike. I trip, fall, and stand up again. My knee stings and hot liquid trickles down my shin. My heart is about to beat free of its confinements, but I don't stop until I'm on the bike.

My legs quiver as I cycle through the forest Dad and I call our world.

His world is different from mine.

His world has duct tape and vacant eyes.

And blood. A lot of blood.

The need to puke my guts out assaults me again, and I nearly give in to it. But I don't.

I drown in the sound of the bike's tires and the crunching of the dry leaves and the fallen branches.

I don't look behind as I pedal the fastest I can. No idea what I'll do now. What if… What if Dad was helping her? What if —

I frantically shake my head at that thought.

The scene was clear. There's no mistaking that no matter how I flip it.

I halt at the edge of the road, catching my breath. My nails dig into my palms and I bite my lip as more tears soak my cheeks.

Dad is...

No. I can't say it.

I reach into my back pocket and retrieve my phone. Alicia. I need to call my sister. She'll tell me what to do.

The phone doesn't ring.

Damn it.

Wait. Now that I think about it, Alicia mentioned that her son, Aiden, is missing. Did something happen?

My thoughts jump all over the place, unable to stay in focus. The inability to think straight is paralysing. So much is going on in my brain and I couldn't comb through everything, even if I tried.

All I know is that I need to get in touch with my sister. I need to make sure her family is safe, and I need her to tell me what to do.

My fingers hover over the number titled 'Jonathan: Emergency Only.' Alicia said to only call him if it's a life or death situation and I'm unable to reach her.

This one definitely is.

My toes curl into my shoes as I hit the number and the phone rings. I haven't met Jonathan even once since the wedding nine years ago. Alicia comes to visit alone and we usually keep up through calls. When I tell her to FaceTime, she says that's for the younger generation, not her.

"Hello." A strong voice brings me out of my reverie.

"H-hey...I...I'm...Clarissa...A-Alicia's sister."

"I know who you are."

Oh. He remembers me. I don't know why I thought I had to explain myself some more.

"I-is Alicia there? I'm trying to reach her and..."

"She's dead."

REIGN OF A KING | 129

My heart nearly hits the ground for the second time today. "W-what?"

"The funeral is tomorrow. I expect you to be there."

The line goes dead.

My heart follows soon after.

He...can't mean what I think he does, right?

I call him again, but there's no answer.

No, no, no.

I flip open my browser and search Alicia King. That's what I usually do when I miss her. I study her pictures with Jonathan and their son on the internet from fundraisers and parties.

The results that enumerate in front of me aren't of those joyful events, though.

'Breaking News: Alicia King found dead after a tragic accident.'

'Jonathan King is a widower after the death of his wife, Alicia King.'

'An accident takes the life of Alicia King, Jonathan King's wife.'

The first droplets of rain hit my screen and more soon follow.

My legs abandon me and I drop to the ground as I see the pictures of Alicia's white car, the one she used to take me all over town with as we shopped and ate.

Then the images of a body covered in a white sheet appear.

The rain blurs my vision as I scroll through the articles, all from today.

Alicia is dead. My sister is dead.

No.

No...

Alicia. You can't leave me.

She promised we'd see each other more often if I chose to study in a university in London once I was eighteen.

I was counting the days, crossing them off my calendar until I got there.

A sob tears from my throat as a sense of grief sneaks up on me quietly and grips me in its clutches. All our moments together play like a distant song at the back of my head, and the fact that I've lost her forever engulfs me in a wave of darkness.

A bleak world.

A strangled heart.

This can't be happening.

Alicia can't be gone.

It's a lie. It *has* to be.

Still, my tears blind my eyes no matter how much I bargain with my head.

I stare up at the sky, at the stormy clouds and the pounding rain. At the howling wind in the trees and the desolate road.

That's how it feels inside. Barren. Hollow.

Wake me up, please. I can't breathe. Someone wake me up.

My phone vibrates and I startle as a picture of Dad lifting me in his arms on my sixteenth birthday flashes on the screen.

My Hero.

I named him my hero, but he never wore a superhero cape. Not even close.

I stare behind me, my tears coming to a screeching halt. I hop on my bike, throw my phone in the basket, and pedal down the road the fastest I can. The rain soaks me, my dark hair sticks to my forehead and my mouth, but I don't stop my high speed.

The phone flashes with a text from Dad.

My Hero: You were here, weren't you, my little muse?

Muse. That's what Dad calls me sometimes. When I asked him why he uses that nickname, he said it's because I inspire him to be a better man.

My breathing catches as I stare behind me. No one is following me, but I feel as if someone is.

The phone flashes again, and this time I do answer, putting it on speaker as I continue my escape.

"Clarissa." His suave, welcoming tone suffocates the air. The Yorkshire accent is barely there. "You know I don't like it when you don't answer my calls."

"W-why…? Tell me why, Dad."

"It's not what it seemed, Muse. Wait for me at home. We'll talk when I get back."

"Why, Dad?!" I shriek. "*Why?*"

"Because I can. I'll be there in a few."

The line is cut off. Just like that. It's completely cut off.

I open my mouth to scream, but it remains slack and nothing comes out. I contemplate pedalling straight off the edge of a cliff.

Maybe if I do, I won't feel Dad's betrayal and Alicia's loss.

Maybe I can erase today from my memories and I can call Alicia and she'll pick up. I can solve a puzzle with Dad and make him pizza afterwards and we'll binge-watch true crime on Netflix.

But driving myself over the edge won't solve anything.

It won't bring back life to the dead woman he drug across the ground.

I pedal all the way to the town centre, ignoring the screams of my exhausted leg muscles and the funny way people look at me. Some greet me, but I don't reply. I can't.

There are only a few words in my mouth, and none of them are meant to be said back as a greeting.

I stop in front of a shabby building, throw my bike aside, and forge in. I hesitate at the threshold, but then I recall Alicia's soft voice.

'*The silence of an accomplice is similar to committing the crime.*'

Alicia, whom I can't see again. Alicia, who was stolen from my life as if she never existed.

I barge inside and a few officers pause at my entrance. I must look like a mess, soaked in rain, my clothes glued to my skin, and my face must be pale, lips blue from the cold.

A black officer approaches me, his eyes firm but welcoming, "May I help you, Miss?"

"I…I want to report a murder."

TWENTY-ONE

Jonathan

AURORA ISN'T HOME WHEN I GET BACK.

She isn't answering her phone either. And my last email is still without a reply.

I'm not to be ignored. If she's throwing one of her fits or acting out, I'm going to take it out on her arse.

Only, she's not the type who throws a fit without a solid reason. This morning, she came all over my fingers after she licked her plate clean.

When I let her go, she smoothed her skirt and grumbled that she needed a change of clothes as she headed back to her room.

There was no need for a fit.

No matter how she feels wronged, Aurora realises how much she needs the touch only I can provide. She knows that she can't fight herself when it comes to me. The harder she denies it, the faster her body falls under my command.

There's euphoria in the way she falls, even when she doesn't want to. I'm slowly shaping her to be my perfect submissive, but at the same time, I don't want to extinguish her fire. I also don't want to erase the way she glares up at me every time she comes down from her high.

She hates that she can't resist of her trance when it comes to me. And because she can't do anything about it, she directs that hatred towards me.

I'm fine with it. As long as I have her in my grasp.

It started with the need to unravel her and the blasphemy of thinking she could keep a secret from me.

Now, it's more.

I don't even understand it myself, but I'm ready to see it until the very end.

Which brings me to her flat.

A quick inquiry with Harris told me all I needed to know. She had a visit from Maxim's solicitor and she escaped to here.

I hit in the code and go inside. The security came to ask who I am, but after a talk with Harris, who's now waiting for me in the car, he backed away.

The flat is dark except for the TV which shows a black screen but it's not turned off. An automatic light flashes at the entrance as I step inside.

Aurora's flat is medium-sized with countless pictures of watches on the walls. Her taste is mostly in black and white. Her sofas are black. Her walls are white. The hanged watches are black, the carpet is white.

The colour scheme hints at something different than her taste, highlighting her internal chaos.

At first, I don't see her, but then I make out a body curled into a foetal position on the floor.

I pause, trying to get a better view of the scene before me. Something inside me moves. No idea what it is, but it just moves.

I stride to her and crouch in front of her motionless body. I exhale deeply when I notice the rise and fall of her shoulders.

Her pale hands hold her knees to her chest, fingers twitching involuntarily and limbs spasming. Her black strands block her vision, so I lift them up with two fingers.

Aurora's eyes are screwed shut so tight, almost as if she's afraid to open them. Her lips are clamped in a line, her pink lipstick smudged. Mascara and dried tears cover her cheeks.

"Why…" she murmurs. "Why?"

It must be about Maxim. Is she having nightmares about him, or is she perhaps reliving certain memories?

"Aurora."

She doesn't even stir, so I shake her shoulder. For some reason, I don't want her trapped in that place. That place only injected her with suffering and pain.

"Aurora!"

Her eyes flutter open, but she doesn't see me, not really. It's almost like she's looking through me. The deep, dark blue of her irises are caught in a trance she can't force herself out of.

I run my fingers through her hair. "Come on, wild one. Come back."

She doesn't. For a moment, she stares ahead as if enchanted by something on the TV.

My fingers slide to her neck and I squeeze a little, increasing the pressure in small increments until she focuses on me.

She does, but her eyes aren't quite there. It's almost like she wants to see me but isn't able to do so.

"Alicia can't be gone. Not today." Her voice is brittle, haunted even. "She can't, Jonathan."

I wrap my arm around her back and she bunches my jacket in a lethal grip, her body shaking, breaths trembling.

It comes back to me then.

Aurora received the news of Alicia's death the day she reported her father's crimes. No idea why I haven't thought about that fact before.

All her tragedies happened in one day. One blow after the

other. She was only sixteen and didn't know what life was before it was snatched away from her.

No wonder she needed a rebirth.

Now that a part of her nightmares is back, she's been shoved back eleven years in the past.

I carry her in my arms and she snuggles into my hold, her body still shaking. Despite being considerably tall, she's light as a feather.

The way her curves mould into me feels natural and effortless. Like it was always meant to be.

A whimper tears out of her as she nuzzles her nose into my jacket. "Alicia…"

"She's not here, but I am. I'll always be here, wild one."

TWENTY-TWO

Aurora

"I'LL ALWAYS BE HERE."

Those words trickle in and out of my consciousness. Like a shadow you can see, but you can't touch.

By the time I open my eyes, I don't know whether what I'm seeing is real or a mere play of my screwed up imagination.

The first thing I notice is that I'm not in my flat lying on the floor, reliving my gruesome memories.

My room in Jonathan's house comes into view with its huge space and elegant ceiling. When did I get in here?

"You need to eat."

I startle into a sitting position and that's when I notice Jonathan seated on a chair opposite my bed.

He's in a pair of dark blue suit trousers and a white shirt with the sleeves rolled to his elbows. The top buttons of his shirt are undone, revealing the taut lines of his collarbone and hinting at his chest muscles.

That's the most skin I've ever seen from Jonathan, aside from his veiny arms. It's like he lives in a suit—or was born in one.

Not that he had to get nude before, all he needs is that firm hand to make me fall all over the place.

He's been focused on his phone, but now, he slides it in his pocket and lifts a bowl of soup from a tray on the bedside table.

"You brought me here?"

"Why ask a question you already know the answer to?"

Did he listen to Alicia's voice message? Worse, did he see me at my lowest on the floor?

"How…how did you get access to my flat?"

"I have my ways." He offers me the bowl. "Now, eat. You haven't had anything since this morning and it's nine in the evening."

How the hell does he know that? I don't bother asking, because he'll just say he has his ways again or bluntly ignore me.

My nose scrunches at the scent of food. "I'm not hungry."

If anything, nausea is about to hit me for no apparent reason.

"Is this part of your rebirth? Skipping meals?"

"So what if it is?"

"You cannot escape Maxim by stopping everything you used to do when you were with him. You do realise you're only fooling yourself, right?"

My nails sink into the duvet as black rage bubbles in my stomach. "You know nothing about me to say that, okay? Nothing! And I told you not to say his name."

"There, clear evidence that your rebirth never took off. If you're a mess after a meeting with his solicitor, how do you intend on facing him when he resurfaces? Because he will resurface, Aurora. If it's not with parole, then it'll be with something else. People like Maxim don't like to be pushed to the shadows. He'll steal the limelight and he'll come after you. So instead of running away from the ghost of his name, get your shit together. Flight mode never works, so you might want to start trying the fight mode."

My lips part as the weight of his words strikes a deep, dark corner in my chest. It's almost like he was with me during the years I looked over my shoulder, expecting the ghost of my past to catch up to me.

In fact, I still do. It's a curse without a solution.

Some of my nightmares are about vacant eyes, but most of them are about me pedalling down that road and I always, *always* get pulled back into the forest's clutches by a dark hand.

"Now, are you going to eat or would you rather I make you?"

I snatch the bowl from between his fingers and don't bother with a spoon. I drink it all in one go as if I'm chugging down alcohol.

Once I'm finished, I slam the empty bowl on the bedside table and wipe my mouth with the back of my hand. "There. Done, your majesty. Leave me alone."

"What did I say about that mouth, Aurora?"

"What are you going to do about it? Fuck me? Oh, wait. You only like to spank and finger me."

His expression shifts from disapproval to what seems like… amusement? "Does that bother you so much?"

My cheeks heat. "It does not."

"If it didn't, you wouldn't have mentioned it in an angry fit."

"You flatter yourself."

"Is that so?"

"I absolutely couldn't give two fucks about that."

"Fascinating." He stands up and I expect him to leave, but he unbuttons his shirt, slowly and with utter confidence.

"W-what are you doing?"

"What does it look like I'm doing?" He shrugs off his shirt and the urge to hide under the covers hits me without a warning.

Since I've never seen Jonathan naked, I don't know what to expect, but the firm chest with lean muscles is certainly not it. Who knew the prim and proper suits covered this view? But then again, Jonathan has always had rugged, brutal characteristics. Why would his nudity be any different?

He's so fit and well-built for his age. His skin is sun-kissed and honed to perfection. Almost as if God took extra care when he was proportioning him.

His fingers undo his belt and while I should look away, I don't. I'm glued to the unapologetic masculine beauty that is Jonathan King.

He slides his trousers down firm thighs, leaving him in black boxer briefs, and takes his time setting his clothes on the chair. It's almost like he's teasing me on purpose.

My spine snaps upright, and my toes curl underneath the sheet in anticipation of what's coming next. By the time he removes his boxer briefs, I'm ready to hide for real, for a different reason from earlier.

Holy. Shit.

His cock isn't only hard and thick, but it's also massive. No kidding, I've seen my fair share, but Jonathan wins the crown. Literally.

Oh God, does he expect to fit that *thing* in me or something? Even though being aroused is no longer a foreign concept to me, I don't think I could ever take him inside me.

Not in this lifetime, at least.

"Do you like what you see?"

I shake my head frantically, and I mean it. I might be in awe at his size, but I want to continue being in this phase while staying far apart.

Then why the hell are my thighs clenching?

Jonathan smiles, and the motion reaches his dark, stormy eyes, lightening them a bit.

Woah. I didn't know he could smile, let alone do it so lethally.

That smile could kill. It's not only the beauty in it. No. It's the sheer promise it carries.

"The reason I didn't fuck you is because I needed to get you ready, but since you want it so bad…"

"I don't." I meant for my voice to be firm, but it's similar to a moan.

What the hell is wrong with me? Do I…*want* this?

Before I can figure out an answer, Jonathan yanks the cover away. Now I have no defence line. Without his tailored clothes that somehow tame his raw self, he appears like the roguish predator he actually is. The slight stubble on his jaw gains a dark shadow within seconds.

He crawls atop me and undoes the buttons of my blouse, as slowly as he did his and with the same level of confidence.

It falls from my shoulder, exposing my black satin bra. Jonathan's fingers trail over the material, eliciting a shudder at the base of my spine.

"Next time, I want red. Like that lipstick." He snaps it open, pulls it off me, and throws it beside us.

I'm breathing so harshly, I'm surprised he doesn't notice. Every inch of my skin is attuned to his touch, and my entire body is homed in on his presence.

I take in his woodsy scent with every inhale and purge some of my inhibition with every exhale.

Somewhere in my mind, I recognise this is wrong, but I can't think of the reasons why right now. They're trapped, unreachable. Almost invisible.

He unbuttons my trousers and slides them down my legs, then throws them on top of the pile of clothes.

We sit opposite each other, completely naked. Or more like I'm sitting while he hovers over me like a dark promise in the middle of a moonless night.

"You're now the property of Jonathan King, wild one."

"I'm no one's property."

He narrows one of his eyes. "If you have nothing useful to say, shut that mouth."

"I mean it. I might have agreed to this deal, but you don't own me, Jonathan. No one does and no one ever will."

He grabs me by the hips and flips me over. I yelp as my front hits the mattress and he lifts my arse up in the air.

"I was going to give you what you crave and fuck you, but I changed my mind."

"W-what?"

His hand slaps my arse. Hard. I moan into the pillow, my voice wanton, even to my own ears.

"You'll beg for it."

"Screw you, Jonathan."

He spanks me again, this time circling a finger on my slick folds until a whimper escapes my throat. "Add a please and I might."

Ugh. Damn him.

His length slides up and down my wetness, slow and unhurried. The sheer confidence he exudes with his movements turn me into a puddle. My nails dig into the sheets, trying to find refuge in Jonathan, and failing miserably.

His assault continues, getting more ruthless by the second. The crown of his cock aligns with my entrance and I tense with anticipation, but he removes it all too soon.

He thumbs my clit just to back off.

He spanks me just to push me into the highest throes of lust.

The small bursts of excitement, arousal, and then disappointment hit me over and over again. I've never been this turned on in my entire life. It's torture in its deadliest form and all I want is more.

"I hate you," I mutter.

"But your cunt wants me." He glides his cock up and down my folds, teasing. "See how much it's soaking wet for me? I didn't even inflict any pain."

"Jonathan…" I whimper.

"Say the words, Aurora."

"I…ugh…"

"Those aren't it. Try again."

"J-just do it."

"Not quite there."

"Fuck me, you arsehole."

"And?"

"*P-please* —" the word catches in my throat as Jonathan thrusts inside me in one brutal go. Just like everything about him.

Holy…

My body bucks off the bed as he fills me in a way I never thought I could be filled. The stretching sensation leaves stinging pain that hurts so good. Our bodies aren't only joined, they're so absorbed in one another as if falling into an unknown dimension.

"Fuck." His long, masculine fingers with perfectly manicured nails savagely grip me by my hip. It feels so bare and weak under his grip. So vulnerable. That hand can bring me so much pleasure, but its price is always pain.

"Do you feel how your tight cunt traps me inside? It's made for me."

I want to tell him to shut up, but I can't speak. Besides, his dirty words tighten my nipples even more, which is almost impossible, considering they were already hard.

Jonathan pounds into me slow at first, rocking his hips in moderate circles. Then just when I get used to the rhythm, he picks up his pace.

It's so relentless that my body physically slides on the mattress. I soak in every thrust and every jerk of his hips.

Something inside me unlocks and a needy moan rips in the air. That's when I realise it's mine.

Jonathan wraps a fistful of my hair around his hand and pulls me up by it so that the slick warmth of his chest covers my back. The position is uncomfortable, but the angle of his cock gets deeper, hitting that most pleasurable spot inside me.

"Oh…oh…t-there…there…"

"Here?" He does it again and I nod frantically.

He slaps my arse, then reaches out with the same hand and closes it around my throat. "As much as you say you hate me, your body unravels around me, Aurora. This body is my fucking property."

I don't have the energy or time to answer as I'm shocked into an orgasm, instinctively screaming out his name. It's so different from the other ones. This one goes on and on, and I feel like I'm going to faint or something.

Do people ever faint during sex?

Jonathan's grunt fills the air as he pulls out of me and comes all over my arse.

The hot liquid burns a little against the sting of his handprint on my flesh. I bite my lower lip, relishing the sensation.

Is it supposed to feel as if I've ascended out of my body and have just now come back?

This must be what it means to be fucked.

Literally.

Figuratively.

When I think Jonathan will release me, he pulls me up by the hair, his hand still caging my throat, and whispers hot, sinister words at my ear, "The only reason you haven't been owned before is because I hadn't come along yet."

TWENTY-THREE

Aurora

THERE'S SORE AND THERE'S THE INABILITY TO MOVE.

I'm in the latter category.

No kidding.

I rolled to my side to silence the alarm and stopped when stinging pain exploded through my whole body. It's worse between my thighs and on my arse.

That was half an hour ago.

I probably need to call in sick or something. Jonathan broke me with his cock. I knew that thing wasn't supposed to be anywhere near me.

Whenever I shift and feel the sting of pain, memories from last night rush to the front of my mind and my core tingles as if he's still inside me. Like he's still owning every inch of me and driving into me with feral power.

The control and ruthlessness he emanated still cause hot blood to rush through my veins. I never knew I needed that savage brutality until I had Jonathan—or he had me, to be more accurate.

I kind of passed out after we were finished. I don't recall how my arse was cleaned from his cum, but I faintly remember moaning at the feel of soft cloth on my behind and between my legs.

Then there was the distinctive click of the door as his woodsy scent disappeared from around me.

It's not that I want him to cuddle me or anything. We have separate rooms for a reason, and while I'm never allowed in his, I liked the arrangement of having my own space.

So why do I feel abandoned?

That's stupid—utterly so. What the hell was I expecting? A bloody connection or something? I've already decided that it won't happen in this lifetime. Just because Jonathan revived my body, doesn't mean I'll want other things from him.

I stopped wanting things that day when I stared up at the pouring sky and begged to be woken up, yet never was.

My guilt doesn't help either.

The fact that I desire Jonathan when I shouldn't cuts through my ribcage like the knife from that day. But this phantom pain is more stabbing than the real one. It's not only a betrayal to my mission to unravel the truth, it's also a betrayal to Alicia and to who I am.

For the life of me, I can't stop my body from craving him, no matter how much I try to.

And I have tried.

Maybe you're not trying hard enough.

Sighing, I reach for my phone, I'll call in sick and work from here. Layla will shower me with her 'daddy' jokes if I go to work walking like I've been thoroughly fucked.

Not that I can even get up, let alone shower so I can go to work. Maybe it will get better with time.

The door opens and I think it's Margot. But then I recall she always knocks before entering my room. The only one who barges in without warning is the tyrant of the house.

Sure enough, Jonathan strides inside with that infuriating confidence that he wears like a second skin.

He's dressed in an elegant black suit, his jacket closed. Who knew there was an entirely different world hidden underneath that brutally elegant look? The cloth moulds to his well-built frame, outlining his hard muscles. Muscles I ogled last night, touched, and grabbed onto while —

I shut the door on those thoughts, refusing to get caught up in him all over again.

"You're five minutes late for breakfast and you didn't answer my email."

People normally say good morning, but Jonathan reminds you of how you breached his rules.

The man is such a charmer. And I mean that in the most sarcastic way possible.

When I don't reply, his tone shifts to that authoritative one. "Have you become a glutton for punishment, Aurora? Is that it?"

I face away from him. "I'm not feeling well."

"What do you mean you're not feeling well? You were fine last night."

"Well, I'm not today."

"You still have the attitude, so you can't be too unwell."

The bastard. "Well, I am. Now, leave me alone."

"You need to quit the habit of chasing me out, Aurora. That will never happen unless it's on my terms. Understood?"

I purse my lips but say nothing.

"What did I say about answering my questions?"

"Fine. Okay. As you wish, your majesty."

"I thought you weren't feeling well, yet it seems like you fancy a mouth fuck."

"I'll never let you do that." I might like the pain he lashes out, but degradation is another thing altogether.

"I'm the one who decides whatever the fuck I want to do with you. After all, you're my property."

"I'll never do it willingly, so if you're in the mood to force me, go for it."

He narrows his eyes, but seems to let it go. It's the deceptive type of reassurance he shows now and again. As for what he'll actually do? Yeah, no one knows that.

"Now tell me, why are you feeling unwell?" He sits on the edge of the bed and places his knuckles on my forehead. "You're not warm."

If I wasn't before, I am now. I suck in a breath at the way his skin burns on mine and swiftly pull away.

"Can't you leave me alone?"

"That's a no. You should've learnt by now that I always get what I want, so you might as well tell me."

"Arrogant prick," I mutter under my breath.

"I heard that. And I'm not arrogant, I'm goal-oriented. Arrogance comes from false beliefs I don't have."

That is true. Jonathan is the type who never starts anything unless he already knows the end result.

"I'm waiting, Aurora."

"Don't you have work?"

"You also have work and your black belt friend must be throwing a search party, but you're not making a move to go. This is your last chance to freely divulge information before I resort to my methods."

"And what are those? Spanking me?"

"Not in your current situation, but I'll take a rain cheque on that."

"You're impossible, did you know that?"

"That doesn't answer my question. You're wasting both our time."

"I'm sore, okay?"

He pauses, but his expression remains blank, non-existent even. "Huh."

Huh?

I don't know what I expected, but 'huh' wasn't it.

"How sore are you?"

"Enough that I can't move."

"Should you see a doctor?"

"No. It's not as bad as that."

"Then what do you need?"

"Rest, Jonathan. Ever heard of the word, or was that erased from your workaholic dictionary?"

"Very funny." His face is caught in that snobbish state, which means he doesn't find it amusing at all.

He pulls the covers off my body and I yelp as he wraps his strong arms around my back and picks me up. The room tilts off balance as he carries me effortlessly, bridal style.

There's a faint recollection of us being in this same position before. Did he also do it yesterday?

Were those words that came to my mind his?

I must be imagining things. This is Jonathan, after all. He doesn't feel—at all. Even if he does, he's perfected the art of deception so well, no one sees past his cool façade.

I wince, but the palpitations of my heart take me more by surprise. "Jonathan? What are you doing?"

"Finding a solution." He marches to the bathroom, and I catch a glimpse of us in the mirror. Me, entirely naked and small in his arms. Him, suited up and looking every bit the king from his last name.

My hair is dishevelled and my eyes are slightly puffy from sleep. I don't only look fucked, but also like I enjoyed every second of it.

Jonathan gently lowers me into the bathtub and I wince as my hip bone touches the cold surface.

His attention slides to me at the sound I make. "Endure it for a bit."

"Is that your answer to everything?"

"You have to endure it to get past it, Aurora. That's how it works."

That's an interesting philosophy, but… "That doesn't mean it goes away, you know."

"That's why you have to endure *and* take action. It doesn't make a difference if you only endure. If anything, that'll hurt you in the long run." He turns the tap on the slightest bit, tests the water on his fingers, and lets it fill the tub. And me.

My muscles relax a little as the cool water loosens the ache between my legs and the soreness in my arse.

He reaches over my head to the countless bath products and retrieves one that was already here when I moved in.

"I use the apple one." I motion to the bottle beside it.

"Always an objection." He shakes his head, although he does comply and pours the apple-scented one.

Then he watches with unnerving silence as the water fills the tub and the bubbles cover me to my breasts.

I squirm under his scrutiny. While I'm good with handling silence, I'm rubbish when it comes to Jonathan's. Considering his reticent nature, it always feels like he's communicating something with silence.

And it's not usually good. Jonathan's silence is the type that's meant to keep you on your toes.

"You can go. You don't have to keep watching me."

He doesn't move or say anything. He remains at the edge of the bathtub, his arms crossed over his chest, and studies me intently, as if reading imaginary words off my face.

The intimidation that is Jonathan King knows no bounds. It's like he was born to play the role of a bastard with no soul.

The fact that he has his emotions trapped in a vault, or worse, they don't exist at all, makes him unpredictable.

There's no way in hell to figure out what he's thinking about, and I guess that's what turns me into this confused ball whenever he's around.

Despite steering clear of puzzles, there's no denying how much I love solving them. The idea of digging my fingers into something and figuring it all out fills me with a rush of adrenaline.

The thought of never being able to do that with Jonathan is what's throwing me into an endless loop with no way out.

"You have work, right?" I mutter.

"It can wait."

"Did you just say work can wait? Isn't that like blasphemy in your work god manual?"

He raises a brow, probably because of my sarcastic tone, but he doesn't comment on it. "I own the work. It's not the other way around."

"Are you telling me that you could stop working tomorrow if you choose to?"

"I could, but I won't. There's no fun in hanging around when you can use those hours to be productive."

"More like destructive," I mutter to myself.

"If you have something to say, say it out loud. Hiding makes you seem like a coward, and you're no coward, Aurora."

His words send a tingle of pride down my spine. Not that I need Jonathan to tell me I'm no coward, but the fact that he's probably always thought that way about me says something. No idea what, but it does.

He reaches a hand to my face and I stiffen. Is he going to stroke my cheek?

Now that I think about it, Jonathan hardly touches my face—if ever. The only time he's done so was earlier when he checked my temperature. He's never attempted to kiss me either. Not that I would peg Jonathan as the emotional type who would do that, but —

Why am I even thinking about it? First, the tightness in my chest because he left last night. And now, the fact that he didn't touch my face or kiss me?

Instead of touching me, Jonathan reaches behind me and shuts the tap. My stomach sinks in with something different to relief.

He removes his jacket and lays it on the towel hanger, then undoes his shirt's cuffs and rolls his sleeves up to expose his taut arms with masculine veins.

By the time he crouches beside me, I'm watching him as if he's an alien. "What are you doing?"

He flops a hand in the bubbly water, right between my legs like he knows exactly where that is.

His strong fingers grab my aching thigh and rub long circles with a tenderness that I never thought Jonathan was capable of.

My muscles loosen with every passing second and his touch turns more soothing, pleasurable even. My head lies against the edge of the tub and my eyes flutter closed.

My legs open of their own accord the more Jonathan massages my inner thighs, his fingers inching towards my sensitive core, but not touching.

A low moan fills the air and it's with utter horror that I realise it's mine. I sink my teeth into the cushion of my bottom lip to keep any further sound from escaping.

Jonathan's pace slows, but he doesn't stop. "You like this."

I remain silent, refusing to admit my depraved thoughts.

He grips me by my sex, making my eyes shoot open. The intensity that greets me in his darkened features turns me breathless.

"If you like something I do to you, I expect you to say it. You don't get to deny it while still enjoying it. We've already established that you belong to me."

"You've established that. I never agreed to it."

"Yes, you did. Not with words, but it was written in big capital letters when you screamed my name as your cunt strangled my dick. It's right here with the way your folds are inviting me inside even when sore."

My cheeks redden at the explicit image he paints in my head. Damn him and how easily he can rile me up.

When I say nothing, Jonathan removes his hand from between my legs and stands up. He pulls out a towel and dries his hands on it with sure, firm movements.

"T-that's it?" I don't know why the words escape my mouth. I was supposed to ask that to myself.

"That's it. You don't deserve something you don't admit to enjoying." He throws me an indecipherable glance. "I expect you in the dining room in fifteen minutes. Every minute you're late will be taken out on your arse."

And with that, he leaves the bathroom.

A frustrated scream bubbles up in my throat, but I trap it inside and flop under the water, letting it cover me whole. Not that it does anything to cool the flames he left behind.

Damn Jonathan King to the darkest pit of hell.

And because I want to strangle him—not in a sexy kind of way—I waltz to the dining room five minutes late.

The bath actually helped. My muscles are less sore, but they still ache and I feel him inside me with every step I take.

I'm dressed in my light pink sleeveless dress, my hair is loose, and I put on red lipstick. I need all my confidence today. And maybe I want to get on Jonathan's nerves as much as he gets on mine. After all, he does stop and stare whenever I paint my lips red.

By the time I join Jonathan, he doesn't appear in a good mood. He watches me with that furrowed expression that usually means disapproval.

"You're five minutes late."

"I had to get ready."

"Excuses only make your case worse, not better, wild one."

I lift a shoulder and pull my seat. Jonathan tuts and I sigh. Of course.

Making a detour, I go straight to him and sit on his lap. I hate how familiar—and dare I say, comfortable—this seat has become.

"Why do you always call me that?" I murmur in an effortless attempt to not focus on his presence at my back.

"What?"

"Wild one."

"You've been wild since you were a child."

"I was not."

His lips twitch in that almost-smile of his, but he returns to a neutral expression soon after.

Jonathan grabs a small piece of bread and places it at my mouth. "Now, eat."

I wrap my lips around it, but when they brush against his finger, a jolt of electricity blooms between us.

Our gazes bind and it's like they can't get unlocked. Jonathan's dark grey eyes almost turn black as I keep my lips on his finger for a second too long.

Heat spreads beneath my clothes, forming goosebumps over my skin and ending straight between my thighs.

"Careful, Aurora. You're tempting me to fuck you right here and now. After I punish you for those five minutes of tardiness, of course." The raspiness of his voice and the words he says turn me into a bundle of inexplicable emotions.

I don't remove my lips.

Shit. It's like I'm opening my legs for him all over again. The fact that I'm still sore doesn't even matter anymore.

Jonathan's lips turn up into a seductive smile that worsens the state of my ruined knickers. "Is that an invitation, wild one?"

The piece of bread has melted in my mouth, and I swallow it, the sound loud and intrusive in the middle of the silence.

Before I can say anything, the door to the dining room barges open.

"Well, well, what do we have here?"

TWENTY-FOUR

Aurora

F OR A SECOND, I'M TOO STUNNED TO REACT.

I'm now used to having meals alone with Jonathan and his devious mind and wandering hands. Margot and Tom never interrupt us, which I assume is due to Jonathan's orders.

So the moment I hear that familiar voice, I get caught into a denial game, thinking this is a play of my imagination. Or even that Harris decided to be an arsehole today.

But it's neither Harris's face nor his voice. It's…

Aiden.

My nephew whom I've never officially met, despite begging Alicia to bring him over during her visits to Leeds. She said she would but had never kept that particular promise.

My nephew who called me 'Mum' upon first meeting me because he didn't know I existed in the first place.

He walks inside, a hand shoved in his dark jeans pocket. His strides are purposeful and confident. Just like Jonathan. He's also a carbon copy of his father, looks-wise. The dark hair and the grey eyes. The proud nose and the chiselled jaw. Even the permanent disapproving look is the same.

And it's now directed on me.

That's when I realise the compromising position Aiden has walked in on. I'm sitting on his father's lap, lips wrapped around his damn finger.

I startle, trying to stand up, but Jonathan holds me tight by the hip. I beg him with wild eyes to let me go. He might be too assertive to care about what his son thinks, but I do. So much so that every second he holds me against him, I'm close to the point of hyperventilating.

He must see the panic on my features, and since Jonathan doesn't really care about others, I suspect he'll never let me go. But then, his fingers loosen from around my waist and I use the opportunity to get off his lap.

My breathing shortens as I smooth my dress and touch my hair in a shameful attempt to pull myself together.

This isn't how I wanted to see Aiden again.

Besides, there's a tiny part of me that didn't actually want to meet him. Jonathan was right, the guilt I feel towards Aiden is too big to be translated into words.

I figured that since I moved here, I'd have to confront him eventually, but I never thought it would be under such circumstances.

If he didn't hate me before, he sure as shit must now.

I should've asked Jonathan when he'd return from his honeymoon. Maybe I would've been more prepared if I had. Or at least not been sitting on his father's lap, sucking on his fingers.

Aiden stops a seat away from his father, his lips set in a line, hot fury emanating off him in waves. "What, and I can't stress this enough, *the fuck* is going on here?"

I swallow. "It's not —"

"Did I talk to you?" Aiden cuts me off, his attention still zeroed in on his father.

Fine. I deserve that. Doesn't mean it hurts any less, though.

Aiden is the last thing Alicia left behind. Aside from me, he's the only one who shares DNA with her.

And despite looking like Jonathan, I can feel the touch Alicia left in him. That might sound creepy, though, so I don't dare to voice that thought.

"I'm waiting, Jonathan." Aiden plants his hand on the table, meeting his father's gaze as if he's a rival.

Jonathan's expression remains neutral. The same blankness he wears so well doesn't waver. It's almost like his only son didn't just walk in on him in a sexual position with his aunt.

This is so fucked up.

"I do not answer to you." Jonathan takes a sip of his coffee ever so leisurely.

"You answer to your dick then? Is that it?"

My eyes widen, flying straight to Jonathan, kind of afraid about the wrath he'll strike on his son. The older King continues sipping from his mug of coffee as if Aiden didn't just say what he did. If he hadn't spoken aloud, I'd suspect Jonathan didn't even hear him.

"How dare you bring this whore to the place Alicia called home?"

I bite my tongue, but I can't let this slide. I *won't*. I may feel guilty towards Aiden, but I won't allow him or anyone else to treat me this way.

Squaring my shoulders, I glare at him, but before I can say anything, Jonathan stands up abruptly, slamming both his hands on the table and meeting Aiden's merciless gaze with one of his own.

However, Jonathan's is more intense and the tic in his jaw enunciates it to a frightening level.

"Enough. This is the first and last time you disrespect her under my roof. Do it again and you'll have me to answer to."

I grab my watch to stop my shaky fingers from moving. I never thought I'd need Jonathan to stand up for me until I saw it myself.

Not that it forgives anything he's done—and continues to

do—but the fact that he won't allow anyone, even his own son, to speak to me that way means something.

I don't know what it is. But it does.

"Remember what you told me last year?" Aiden's left eye twitches. "The part about how I have no respect for my mother's memory? Who, between the two us, doesn't have respect for her, Jonathan? Huh? Because I sure as shit am not sitting with her doppelgänger on my lap."

His words slam into me, even though Jonathan remains unaffected. My fingers continue their quivering and I clear my throat. "I…I'm going to go."

"Stay. This is my house and if he doesn't like what he sees, he'll be the one to leave," Jonathan says with his usual authoritative tone of voice, then addresses Aiden, "After all, you didn't hesitate to marry Ethan's daughter."

"Elsa. Her name is Elsa, Jonathan, and she had nothing to do with whatever feud you have with Ethan."

Stepping backwards, I inch towards the door. Not only do I not want to be caught in the middle of a father-son quarrel, but I also don't want to be the cause behind it. I don't want to witness the two people Alicia loved more than the world itself go at each other's throats.

It's almost like a fight between a king and the rebel crown prince.

By the time I'm at the door, Jonathan throws me a disapproving glance, probably because of the way I'm leaving after he insisted I stay.

We're different, he and I. While he doesn't care about yelling at Aiden, I do. The scene breaks my heart.

Jonathan is an emotionless man. Or more accurately, his feelings don't resurface, so I didn't expect him to have a sappy father-son relationship with Aiden. But I also didn't expect this hostility either. I thought Alicia's early, unexpected death would've brought them together. Apparently not.

That sure as hell doesn't help my guilt trip towards Aiden.

Maybe things would've been different if I'd been there for him since the funeral.

Or if I hadn't fucked his father.

I hang my head as I grab my bag and make a beeline towards my car. My phone dings and I smile as Layla's name appears on the screen.

Layla: Are you late because of daddy kink?

Layla: Say yes and I'll pay for lunch for a week.

Layla: It can even be a lie. Just say yes.

I smile and shake my head. Despite being a devout Muslim who prays five times a day, fasts during Ramadan, drinks no alcohol, has no sex before marriage, and eats no pork, Layla has the wildest fantasies, I swear.

What I love about her the most is that she isn't afraid to let those fantasies show or to even joke about them. She also doesn't judge how others live their lives as long as they don't judge hers. She's never once tried to apply her beliefs on me. Back at uni, she accepted me the way I was, scars and all, and never probed hard about my past.

The first time she brought me to her home for Eid and her family welcomed me to their table, as if I'd always belonged there, was when I found some sort of balance after struggling with it for so long.

Aurora: No.

Layla: You're so cruel. How could you kill the fantasy so brutally? *crying emoji* X3

Biting my lower lip, I type.

Aurora: But I am sore.

Layla: I knew it!

Layla: Details, mate. Details! You can't keep me hanging like that. The suspense is killing me here.

Aurora: I'll be in the office in a bit.

Layla: Fine, I'll be productive until you come. By the way, why did you leave early yesterday? Are you okay?

The memories of Stephan and the panic attack I had nearly assault me all over again.

But since Jonathan flipped me on my stomach and fucked me so thoroughly, those have been the least of my worries.

Go figure.

Ever since the day I walked into that police station and uncovered the murder of not only one woman but seven, *he* has been in the forefront of my mind.

He has been the first thought I wake up to every day and the last thought I sleep to every night.

Until last night.

Actually, it started after Jonathan taught me in the roughest way that my body is, in fact, not dead.

I slide into my car and place my bag on the passenger seat. When I lift my head, I'm startled by the shadow perching against my window.

Aiden. His features are still closed off like earlier. If anything, his quarrel with Jonathan seems to have turned him angrier.

Swallowing, I lower the glass. The low sound echoes in the deafening silence.

"I want you gone," he says ever so casually, as if it can be done by merely giving a vocal order.

He's Jonathan's son, all right.

"I can't."

"What do you mean you can't? Just disappear like you've been doing so well for the past eleven years."

"I understand that you don't like this situation, I don't either, but —"

"If you don't like it, then leave. No buts are needed."

I grit my teeth. "If you'd let me finish my sentence, I would've told you I don't have a choice."

"Even if this is one of Jonathan's games, surely you can find a way out. I don't care what it is as long as you stay as far away from this place as possible." His gaze meets mine with distaste. "You might be Alicia's doppelgänger, but I can't even stand to look at you."

"Why not?" My voice softens.

"Because you're fake. You might resemble her, but you'll never be her."

"I've never tried to be Alicia."

"Is that why you're fucking Jonathan?"

I purse my lips to not snap at him for speaking to me this way. He must've inherited the entitlement gene from his father.

"He gets bored easily, you know. The moment he finally sees that he can't get Alicia back through you, he'll throw you out as if you never existed."

"That's exactly what I want, Aiden."

He watches me peculiarly for a bit, then steps back. I take it as my cue to leave the property.

I have no doubt that I'll face Aiden again. No idea how that will go, but I'll make sure not to be caught in that position with Jonathan a second time.

As I drive to work, I feel eyes following me.

At first, I chalk it up to paranoia since I've had many false alarms in the past. Especially after the attack.

But as it stays persistent and strong, I realise that maybe, just maybe, this isn't a false alarm after all.

TWENTY-FIVE

Aurora

A FEW DAYS LATER, I'M ATTENDING A DOUBLE CHARITY DINNER organised by Layla's local mosque and a church for orphaned children's associations.

We do this annually. Layla and I help her mother and their neighbours cook, and then we try to invite as many rich people as possible. Meaning, many of our clients. Some appear, some send cheques, and others ignore us altogether.

It doesn't stop us from trying, though. We still send invitations to our contact list every year and try to retarget them.

It's the one time I'm not ashamed to spam. If someone has given me their business card, they should expect an invitation for this.

The hall we rented for the event is big enough to fit not only our invitees, but also the orphaned children, their support, and the associations who will benefit from the money we'll raise tonight.

The priest is talking about the importance of giving. The imam spoke earlier about how vulnerable children are and how much they need our support.

Layla and I are at the entrance, welcoming the invitees and giving out directions to whoever needs it.

Inside, her parents are doing background work since they're a part of the organisation committee. Layla's family is all about activism. Her eldest brother is a part of Doctors Without Borders, and the rest of her family participates in charities like these or ones that support passed soldiers' families.

Layla even made an effort and actually wore a dress. An elegant floral scarf that I gave her for her birthday covers her hair and I kind of had to hold her down, with the help of her mother, to put some makeup on her face. She hates staying still for more than a minute.

I, on the other hand, have opted for a dark blue knee-length dress and left my hair loose. I brought my clothes with me and changed in Layla's house so that I wouldn't have to go back to the King mansion.

"Look at all the people who showed up!" she whisper-yells, her voice filled with so much enthusiasm.

"I know."

"Imagine all those little faces happy. I wish I could adopt them all…wait, maybe I can."

"Remove that crazy idea from your head right now, Lay."

"Don't be a fun-ruiner." She pokes my arm. "Why are you in a pissy mood lately?"

"I'm not."

Okay, maybe I am a little. Aiden's visit has left a sour taste in my mouth, and I don't know how to fix it. If I make an attempt to meet him, he'll probably chase me out with a bat.

Now, every time Jonathan touches me, I stiffen, thinking about Aiden's words and how true they are. But then, the pull drags me under and I get lost in Jonathan's touch and those damn hands I've become addicted to.

It's only when the spell breaks that I go back to the internal guilt trip, blaming myself for how I'm not even close to solving Alicia's death.

REIGN OF A KING | 163

I manically check with Paul in case I've received any more wooden box packages, but nothing appeared in my inbox.

Layla pokes my side. "Are you perhaps missing Johnny?"

"Lay!" I hiss, then smile as one of our clients greets us. As soon as she heads inside, I go back to glaring at my friend.

"What? You're usually with him around this time."

"I don't miss him when I'm away from him."

"Is that why you keep checking your watch?"

"Suck my dick, Lay."

She feigns a gasp. "Blasphemy. The priest will soak you in holy water."

I rub my arm and flip her off discreetly so no one sees. She laughs, bumping my shoulder with hers.

"He must be missing you, though. Imagine a grumpy Johnny sitting in his castle alone without you to entertain him. He must be waiting for you while drinking and sighing like an old man."

"I didn't tell him where I was going."

She gives me a funny look.

"He's not the boss of me, okay? He doesn't need to know where I am at all times."

"It's not that…" Layla trails off when her gaze moves ahead. "Oh em gee, Daddy."

At first, my heart stops beating when I think it's Jonathan. My stomach dips and my forehead breaks out in a sweat. Then I follow her gaze and a sense of disappointment and confusion hit me at the same time.

Ethan and Agnus. They came. I didn't expect much when I sent the invitation to the address on Agnus's business card that I kept.

They're both dressed in dapper suits, accompanied by a blonde girl wearing a white dress and carrying what seems like a heavy basket.

Ethan offers to help her, but she shakes her head.

Elsa—Aiden's new bride.

My breathing hitches as I stare behind her, expecting to find

Aiden's grim features. But he's not with them. A sense of relief mixed with the same disappointment from earlier grips me in its clutches.

"Layla, Aurora." Ethan smiles at us, shaking our hands respectively. Agnus follows suit.

"Hear that?" Layla whispers. "Daddy remembers my name."

"He's not your daddy," I murmur back, poking her side the hardest I can.

She winces but continues smiling as she peeks at Elsa. "And you are?"

"She's my daughter." Ethan's voice drips with pride as he wraps an arm around her shoulders. "She wanted to join, if that's okay."

"Of course, the more the merrier." Layla offers to take the basket from Elsa.

"Aunt and I made them. There are cupcakes and different lollipops for the children," Elsa speaks to Layla but keeps stealing glances at me. The ring on her finger is blinding, and I pause as I recognise it. Alicia's ring. I'd recognise it anywhere, considering she had a habit of touching it whenever she was absentminded.

The reminder of the time I spent with my sister comes rushing back in. The emotions. How much I miss her. It all hits me hard. I force myself to shut the door on those thoughts and steady my breaths.

"I'm sure they'll love them." Layla struggles to hold the basket. With her petite body, she's like a toddler carrying a teddy bear twice her size.

Ethan steps in and takes the basket from her, helping her place it on the counter.

Layla pretends to faint behind his back so only I can see her, then mouths, "Daddy." That dork. It takes everything in me not to burst out laughing.

"I must admit, I didn't think you'd show up," I tell Agnus.

"We do attend charities," Agnus says in his eternal cool voice. He's iceman. No kidding. He retrieves his phone, stares at the screen, and gives Ethan a knowing look. "I have to take this."

He nods at us and disappears around the corner, making way for old ladies who come in carrying baskets similar to Elsa's.

Once finished, Ethan motions at me. "Elsa, this is Aurora."

"We've met before," she whispers. "At the wedding."

I fidget, struggling to maintain a smile. "Right. Sorry about back then."

Elsa shakes her head. "I'm the one who's sorry about what Aiden did afterwards."

"He told you?"

"He doesn't have to. I could feel he went searching for trouble as soon as we were back from the honeymoon." She touches her ring finger. "I just want you to know that losing Alicia has changed Aiden drastically, and it's not necessarily for the better. Seeing you and knowing you existed after such a long time didn't sit well with him. It's not that he hates you, it's that..."

"He hates how much I look like her. I understand."

Her electric blue eyes light up. "You do?"

"It's not easy to see a ghost." I know that more than anyone else. "Where is he?"

"He's with my doctor."

"Your doctor?" I throw a curious glance between her and Ethan.

"I have a heart condition, and Aiden basically possesses my attending physician. Whenever he doesn't answer the phone, he barges into his workplace or house." She rolls her eyes. "Like today."

Ethan squeezes her shoulder. "He only wants to make sure you're fine, Princess."

"I know that, Dad, but he can be so extra. Dr Albert hates me because of it."

It strikes me then. The difference between Jonathan's behaviour and Ethan's. My tyrant disapproves of Elsa and doesn't shy away from expressing his opinion. On the other hand, Ethan doesn't seem to disapprove of Aiden—despite his menacing feelings towards Jonathan.

One is definitely more parental than the other.

"Tell you what, Aurora." Ethan meets my gaze, still holding his daughter by the shoulder. "We plan to have a family dinner with Aiden and Elsa this weekend. How about you join us?"

I gulp. This could be either my last chance to try and fix things with Aiden, or to completely screw it up.

"Please come," Elsa says. "I'll make sure Aiden behaves."

I smile at the enthusiasm in her tone and face. There's something about her that's both bold and innocent. I wonder how she gets along with a hot-headed person like Aiden. He's so much like his father, it gives me whiplash.

"I will love to."

"You will *not*."

My back snaps upright and I nearly yelp like a damsel in distress at that strong, authoritative tone.

The entire atmosphere shifts from familial and fun to stormy and dangerous in a fraction of a second as Jonathan strides to the middle of the scene as if he's the master of it.

The priest's words and the slight chatter coming from the inside filter and vanish into thin air. Even the people greeting and passing us by might as well be invisible right now.

My entire attention is attuned to the man standing before me in his pressed black suit, diamond cufflinks, and dark leather shoes that I could see my face in if I squint hard enough.

There's something about Jonathan's presence that throttles and pins me in place without him having to touch me. The fact that it's effortless on his part makes him even more frightening. He's a man in power and he's well aware of the fact.

All I can do is watch as he dominates the room and everyone in it. Or maybe it's only me.

His black hair is styled back, revealing that strong forehead and his too-sharp jaw.

He is too sharp.

Everything about him is, from his suit to his face and down to his damn character.

He looks perfect tonight—masculine, groomed, and out to ruin lives. Which is funny since I don't ever remember seeing Jonathan dishevelled.

Being presentable seems to be his default mode. It's an extension of his infuriating confidence and how, if he chooses to do so, he can own any place he walks into.

Then I recall that he shouldn't be here. I didn't even tell him about the charity event.

"What are you doing here?" I pull myself out of the trance his presence never fails to trap me in.

He places a hand to his pocket. "I was invited."

"No, you weren't."

"Black Belt." Jonathan raises his brow at Layla.

My eyes snap to the culprit beside me, and I whisper-yell, "You invited Jonathan?!"

She fakes a smile at Ethan, who's meeting Jonathan's glare with one of his own, and then at Elsa who seems suffocated by the tension.

Layla pulls me by the sleeve of my dress into a corner and says in a low voice, "To my defence, I didn't think he'd come."

"Why would you invite him in the first place?"

"Why do you think? His bank account and the amount of money he writes on cheques."

"I thought you hated Jonathan."

"I don't hate his money. Come on, mate. Think of the cause."

"Ugh. Fine. But one of these days, I'm going to kill you, Lay."

"I know you love me. Besides, you don't have to check your watch now that he's here."

I hit her shoulder so she'll shut up and she hits me back before we re-join the others.

"Sorry about that." Layla grins. "Some differences in logistics, but it's all cleared up now. Aurora is happy to have you amongst us, Johnny."

He narrows his eyes on me even as he speaks to her, "The name is Jonathan."

"You call me Black Belt. Why should I call you by your full name?"

Ethan and I smile, but Elsa stares frantically at Layla as if begging her to take it back. Jonathan's bored expression doesn't change. He watches Layla and everyone else like they're disposables—if they have something to offer him, they're good, if not, they're out.

Right now, he seems to be weighing Layla's worth, contemplating whether he should let it slide or crush her to pieces.

Elsa and I simultaneously release a breath when he doesn't press the matter. Lay seriously needs to keep her mouth shut. Sometimes, it's like she doesn't care who she's talking to. The girl is too fearless for her own good.

"I'll send you the address to the house," Ethan tells me as if we were never interrupted.

"Thank you."

"I said —" Jonathan's face remains blank, but his tone gains a firm, final edge "— she will *not* be there."

"Is that so, Aurora?" Ethan asks.

"Maybe we should reschedule," Elsa suggests. "Next week?"

"She'll not be there next week either," Jonathan shoots her down.

"There's no need to reschedule, I'll be there."

"I'm happy to hear that." Ethan's lips curve in a slow smile.

Jonathan towers over me, his woodsy scent closes imaginary hands around my throat and squeezes. He speaks low so only I can hear him, "Did you hear what I said? You will *not* be there and that's final."

"Last I checked, you're not my keeper." I bypass him and motion at Ethan and Elsa to follow me, leaving Jonathan with Layla.

That should be fun.

I spend the rest of the evening trying to ignore Jonathan's looming presence. He somehow ends up in circles of people who buzz around him like bees to honey. It's almost as if he's stealing the lime-light away from the children with his presence.

Pretending he's not there, I continue networking and introduc-ing the associations' representatives to the donors.

When I was young, I took everything for granted, and because of that, I need to revisit my choices and try to make a difference.

No matter how small that difference is.

Charity is all about giving, and I always feel like I haven't done enough of that—giving, that is.

I've taken and taken and haven't even stopped to look back once. Now, I have the choice to do something different.

Layla's mother, Kenza—which literally means treasure—is a plump woman in her mid-fifties with pale skin and dreamy hazel eyes. When she catches me roaming around, she hugs me and rubs my arm. She has a French accent she acquired from her time living in France. Like Layla, she covers her hair with a hijab, but unlike her daughter's hip-hop style, she wears modest, elegant dresses. "I'm so happy our Layla got to know you, Aurora."

"I'm so happy you gave birth to her."

"Believe me, so am I." Then she leans in to murmur, "Don't tell anyone, but I hate boys."

"Your secret is safe with me."

"Seriously. The only reason I kept giving birth was so I'd get a baby girl. Though she did turn out to be like her brothers, didn't she?"

"Sort of."

We laugh and she reaches into her pocket. "Hold on, Layla has been teaching me how to take selfies."

She pauses when she doesn't find her phone. "I lost it again."

"Don't worry, I'll help you find it. I'll call you."

"It's on silent mode."

"Where was the last place you saw it?"

"At home. No. At the storage room. Or was it in the bathroom?"

I laugh. Kenza plays a constant lost and found game with her phone. "I'll go check the storage room and you check the bathroom."

We part ways and I head to the small supply space that was originally filled with cleaning equipment. Now it contains all the baskets and gifts people have brought in for the children.

Something glints on the ground and I get on my hands and knees to check it out. Nope. Not the phone. It's a lollipop wrapper.

I'm about to stand back up when the door clicks behind me and Jonathan's strong voice fills the space.

"I like the view."

TWENTY-SIX

Aurora

MY SPINE JERKS UPRIGHT AT JONATHAN'S NOW VERY recognisable voice.

It doesn't matter how much I hear it or how much time I spend in his company. It will always hold a frightening edge that's meant to be obeyed.

Worshipped even.

Despite my earlier retorts, I admit taking refuge in the public setting. Now that we're all alone, I have absolutely no defence against my tyrant.

I scramble to my feet, realising the position I'm in—on my knees with my arse in his full view.

The moment I stand up, a scorching warmth appears at my back like a volcano nearing an eruption. I don't even get to turn around as Jonathan grabs both my wrists and pins them with one hand at the small of my back.

My breathing shortens and that now-familiar heat shoots through my limbs and settles between my legs.

"Do you think it's okay to defy me, Aurora?" His voice lowers as his lips graze the shell of my ear. "Is that it?"

172 | RINA KENT

"I...I don't know what you're talking about."

"Oh, but you do. That's why you're doing it on purpose. Do you like to see me lose control?" He pushes his hips forwards and I suck in a crackled breath at the feel of the hard bulge nestling against my arse.

"Or do you perhaps like to be punished?" His other hand yanks my dress up. Shivers cover my skin, but it has nothing to do with the cold air and everything to do with how he grabs my arse as if that's what he was always meant to do.

"I did nothing to be punished for," I speak firmly, even though my legs have turned into jelly.

"Nothing to be punished for?" His hand comes down on my arse and I yelp, my thighs shaking and coated with the evidence of my arousal.

"N-nothing," I breathe out.

Slap.

I gasp, the sound ending in a moan. "...aaah."

"You're mine, so act like it, mean it, fucking breathe it if you have to. You do not get to defy me in public again. Do you understand?"

My quivering lips set in a line, I refuse to give him an answer.

Slap.

"I said. Do you understand?"

A full body shudder goes through me and my hands curl into fists in his hold, but I still don't say a word.

"We can do this all night." He grabs my arse with false tenderness, and I nearly moan at the sensation before he slaps the skin again.

A whimper rips out of me, and I hate how needy it sounds. I hate that no matter how sore my behind is, I can't help wanting more.

His voice drops in range as he murmurs in my ear, "If you don't say the words, I'm going to spank your little arse until everyone hears your cries. Is that what you want, wild one?"

"N-no!"

"Then say it."

"Fine," I hiss.

"Glad we agree on that."

More like he coerced me into agreeing. Arsehole.

"Now, what did I say about staying away from Ethan?" He tightens his hold on my wrists. "When we go outside, you'll tell him you won't make it to the dinner."

"No." The word is barely audible, but it's there. The most horrifying part is that I didn't say it because I won't allow Jonathan to dictate my life.

It's more like a challenge. At this point, all I want is the lash of his hand and the way he elicits these weird sensations from deep inside me.

If provoking him is what it takes to bring out his true self, then so be it. I've become a pro at it in such a short time.

I have no idea why I'm so addicted to this side of Jonathan. Perhaps it's because this is one of the rarest times he shows what's actually inside him; I want to be the only one who gets to witness the great Jonathan King at his most raw, truest form.

"Aurora." The warning in his voice is loud and clear.

"You don't get to tell me what to do."

He spanks me again, and I get on my tiptoes from the force of it. My thighs are shaking from the amount of clenching my core has been doing since he walked in.

But that's not all.

With every hit on my arse, it's like he's thrusting his fingers deep inside of me and owning me whole with no way out.

"Are you going to refuse Ethan's invitation?"

"No."

Slap. Slap. Slap.

I'm gasping for air by the time the multiple lashes are over.

My unsteady legs are splayed wide apart, my wrists are

imprisoned behind my back, my arse burns, and my pussy pulses with the need for more.

I don't know how much more. I seriously don't know my limits anymore. Not that I've been an expert on those since the beginning. All I know is that being with Jonathan has stretched them pretty far, even for me.

"Let's try this one more time." He grips my arse threateningly, and although my underwear is still in place, I feel his touch all the way to my bones. "Are you or are you not going to refuse the invitation? This time, say the right words."

"N-no."

I brace myself for the onslaught of his hand, but it doesn't come. I glimpse at him over my shoulder to find one of his eyes narrowed and pointed at me.

"You're doing this on purpose, aren't you, wild one?"

"No."

"How come I don't believe that?" He places his fingers at my core and I swallow as they meet my folds over the cloth. "You're soaked and begging for more."

He slides the ruined underwear down my legs and I don't hesitate to step out of them. I watch with bated breath as he bunches the knickers and shoves them in his pocket.

"Why did you do that?" My voice is needy and all sorts of messed up.

"I'll answer that if you tell me why you won't refuse Ethan's invitation."

Because of his damn son, but I don't voice that. I meant it when I said that Jonathan doesn't get to tell me what to do.

"That's what I thought." He pushes me so that I'm bent over the table meant for supplies.

My chest touches the hard surface as he holds me down by my wrists. My throbbing nipples turn painful with the mere friction. I hear a belt snapping behind me, but before I can focus on it, the sound of a slap fills the air.

I bite my lower lip, eyes closing to engrave the sensation.

"One final chance." His words echo around me like a dark promise, and I hate that my first response to it is wanting more.

He's turned me into a mess who can't get enough. He was right the other day. I've become a glutton for his punishment and rough handling. I've become attuned to him on a scary level.

"You want to be fucked here and now?" His voice lowers with lust and something else I can't put my finger on. "You don't even care that we're in a religious setting, or that anyone can walk in. You're quite the exhibitionist, aren't you?"

His words should be a turn off, but heat engulfs my body and burns the last of my inhibitions.

Jonathan thrusts into me from behind, his huge cock filling me whole with a slight tinge of pain. The position gives him access to parts of me I didn't know existed.

"You're quite the adventurous one." His raspy voice adds more punch to his callous presence at my back. "Wild. Unstoppable."

He pounds into me with an urgency that slams my thighs against the edge of the table. With my hands bound behind my back, I can't do anything.

Not that I want to.

The sense of helplessness adds to the pleasure gripping me by the throat. There's something so utterly addictive about the way he takes from me, leaving me barren and with no way out but back to him.

The sheer power of Jonathan King turns me helpless, speechless, almost like I'm levitating and living an out-of-body experience.

He slaps my arse, and while the sting may start there, it ends up straight between my legs.

"Oh... Aaaah... J-Jonathan..." My voice shifts into a loud moan as the orgasm brews in the distance. My stomach tenses and my fingers curl, nails sinking into his or my skin—I can't really tell anymore—in preparation for the impact.

It's coming. The sensation builds on the horizon, mounting and magnifying, about to hook into me and snatch me into its barbarous clutches.

His hard chest covers my back, fully, entirely, as if he's about to suffocate me.

He doesn't.

His lips find my earlobe. They're hot and firm like a blade. He whispers in a voice filled with raw possessiveness, "My name is the only name you're allowed to moan. The only name you're allowed to think about or even dream of."

I'm too delirious to make sense of his words, let alone form a response.

He thrusts harder, hitting my hip bone against the table with the force of it. There's nothing normal or ordinary about the way Jonathan powers into me.

He doesn't just fuck, he owns. He stakes his claim with each long thrust. His fingers wrap around my throat and he squeezes until he's all what remains in my conscious.

"Show me how you come for me, wild one."

The explosion of an orgasm takes me under in a fraction of a second.

I don't have a choice in it.

The softness of my body is attuned to the power in his, to the way his hips jerk forward with dominant resonance. To the way he grips my wrists, to how my arse stings from the feel of his hand on my flesh.

I'm panting, fighting and scrambling for breath by the time I fall down that cliff. I'm rolling in the dirt with no landing in sight.

And honestly, screw landing. I can stay suspended in this alternative reality all day.

"That's it. Good girl."

Jonathan follows soon after, this time, spilling inside me. I don't tense or think about it. That possibility doesn't scare me.

Everything ended before it even started in that regard.

"Fuck." Jonathan pulls out, his hot cum streaking down my thighs. "Are you on birth control?"

I pull up to a standing position, even though my legs hardly hold me upright.

Jonathan releases my throat and my hands to tuck himself in. My wrists feel sore, empty almost, at the loss of his grip.

"You should've thought of that before, don't you think?" I smooth down my dress.

"Answer the question, Aurora." His face carries the same mask of unemotional blankness, but there's a tic in his jaw.

Jonathan lost control by coming inside me, and he doesn't like losing control. However, that's not the only reason he's ticked off. He doesn't want any type of accident—a child. Which is understandable, considering he has Aiden, who is nineteen going on twenty, and his nephew, Levi, who's a year older than his son.

That doesn't mean I'm not pissed off myself, though. "Maybe I am, maybe I'm not."

"If you don't quit provoking me, I'm going to spank your arse until you can't sit straight."

"Already done." I extend my palm. "Give me my underwear back."

"How about no?"

"Jonathan!"

"You can't give me attitude and expect to get things from me." He tilts his head to the side. "You'll go back in there with nothing underneath your dress, and you'll think of me every time you squirm in your seat."

"You can't do that."

"Consider it already done." He reaches a hand and wipes something at the corner of my mouth, a sadistic smirk grazing his sinful lips. "Also, you might want to freshen up. I don't mind dragging you outside looking like this, but you might."

"What are you talking about?"

"You look thoroughly fucked, wild one."

I push his hand away, a flush of heat ascending to cover my already flaming cheeks.

Jonathan chuckles as he steps out the door. The sound of his rare laughter resides in the room long after he's gone.

Why did he have to laugh, damn him?

I use some tissues to clean up and then sneak behind everyone's back to get to the bathroom. He's right, my hair is in a state of disarray and my eyes are puffy and watery. My lipstick has smeared a little from how I bit my lips.

It takes me a good ten minutes to make myself appear somewhat presentable.

When I go back, Kenza has already found her phone. She jokingly tells me she thought I was the one lost.

If only she knew how true that statement is.

We sit in tables of five for dinner. The dick, Layla, puts me with Jonathan, Ethan, Elsa, and Agnus. And Jonathan is right beside me.

"What?" Layla said when I almost strangled her. "I can't deny requests made by those who write large cheques. Think of the cause, mate."

She's now waving at me from her table, where she's seated with her parents and two old ladies from their community. Layla's doctor brother is in Africa, her two British Army brothers are captains in Afghanistan, and her fourth brother couldn't make it tonight.

While she gets to sit in a familial atmosphere, I'm stuck here. To say the atmosphere is tense at my table would be like saying my life is normal.

It doesn't help that—true to Jonathan's words—I can't sit

straight. My arse stings and the lack of underwear makes the friction at my core unbearable.

Usually, after one of Jonathan's sessions, I sleep on my side or on my stomach until the burn goes away. Not now.

Agnus focuses on his mobile phone, seeming oblivious to the war of gazes going on between Ethan and Jonathan. If this were a few centuries ago, they would've gotten their swords out and gone at it right here, right now.

Elsa seems as bothered by the tension as I am. She digs into the couscous Kenza cooked and plasters on a smile. "This is so delicious. How do they make it?"

"Kenza says it's a family secret. She won't give away her special recipe." I pick up my spoon and pretend I'm a functioning human and that Jonathan isn't sitting beside me like a gloomy shadow straight out of a horror film.

"Do you like cooking?" Elsa asks me.

"Not really," I tense as I say the words.

Jonathan leans over to whisper so only I can hear him, "One of the habits you gave up for your rebirth?"

"Shut up," I hiss, then smile at Elsa.

Ethan takes a spoonful of the food and chews leisurely. "Alicia used to love these types of exotic dishes, too. Didn't she, Jonathan?"

My tyrant remains unaffected, as if he were expecting the blow.

It's Elsa who gasps, "Dad!"

"Was he supposed to ignore the elephant in the room?" Agnus speaks for the first time in the last hour, but he still doesn't lift his head up from his screen.

Elsa glares at him from across the table like she wants to jump or punch him. Or both.

"It's okay," I try to calm the atmosphere. "I know I look so much like her."

Ethan continues chewing, his attention never straying from Jonathan. "Is that why? You do know she's not her, right?"

My grip tightens around the spoon as Ethan's hostility rolls off my skin. It's not that he's attacking me directly. He's saying those words to provoke Jonathan, and yet, I'm the one who's stung by them with no warning.

But why?

I'm not Alicia. I don't *want* to be Alicia.

Why can't everyone stop comparing me to her? Or is this perhaps the karma I have to endure for abandoning Aiden when he was a young boy?

I was only sixteen at the time. I didn't understand anything past the need to run, to shed my armour, and get the fuck out of Clarissa Griffin's skin.

If I had the chance to do it all over again, I'd be there for Aiden. However, that means being in Jonathan's entourage from such a young age. So thinking about it again…no, thanks.

I can barely handle him now. If at all.

A strong hand wraps around my thigh under the table and I jolt as I recognise the warmth of his firm grip.

Jonathan's face has the usual coolness of a mountain so high, it's toying with the clouds and reaching for the sky. "I don't see why that's any of your business."

"Inquiring minds want to know, Jonathan. After all, Alicia left too soon."

"Dad…" Elsa pleads.

Jonathan's hold on my thigh tightens, his fingers digging into the skin. I wince, placing my spoon next to my plate. I'm in no mood to eat.

I stare behind me in a helpless attempt to have Layla get me out of here.

My attention is stolen by a petite girl in a dirty hoodie and torn shoes, who's carrying a crying baby in her arms.

Sarah.

My fingers shake as the recognition settles in the pit of my stomach. She's eleven years older now. Back then, she was around ten, her blonde hair cut to beneath her chin and her huge green eyes filled with tears as she held the sign.

'JUSTICE'.

Everyone else hit me with eggs, food, and even used condoms. They called me names. They pulled on my hair and scratched my skin.

They called me an accomplice.

She didn't.

She held on to my sleeve and whispered the words that broke me to pieces, "Please, can I have my mum back? I have no one but her. Please, I'll give you everything I have."

Then she was pushed away by someone who threw a bucket of black dirt on my face.

It's been eleven years, but I've never forgotten that girl. I dream of her sometimes, of her green eyes and her silent pleas. Of the desperation in them, of the innocence that Dad killed along with her mum.

Even now, as I recall that scene, my skin prickles and my ears start buzzing with a shrill beeping sound.

They're coming after me.

They'll kill me.

'Do you blame them, though?'

The words I heard from the officers who were supposed to protect me rush to the forefront of my brain. Even they thought I didn't need protection. If it had been up to them, they would've thrown me out of the car into the hands of the protestors.

A harsh grip on my thigh brings me back to reality. I've been clutching my watch, hands fisted in my lap.

Jonathan throws a quizzical glance in my direction. That says something, considering how engrossed he was in his verbal war with Ethan.

"I..." I stand abruptly, forcing Jonathan to release me. "I need to go."

I don't wait for their reply as I rush from there. My eyes meet Sarah's before I duck down, then practically jog towards the back entrance. That girl can't find me. None of them can.

My steps are a frantic, jumbled mess. I trip and nearly fall, but I hold myself up and continue my escape out of here.

My car is nowhere in sight. My vision is blurry. I didn't even bring my bag or my keys.

They're coming for you.

Run.

Run.

Instead of doing just that, my legs lock and I couldn't move even if I tried. I spot Moses, Jonathan's driver, smoking in front of his car.

I don't think about it as I half-jog in the direction of the Mercedes, open the back door, and slide in.

A breath heaves out of me the minute I'm out of the open. She can't find me in here.

They can't find me.

Despite that, I stare out of the tinted windows, making sure no one followed me.

"Good evening, Ms Harper."

I yelp, my hand clutching my heart at the voice coming from my right.

Harris sits beside me, his tablet in hand as usual. He's wearing a shirt tucked into his trousers with his jacket lying beside him.

He adjusts his glasses with his index and middle finger. "I apologise for startling you."

"What..." I clear my throat. "What are you doing here?"

"Shouldn't I be asking you that?"

"I meant, what are you doing outside of the charity event? And since you're here, shouldn't you go inside?"

"No. This event wasn't on the schedule. I'm preparing a draft for a meeting that we're going to have with our Chinese partners in a few hours."

I frown. "Then why isn't Jonathan with you?"

"That's my question, Ms Harper. He insisted to come here instead of preparing for the meeting."

Oh.

Is it because Ethan is attending? Or maybe it's because of me?

Don't even think about it, Aurora.

An awkward silence falls over the car as Harris focuses back on his tablet. I squirm and wince when my arse burns, remembering my lack of underwear since the tyrant, Jonathan, confiscated it.

Instead of thinking about that, I tilt my head to study Harris. He must be somewhere in his thirties. Always clean-shaven, prim, proper, and with a snobbish nose that he uses to judge everyone.

"How long have you been working with Jonathan?"

"Around ten years," he says without lifting his head.

"That's a long time."

"Probably."

"Do you like working for him?"

"Yes. He's efficient."

"Efficient?"

"Gets things done no matter what the method."

"There's another word for that—brutal."

Harris lifts a shoulder. "Fear is a good motivator for humans."

Ugh. He sounds so much like Jonathan. Machiavellian, with few to no morals, and cold. No wonder he likes working for him.

"And, Miss…" He finally looks at me. He actually has beautiful blue eyes behind those glasses.

"Aurora's fine."

"Quit distracting him, Aurora."

"W-what?"

"He's been making a lot of useless stops, like the one today, since you came into his life. I don't like it."

"You don't like it?" He sounds like he's Jonathan's wife.

"Yes. It takes away from his efficiency."

"Well, maybe he shouldn't be such a robot. And that applies to you, too, Harris. Loosen up."

"I am loosened up."

"Have you looked at yourself in the mirror lately?"

"What's wrong with my face?" He seems genuinely offended.

"Emotions. Ever heard of them? Or did Jonathan confiscate them with your smile?"

"I can smile." He shows me a menacing one.

I burst out laughing and he frowns, bemusement written all over his features.

For a moment, I forget about the past and insert myself in the present.

Because right now? I'm in the mood for a duel.

TWENTY-SEVEN

Jonathan

MY GAZE FOLLOWS AURORA AS SHE PRACTICALLY FLEES THE scene.

She didn't stop and search for her wingman, Black Belt, which means she's more agitated than she shows.

And it's all because of the bastard sitting across from me, eating as if he didn't bring up what he shouldn't have.

Not in front of her.

Not in front of anyone.

Aurora might act strong and aloof, but the memory of Alicia burns her. I don't miss how she sneaks into her room any chance she gets. Alicia's death is a reminder of the darkest day of her life. She doesn't need to be hit with the reminder that she also looks so much like her.

So what if she does? They're nothing alike.

Ethan will pay for bringing up the past and causing her to leave.

"I heard you're acquiring a horse." I lift the spoon to my mouth and take my time to savour the food.

The fact that I threw a bone in there is enough to get his attention. Ethan slows his chewing and glares at me.

Keeping my nonchalance up, I continue, "Arabian stallion. Impressive."

Agnus pauses reading what I assume are reports on his phone. "You shouldn't know about that."

"Apparently, I do. You're not the only one with inside intel, and guess what, Ethan? Consider it bought by me."

"You don't even like horses." Ethan rests his hands on the table.

"Doesn't mean I can't have it."

"Then I might consider that piece of land in Northampton you've been keeping an eye on." Ethan eats another spoonful of food. "I don't even like properties in Northampton, but that doesn't mean I can't have it."

"Take something of mine and I'll take ten in return. Even your daughter holds the King name now."

Elsa lowers her head and continues eating in silence, choosing to stay in the awkward zone. That's the difference between her and Aiden. If my son were here, he would've taken her out an hour ago. He has no patience whatsoever for things he thinks are none of his concern.

"How about Aurora?" Ethan raises a brow.

The decades I have spent to perfect my façade come into use now. I pretend not to be affected, even though I want to jam a knife in both his eyes so he doesn't look at her anymore. And I might as well include his mouth so that he doesn't say her name again.

I conjure all my self-restraint to not throw him down and punch some sense into him. Instead, I ask in my seemingly detached tone, "What about her?"

"Is she part of the game now?"

"Dad…" Elsa looks at him with pleading eyes. "You said no more games."

"I can't back down from a challenge. Isn't that right, Agnus?"

His lap dog nods once, still focused on his phone. He hasn't touched his food since we sat down. Agnus is the type of freak who rarely eats and survives on Ethan's graces, or something of the sort.

I should've known that, when news came out that Ethan was dead eleven years ago, Agnus wouldn't have stopped there.

He practically brought him back from the dead.

"There's no game," I say in my most lethal tone.

"Does that mean Aurora is off-limits?"

"She is." There's no hesitation, no second thoughts, and fuck if I know what that means.

"Does she know that, though?"

I stand up, slamming my spoon down. Elsa startles, but holds her ground as she stares at the surrounding people whose attention shifts to our table.

I lean over so that I'm glaring at Ethan head-on. He returns it with his own cool gaze.

He's always been the type who likes to stir up trouble from behind the scenes. When we were in university, people saw me as the ruthless one and Ethan as the guy next door.

They know nothing about the devilish way his brain works. They only see the façade he wants them to see. He might have spent nine years in a coma, but nothing changed the way his brain works.

Just like me, he loves holding things over people's heads. And just like me, he doesn't hesitate to use it against them.

That's why he approached Aurora first. The fact she looks almost exactly like Alicia gave him leverage. He didn't even need to know how she was related to my late wife. His sole purpose was to use her against me.

He's done it all to appear as her most trustworthy ally. Having Agnus invite her to the wedding, the investment, this charity…and even the dinner invitation—that she will *not* accept.

All of those are methods to worm his way into her life and then destroy me by using her.

However, I'm one step ahead.

Problem is, knowing his intentions doesn't necessarily mean

it'll be easy to stop him. One, Aurora is unpredictable as fuck. If she gets something in her head, she'll do it, my opinion be damned. Two, his game could be bigger than this, and being unable to pinpoint it keeps me uneasy.

"Come near her and I'll consider it a declaration of war, Ethan."

His lips twitch in a smirk, showing his true self. "Careful of your own battalion, Jonathan."

"Stay. The. Fuck. Away," I enunciate every word, pause to make my point clear, then I turn around and leave.

Behind me, I hear Elsa ask him about the truce her father and I agreed to when she and Aiden started officially going out a year ago.

We did that to score an important deal with a duke's family business, but Ethan and I both know there'll never be a truce between us. We'll be ninety years old and in wheelchairs, and we'll still fight to see who gets to own the world.

We've been like that since university. Due to our competitive nature, we clashed in everything. Then after we graduated and embarked in the world of business, our rivalry grew. It started with a simple chess game about who got to own a yacht then extended to gambling subsidiaries and net profit numbers.

We rivalled each other in everything, including how to start a family. Since we were bored with the easy pussy we got, we made a bet to marry mentally unstable women. It wasn't a necessity or even forced. It was by choice.

I found Alicia and he found his late wife, Abigail.

Since then, everything has gone downhill.

That's when I realised the monstrosity of human greed. If nothing satiates you, you'll slowly but surely deteriorate to a worse state of mind, and eventually to your downfall.

That's what happened with Alicia. Her condition wasn't that serious when we first got married and had Aiden. But over the years, her mental state declined and nothing could've saved her.

Aiden thinks I could've. But Aiden doesn't know everything.

And it'll remain that way. For his sake.

I head to the entrance and opt to leave or, more accurately, follow Aurora.

Harris will bitch at me all night about the late-night meeting with the Chinese. But Harris is always displeased in one way or another.

"Johnny!"

I summon the patience I don't have as I stop and turn around to face Aurora's weird friend.

"Call me by my actual name and I might grant you permission to talk to me."

"Relax. You're too uptight. Has anyone told you that?"

Your friend. All the fucking time.

"Do you need something, Miss Hussaini? Because you just wasted a minute of my time."

She rolls her eyes and shoves a pink bag at me. "Aurora left this behind. Her keys are in there."

I take it from her and turn to leave.

"Treat her well!" she calls after me. "Remember, black belt karate."

No idea how a quiet woman like Aurora came in contact with this bizarre existence. They're dissimilar personality-wise, but perhaps their differences are how they grew H&H's capital in a considerably short time.

I stare at the bag in my hand. The fact that she left it and her keys means she didn't go to her car.

Where could she have gone this late at night?

I stop at the entrance and search the car park area. She couldn't have left in a taxi, considering her money is in here. Did she leave on foot?

The problem with Aurora is that I can't tell what she'll do next, and because of that, I can't exactly plot something for her. And if I do, she thwarts it.

Which is both fascinating yet infuriating.

She might share physical traits with Alicia, but all the similarities end there.

Her older sister was demure and predictable. She was the type who told me her schedule for the entire week and never did anything that she thought might upset me.

Where Alicia was soft, Aurora is rebellious.

Maybe that's why she's driving me insane when Alicia never did.

It's unfair to even compare both women. Alicia was the mother of my son and the woman who felt too much, then stopped feeling altogether.

Aurora is...different.

There's no obligation keeping me glued to her. If anything, it's the other way around. I've been trapping her so she doesn't slip between my fingers.

It's the first time in my life that I want to keep something instead of destroying it to pieces.

The first time that I've looked forward to going home instead of spending all-nighters at the office.

The defiance in that woman makes me both insane and keeps me driven.

The more she slips away from me, the harder I cage her in. The more challenging she becomes, the more ruthless my reaction turns.

It's an everyday game. One I can't seem to shake off. But I'll have to one day. I'll have to go back to my usual balance and peace.

However, that day isn't today.

I spot Moses in front of my car, but he's not smoking. That's the only reason he'd step outside since he usually stays inside with Harris.

Unless Harris isn't alone.

I start towards my car and don't bother to ask Moses if she's in there. I know she is. Another one of the infuriating habits I've developed—sensing Aurora's presence a mile away.

The front windows are open, so I catch a hint of the heated conversation coming from the inside.

"...you need to look down your nose sometimes. Why is it always stuck in the sky?" Aurora's voice.

"There's no other better place to be."

"You need help, Harris, okay? I'll forward your details on to my psychotherapist so that he can teach you how to be less arrogant and how to deal with other issues. While you're at it, take Jonathan with you."

My lips twitch in a smile. That woman is... I have no words. I, in fact, have no words.

That's a first.

She left the charity to come bicker with Harris, who, by the way, makes it his mission on earth to win every argument possible. It doesn't matter what you fight him on, he comes with different ways to prove you wrong—even when you're right. He doesn't dare try that tactic with me, though, because he's smart enough to recognise his limits.

I open the back door and Aurora jolts in her seat, eyes widening to a dark blue that matches the colour of her dress. The way she pushes back against the leather suggests that she was expecting her worst nightmare.

Fascinating.

Her lips fall apart, begging for my dick between them. Blood rushes to my groin at the memory of fucking her from behind until she shattered all around me. I place a hand in my pocket, feeling the evidence of her arousal on her underwear.

I can't believe that I not only fucked her without a condom—for the second time in a row—but I also came inside her. There was a voice reminding me that I forgot something, but when I'm inside her, I lose all focus on anything that isn't her.

Needless to say, that's not good, but fuck me if I can find a way to put an end to it.

Aurora releases a long breath. "Oh. It's you."

I narrow my eyes. "Who were you expecting?"

"No one." She stares at her pink-painted nails.

She's lying. No idea why, but I'll find out. Maybe she left the dinner table for some other reason than the tension brought by Ethan.

'Is she part of the game now?'

A wave of possessiveness slams into me like the first clash in a battle. The need to own her all over again grabs me by the balls, demanding release.

Knowing she's not wearing any underwear beneath her dress makes the idea more plausible.

Before I can think of a way to kick Harris and Moses out—or send them away—she reaches for her bag in my hand.

"I'm going back to the house."

"We'll drive you." I keep the bag out of reach and barge inside so that I'm sitting beside her. Harris grumbles something unintelligible, but he takes the hint, gets out, and sits in the passenger seat. Soon after, Moses slides into his driver seat and the vehicle slowly retreats into the main street.

"I brought my car." She reaches for her bag again.

"And I said I'll drive you."

"Don't you have to prepare for a meeting or something?"

"We do," Harris says from the front seat. "Thirty minutes late."

I throw him a glare, but he merely adjusts his glasses with both his index and middle finger and focuses on his tablet again.

"I can go back on my own," she says.

"Or we can drive you."

"Do you ever give up?"

"Not when I can win."

She huffs but doesn't stop trying to reach for her bag.

I grab her by the arm and she freezes as her body half-falls against mine. The storm in her eyes gains an electric spark, almost as if she's slipping from one state of mind to another. It's fascinating how much the colour of her eyes can hint at her state of being so accurately.

"If you don't stay still, I'll consider that as an invitation to finger-fuck you," I murmur against her ear, then bite down on the shell to reinforce my point. "After all, you're naked under that dress."

"Jonathan!" she whisper-yells. "Harris and Moses are here."

"So fucking what?"

She moves those lips to say something, but they remain in that perfect 'O'. Aurora must see that I'm crazy enough to do it.

I'm about to reach under her dress and prove how right her assumption is, but she chooses the smart route and pushes back, clearing her throat.

Her cheeks are a soft hue of pink, and she keeps touching her neck, the one I held her by as I fucked her into the mattress the other day.

She thinks if she touches it enough, she'll be able to cool down. A myth, but I don't correct her.

"Can I brief you now?" Harris asks in his usual disregard. "If Aurora doesn't have an objection."

She makes a face at him, and he counters by readjusting his glasses.

Aurora. Since when did he start addressing her on a first-name basis? I don't like that.

"Start," I say in a harsher tone than needed to break whatever connection they're developing. I'm the only one she's allowed to form a connection with.

Harris passes me the document he prepared and goes on about the points we'll discuss during tonight's meeting. I nod at him, but my entire attention is on how Aurora is trying to look at her nails, her watch, out the window. Anywhere but at me.

That irritating habit of hers of trying to erase me needs to go.

While Harris goes on in his steady voice, I steal glances at Aurora. She seems to listen, too, but her concentration is also occupied by something else. Her gaze is a bit unfocused, and she keeps glancing behind her.

Perhaps it's the same thing that made her leave the charity dinner she organised herself.

Only one thing rattles Aurora to the point of no return. Or, more accurately, one person.

Maxim.

If his solicitor got in touch with her again, I'd know about it. As that option is erased, what's this about?

Since we do have an important meeting, and I already wasted time by coming here, I reluctantly rip my attention away from her and focus on Harris's words. I read the document with him at the same time and highlight the parts where I'll hit hard and demand better conditions.

Something warm lands on my shoulder, and I halt with the marker halfway on the page.

Aurora's eyes are closed shut, her head against my bicep. Her soft features appear relaxed, at peace almost.

I stroke her hair behind her ear and she moans softly, leaning into my touch like a kitten. If only she was this compliant when awake, too.

Harris motions at her without saying anything.

"Continue." I rest her head on my lap and her hand grips my thigh as she resumes her sleep.

I keep stroking her hair while she nuzzles her head into my thigh.

It's a single moment in time. Something that happens with no prior planning, but in this second, I decide something I've never thought about in my life.

Aurora or Clarissa or whatever name she goes with is now fucking mine.

Literally.

Figuratively.

In every sense of the word.

TWENTY-EIGHT

Aurora

I FINALLY RECEIVED ANOTHER RECORDING.

It's been weeks since the last one. Damn weeks. I almost gave up on the hope that there would be something else.

The moment Paul called and told me I had a wooden box package, I drove to my flat so fast, I wouldn't be surprised if a speeding ticket shows up in my inbox.

I sit in the middle of my lounge area, finger hovering over the Play button on my remote.

Unlike the previous times, I'm not so ecstatic about listening to my sister's voice.

It's the guilt, isn't it? It's catching up to me in every step I take. With every orgasm Jonathan wrenches out of me, and every slap of his hand against my arse.

It's been weeks of being dominated by him in ways that make me not only delirious, but also beg for more.

Weeks of scorching hot meals and games where he ends up getting what he wants—which is usually my body.

Weeks of running me hot baths where he loosens me up just so he can fuck me all over again.

And with every week, the fact that he was my sister's husband starts to fade away and becomes white noise.

Every day, I have to remind myself that I can't get lost in Jonathan and that, besides H&H, the sole reason I agreed to the deal is to uncover the facts behind Alicia's death.

The problem is, I started to forget about the deal altogether. In the beginning, I counted the days, but now, I vaguely remember that it's been about six weeks since I started this journey.

Six weeks of rediscovering my body.

Six weeks of *feeling*.

Six weeks of forgetting about the outside world whenever Jonathan is in sight.

Or even in my thoughts.

I haven't been thinking about Dad at all, despite the threat of him being granted parole. And that says something.

It's like Jonathan is sucking my soul into a different dimension than the one we currently live in.

Chasing him away from my thoughts, I hit Play and sit on the sofa opposite the TV.

As usual, there's a long silence before Alicia's voice fills my flat. "I haven't been truthful with you about the past, Claire. You know our mother had a one-night stand with your father, but you don't know why she did it. Her husband, Papa, was an abusive man. And while I escaped his wrath sometimes, Mother never did. That's why she killed herself. I was the one who found her sleeping peacefully in her bed with an empty bottle of pills lying by her side. Her will mentioned two specific things; one of them about you. I'm sorry I never told you about it before, but in my mind, I was protecting you. Her will states that she left all her properties to me. The second and only other item on that list was that I needed to cut all contact with you. Our own mother wanted us apart, Claire, and it was for a reason."

The audio goes dead.

I keep staring at the screen as if it'll magically resume or explain Alicia's words.

Mum wanted us apart?

Granted, I never had a mother. I knew my biological mother had a one-night stand with Dad, and the moment she gave birth to me, she threw me in front of Dad's doorstep and disappeared into the night like she was never there.

My start in this world was just like that. Unwanted. Thrown away. A shame.

When Alicia first came to see me, I was three years old and she was seventeen. I remember it so well, that first meeting. I remember the fascination and how I inched closer to her until her summer scent mixed with marshmallow and vanilla enveloped me. I remember the way we smiled at each other like we always knew we were meant to cross paths.

Alicia said that she found out by chance that she had a sister and confronted our mother to tell her where I was.

After that, Alicia made it a habit to visit me. Mum never did. No matter how many letters I secretly sent her.

With time, I stopped sending them and gave up trying to reach a mother who never once looked in my direction. I reached a point where I was content with having Alicia. She was the only mother figure I ever had.

There was never a day where Alicia pulled away from me. If anything, she's the one who showered me with affection and love.

Mum died when I was five and Alicia was nineteen. Dad told me we weren't allowed to attend the funeral.

I cried that day, not because of Mum, but because of the pain Alicia was going through on her own.

That same day, Alicia came to me and hugged me to sleep as we cried together. It was the first and last time Alicia spent the night with me.

She took me to London twice after that. First, to say goodbye to Mum's grave, and again, on her wedding day.

That second time, she came to my school and picked me up. She bought me ice cream and a beautiful tulle dress with ribbons and lace.

After I attended her wedding, Dad came to London and fought with her.

I listened to their exchange from my position behind Dad's truck. When he drove me away, Alicia was crying.

I wanted to cry, too, because I didn't want to leave her. I wanted to stay with her and her new husband who looked like a god.

Alicia never tried to take me to London again. She came to visit me in Leeds, either weekly or bi-weekly, and we spent time together. Then she would leave at the end of the day and that was it.

Alicia never complied with our mother's will or stayed away, so what did she mean by telling me that?

Was it because of Dad?

Did Mum already know what type of monster Dad actually was?

But she couldn't have. They met a long time ago. Before he started killing...or was it after he started?

My head hurts just thinking about it. I won't get caught up in that loop.

Because judging by the way things are heading, it seems like Dad has something to do with it. To know more, I'll have to ask him, and that means seeing him.

The thought brings a sour taste to my mouth.

I don't want to meet that devil until the day I die. The moment he sees me, he'll kill and bury me in the grave he dug up that no bodies were found in.

My phone vibrates and I startle out of my trance. I expect it to be Layla since we had plans to go over the new accountant report together. We've become stricter about that since the last accountant's backstabbing.

It's not my best friend, though. It's Jonathan.

I swallow. He rarely calls. If ever. He's the type who likes to lash out orders in person or via email.

Clearing my throat, I answer.

"You're late."

"Hello to you, too."

"Late, Aurora," he repeats. "Are you craving some punishment tonight?"

I hate how my legs snap together at the promise. He's turned me into a nymphomaniac, I swear.

"What have I done?" I ask.

"Do you or do you not recall that we have a family dinner tonight?"

"Oh."

"Right. *Oh.* I expect you to be here in ten." He pauses. "And don't wear red lipstick. I don't want the two punks to see you that way."

I smile despite myself. The subtle way Jonathan shows possessiveness always brings me a sense of power.

He shows it sometimes when I bicker with Harris and make fun of his snobby expressionless face. Jonathan usually shuts him down like a toddler. Doesn't mean his right-hand man stops trying to prove to me that he can smile. He can't.

My good mood disappears as the reality of what awaits me sneaks up on me out of nowhere.

Family dinner.

Jonathan decided we'd have dinner with Aiden, Levi, and their wives. I know it's his way of keeping me from going to Ethan's house or having any meals with him, but that doesn't deny the reality of what I'll have to face.

Family.

It's not mine, but it's still…family. Jonathan's, to be more specific.

And from what I've heard, both his son and nephew are replicas of him—cold, ruthless, and calculating.

Aiden hasn't even spoken to me since that day he threatened me to leave. I haven't had any interaction with Levi, although I heard Margot mention to Tom that he sometimes visits during the day when neither Jonathan nor I are in the house.

If I can handle the older King, surely I can take on the other two, right?

Supposing I'm even 'handling' Jonathan. If anything, it's the other way around.

It's like I'm in a loop, the moment I think I see a way out, it resets to the beginning.

And now, I have to sit at a table with two mini versions of him who don't like me at all.

How much worse could this be?

TWENTY-NINE

Aurora

I'M LATE.

I could blame it on the suffocating traffic, but I don't. I needed the extra minutes to come to terms with what I'm about to do.

Not that it helps.

By the time I push the dining room doors open, everyone is seated at the table.

Every. Single. One.

And all their attention shifts to me.

My skin prickles at being forced under the spotlight. Ever since the public show I went through during Dad's trial, attention has become my most loathsome enemy. I did everything not to be the centre of it by staying in the shadows.

Apparently, I wasn't doing a good enough job, considering that Jonathan found me.

The focus in this room isn't like the one I received eleven years ago. The people present here don't want to mutilate me and hang my head on a stick. However, the energy isn't welcoming either.

Jonathan is at the head of the table, as usual. His pressed black suit moulds to his muscles like a second skin. I swear the tyrant only likes to wear black, like his heart. I hate how much it suits him and brings out the darkness of his grey eyes and the sharp lines of his jaw.

His lean, masculine fingers form a steeple at his chin as he leans forward, both elbows on the table. Those fingers were inside me just this morning when he brought me to orgasm to prepare me for the size of his cock and then —

I force myself to avert my gaze from him so I can focus on the others. Aiden sits on his right, watching me with that calculative streak he inherited from his father.

Elsa is seated beside him, her body language the complete opposite of her husband's. She smiles and offers me a tentative wave that I return awkwardly.

On Jonathan's left sits a blond-haired man with piercing blue eyes—or rather, blue-grey. Levi King. Jonathan's only nephew.

I know he's a professional football player for Arsenal, and I've seen pictures of him before, but he's more striking in person. His physique appears harder and taller than Aiden's. Despite his blond look that differs from the other King men, Levi has the same straight nose and an intense gaze that's meant to cut.

He now watches me as if I'm a ghost coming after his life. "Fuck me. She does look like Alicia. Are you sure she's not her, Uncle?"

"Levi." A petite woman with long brown hair and jade green eyes holds on to his bicep and shakes her head. Astrid Clifford. Levi's wife and Lord Henry Clifford's daughter.

The digging around I did before going to Aiden's wedding is sure coming in handy. At least I'm not hit out of the blue by people I don't recognise.

Levi's expression immediately softens as he grins down at her. "I'm just saying it how I see it, Princess."

"Levi," Jonathan warns in his non-negotiable tone. "Change seats."

"This is where I always sit," he argues. "Why don't you tell Aiden to change his seat?"

His younger cousin throws him a glare. "That won't be happening."

"It's okay." I flop on the chair at the other end of the table. I realise that I'm far away from the others, but that's probably the type of distance I need.

From the slight narrow in Jonathan's eyes, I can tell he doesn't like it, but he must also see that there's no point in pressing the matter further. Especially with his family as company.

Jonathan's family.

The notion strikes me like thunder. I didn't sign up for this when I agreed to that deal. It was supposed to be only about him and I and sex. Now, there are family members and everything is complicated.

Silence falls on the dining table for a second too long to the point I start touching my neck, then my watch. I drop my hand when Jonathan stares at me across the table.

He said it before. That showing my tells is a sure way to have my weaknesses exploited.

I wish I was more natural at this sealing emotions thing like he is. It's one of the traits that I admire yet loathe the most about him.

His confidence and the way he flips the world the finger while ruling it is a trait only the top of the top possess.

However, being unable to read him, let alone figure him out, is no fun at all.

Margot and Tom wheel in trays of food, cutting through the silence. Levi grins at Margot and even Aiden directs a smile her way. She returns their welcoming expressions with one of her own.

Whoa. So she *can* smile. She just never shows it to me.

By the time she reaches me, her face has turned back to its blank professionalism. After she serves the soup and the main course, which seems like an exotic type of meatloaf, she and Tom nod, then leave.

204 | RINA KENT

"Aren't you going to introduce us, Uncle?" Levi ignores the soup and goes straight for the meat.

"Aurora," Jonathan speaks. "This is my nephew, Levi. That's his wife, Astrid. You already met Aiden and Elsa."

"It's nice to meet you. Elsa told me so much about you." Astrid grins, and I notice she's wearing jean overalls that make her appear way younger than what I think her age is.

I'm about to take a spoonful of my soup, but I set it back down at her words. "Nice to meet you, too."

"I have a question." Levi pauses with a forkful of meat halfway to his mouth. "How come we never knew you existed?"

"Because she didn't," Aiden says without lifting his head from his plate. "She's a ghost. Or more like a parasite now."

"What did I say about respecting my guests when at my table?" Jonathan's lethal voice cuts through the hall like doom. "If you don't like to be here, off you go."

"And leave her to do whatever she wants?"

"Aiden." Elsa glares at her husband. Despite Aiden's frightening expression, she's not the least bit fazed. "You told me you'd play nice."

"I don't play nice, sweetheart. Especially with imposters."

"I'm *not* an imposter," I say calmly, even though something inside me burns.

"Is that why you came into my mother's house and decided you'd make it yours?"

"I have no intention of taking anything of Alicia's."

"Don't say her name." Aiden's left eye twitches. "You have no right to say her name when you didn't come to her fucking funeral."

"I didn't go to her funeral because I was being detained in a police station in Leeds." My voice chokes. "I reported my father for murder."

The silence that overtakes the dining table now is more due to surprise instead of awkwardness.

It's the first time I've divulged that information willingly, but Aiden needs to know that much about my life. He needs to know that abandoning him that young, despite my bond with Alicia, wasn't a choice I took lightly.

Jonathan stares at me across the table and I expect disapproval, or perhaps surprise. Instead, his lips curl into a smile. A genuine one.

A *proud* one.

Wait. He's proud of me?

Wasn't he the one who said I wouldn't tell Aiden anything? He should be surprised that I did talk. Or was that entire speech a manipulation plot to push me to speak?

Whatever it is, the expression on Jonathan's face encourages me to keep talking.

"I was sixteen at the time, a minor. Since I had no relatives, aside from my father and Alicia, I was taken to a safe house. I couldn't attend Alicia's funeral, even if I wanted to."

"I'm sorry." Astrid's eyes fill with deep sympathy. "Mum died when I was fifteen. It would've killed me if I hadn't attended her funeral."

My lips tremble, but I rein in the tears. All I think about is the nights I spent in that safe house. The fear. The guilt for ratting my dad out. The thoughts of what if I made a mistake. But most of all, I was hit by the grief of losing Alicia and the inability to even say goodbye.

In a way, I still haven't.

"What happened afterwards?" Levi is the first who goes back to eating.

"Statements and trials." I release a breath. "Lots of trials."

"How long did that take?" Aiden asks. "Weeks? Months? It couldn't have possibly been eleven years, right?"

Elsa pins him down with a glare again, but his attention stays firmly on me.

"Due to the nature of the crimes my father committed, I had to be admitted into the Witness Protection Program."

This time, Jonathan is the one who narrows his eyes on me. He couldn't possibly know that I escaped the program the moment I could. After that, I didn't let them write my story for me. I went back to the cottage and wrote my new beginning with my own bare hands.

"You have an answer for everything. Brilliant." Aiden goes back to eating.

"Aiden," Jonathan warns.

"You can't bring her here, to the place Mum called home, and expect me to act all acceptant of her. That woman is *not* Alicia. Why can't you see it?"

"She does look like her, though," Levi mutters.

"Silence," Jonathan orders, and just like that, everyone turns quiet.

He has the power to make anyone listen, even if they don't like him or his decisions.

"Aiden." His attention falls on his son. "When I told you to stay away from Elsa, what did you do?"

"That's different —"

"Answer my question," he cuts him off. "What. Did. You. Do?"

"I married her."

Levi laughs under his breath but stops when Jonathan's deadly attention shifts to him. "And you. Did you hear a word I said about staying away from Lord Clifford's daughter?"

"Nope." Levi takes Astrid's hand in his and kisses her knuckles. "I made her my world."

"Fascinating." The tone Jonathan speaks with suggests he finds this anything but 'fascinating.' "Now, you two expect me to listen to you. Do you know what I call that? Hypocrisy."

Aiden releases a mocking sound, but he doesn't say anything, and I'm guessing it's due to the way Elsa is discretely holding his hand on her lap.

After that, the meal goes peacefully—mostly. I keep to my space as Levi goes on about his upcoming game, and then he gets into a teasing argument with Aiden, who quit football after school.

Aiden merely tells him that he's the one wasting his time, con-sidering a career playing football is short-lived.

I focus on my plate and only answer when either Astrid or Elsa asks me a question, which I guess is their polite way to include me in the conversation.

Jonathan rarely speaks, if ever. He just listens. Like the first days I came to live here.

After that, I made it a habit that we talk. Whether it's about the business column he loves too much, or politics. It doesn't matter that we clash a lot and it ends up in an argument. I don't like eating my food in silence. It's a habit I've been trying to get out of at any cost.

Jonathan motions at my plate across the table. My cheeks heat. God, I can't believe he caught on that I wasn't actually eating.

I force down a few spoonfuls, then pretend I'm not affected by the way Aiden avoids me all night. Levi does throw some remarks my way, but soon retreats with a scold from Jonathan or a touch from Astrid.

By the time dinner is over, I excuse myself, pretending I spilt water on my suit trousers.

A huge breath heaves out of me when I'm inside my room. I slump on the bed and hold my head between my hands.

It wasn't as disastrous as I expected it to be, so that says something.

I think.

No idea how many family dinners I can handle in the future, though. The girls are kind and welcoming, but I can't say the same about their husbands. Especially Aiden. He's out for my life

A knock sounds on the door and I straighten up. "Who is it?"

Elsa opens the door, followed by Astrid, who asks, "Can we come in?"

"Yeah, sure." I stand and lead them to the small sitting area in my room. The few times Layla came here, she said I have a princess's room fit for 'daddy kink', at which I proceeded to hit her with a pillow.

The three of us sit down, Elsa and Astrid next to each other while I'm on the chair opposite them.

When neither of them speak, I slice through the silence, "Is everything all right?"

"Absolutely." Elsa clears her throat. "We just wanted to see if you're okay."

"I am."

"Levi doesn't hate you, you know," Astrid blurts. "He's merely curious about you."

"As for Aiden…" Elsa trails off. "When he was younger, he was taken by my parents as a 'fuck you' to Jonathan, and when he returned, his mother was dead. He was wounded deeply by that, and seeing you brings that wound to the surface. Give him time and I promise he'll get used to you."

Aiden was taken by Ethan and his wife? That must be why Alicia called me and told me her son was missing.

Hold on. Is this why Jonathan can't stand Ethan? Because he kidnapped Aiden?

Instead of voicing those questions out loud, potentially making me look like a creep, I plaster on a smile. "Time is all I have."

"Thank you." Elsa relaxes in her seat. "I knew you'd understand."

"So different from Jonathan," Astrid mutters.

"Word." Elsa exchanges a look with her sister-in-law and they both shake their heads.

"He gives you trouble?" I ask.

"Did you hear him earlier?" Astrid winces. "He hates me because Mum caused the accident that killed James King, Jonathan's brother. He doesn't care that the accident also took her life."

"I'm sorry."

A sad smile grazes her lips as she stares at the inside of her forearm where there's a sun, moon, and start tattoo, the star coloured in black. "I'm better now, I think. But Jonathan still sees me as the reason his brother died. He never stops reminding Levi of how my mum killed his father."

"Or Aiden of the fact that Alicia died because of my dad." Elsa lowers her eyes.

"Wait. Go back. Jonathan thinks my sister died because of Ethan?"

"Well, remember when I told you that Aiden was taken by my parents? Alicia died in a car accident on her way to go find him."

Oh.

I didn't know that.

This, however, explains the aggressiveness Jonathan doesn't hesitate to display whenever Ethan is around, despite his generally emotionless façade.

"Can I ask you something, Aurora?" Astrid's voice is low, hesitant.

"Sure."

"Why...why are you with him?"

"Yes." Elsa leans over. "He's scary in a dictator kind of way."

"And he doesn't know how to feel," Astrid adds.

"He dislikes everything that's not his work."

"And his legacy."

"I get the chills every time he's in the room."

"I told Levi the other day that I age ten years every time we have a family dinner with him."

"Oh my God. Me, too!"

My lips part at their exchange. Jonathan is sure as shit winning the most feared person of the year award.

Their attention falls back on me, eyes expectant, waiting for me to answer their question. They must've wondered this for some time now.

I could choose not to answer them, but I like them. Jonathan is an idiot to not appreciate having them to tame his offspring. So I go with the truth. "I don't really have a choice but to be with him."

"How do you cope?" Astrid asks.

"I'm not scared of him, I guess."

"You're not?" Elsa nearly yells.

"No, not really." I mean, he does frighten me sometimes, but it's not enough to erase everything else about him. Perhaps it's the intimacy factor, or that I just know there's more to Jonathan than he projects to the world.

His page isn't half-written or blank. It's simply encrypted, and no one has dared to crack the code due to the wires surrounding it.

"You're the first person I've ever met who's said that." Astrid's eyes fill with awe. "Well, Levi isn't scared of him either, but he's a King. He doesn't count."

"Aiden doesn't count either," Elsa agrees. "They have their own exclusive code of communication that no one else is privy to."

My heart warms at the way Astrid and Elsa talk about their husbands. I can feel their love for them, and despite the other two's aggressiveness—or passive-aggressiveness—towards me, I could sense how much they care about their wives' wellbeing.

As Jonathan said, they didn't really care about his opinion when they decided to pursue these women.

I'm glad they didn't. It must've taken a lot to go against a harsh man as Jonathan but their efforts are so worth it.

Elsa, Astrid, and I talk about art since Astrid is studying drawing and Elsa is into architecture. Considering I'm a designer, too, I give them pointers about some useful classes I took back at uni.

They're fun to talk to, and soon enough, none of us are cautious or awkward around each other.

I don't know how long we spend in my room. But it's long enough that Levi and Aiden come searching for them.

I make plans to meet Elsa and Astrid for lunch next week, and soon after, they all leave.

I change into my pyjamas and slide under the covers. After checking my emails and texting Layla for a bit, I'm ready to sleep.

Today exhausted the hell out of me. First, work. Then, Alicia's message. Ending the day with dinner.

The door opens and I know who it is before even seeing him. He's the only one who barges in uninvited.

His woodsy scent conquers my space before his presence comes

REIGN OF A KING | 211

into view. My muscles tighten like every time he's in my vicinity. It always feels like I need to be prepared for him.

"Forget about Aiden." Jonathan sits on the edge of the bed. He's in black cotton trousers and a T-shirt. It's one of the rare times I've seen him in house clothes.

"What do you mean forget about him?"

"You're making plans with Elsa to try to get close to him, aren't you?"

Yes and no. I do like Elsa's company, but I also hope I can approach Aiden in the future. Considering his reaction, let's make that the *distant* future.

"You don't want me have a good relationship with your son so that we can't plot against you?"

"I don't want you disappointed, because he's hot-headed."

My heart thumps. Shit. How can he move me with such simple words?

I clear my throat. "You mean like you."

"Kind of. It comes with the family name."

"If I can handle you, I guess I can handle Aiden, too."

"You can handle me?" He stares down his nose at me. "Where did you get that idea from?"

"Elsa and Astrid think I'm doing it just fine."

"Elsa and Astrid are still kids."

"They're not kids. They're married to your son and nephew."

"Who are still kids themselves."

"By the way. You don't have to be a dick towards them. They don't really like you either."

"I don't care about being liked."

"Really?"

He pauses, throwing me an indecipherable glance, then nods. "Being liked doesn't get things done. Fear, on the other hand…"

"This is your family, Jonathan. They're not supposed to be scared of you." My voice raises and I realise I've let my own anger get in the way. I whisper, "I didn't mean to yell."

He reaches a hand to my hair and I freeze as he strokes it away from my forehead. "Maxim was not your fault, wild one. Tell that to your reflection in the mirror every day and you'll end up believing it."

Fat tears fill my eyes and it takes everything in me not to let them loose as I fall into the gentle but firm way he's stroking my hair.

Sometimes, it feels like he can dip his fingers inside me and draw me out. Other times, I can't decide if it's his deceptive gentleness that he only uses to get what he wants.

But at the moment, I choose to drown in the soothing touch he's offering freely. I might regret it later, but later isn't right now.

"Sleep." He starts to stand up, but I hold his hand, stopping him in his tracks.

I'm not ready to give up this warmth yet.

Not tonight.

He raises a brow. "Or would you rather be spanked for not finishing your dinner?"

Although the promise turns my legs boneless, that's not what I'm after. It's something deeper, and it might slice and hurt me harder than any of his punishments do.

I pull down the duvet on the empty side of the bed. "Stay."

He pauses, but he doesn't remove his hand from mine. "I do not sleep with others."

"Just tonight," I murmur.

"Why?"

"Please, Jonathan."

"I'll only agree if you do something in exchange."

The damn tyrant. But he's caught me in a vulnerable moment where I'd agree to just about anything. "What?"

"You won't go to that dinner with Ethan."

Why am I not surprised? But since it's a small price to pay, I nod.

Jonathan slides under the covers with me and I expect him to keep to his half of the bed. Surprisingly, his arm wraps around my back. I rest my head on his chest, using it as a pillow. His heartbeat is strong and steady like the rest of him.

I fit in the crook of his body so perfectly, it's as if this is where I was always supposed to be.

His fingers stroke my hair like he did earlier and I get lost in his woodsy scent. In the way he smells fresh out of a shower.

What I don't tell Jonathan is that I don't share sleeping space either. I've always needed to be by myself to convince myself to sleep and to wake up alone in case I have a bad dream.

But tonight, I don't spend half an hour or more tossing and turning and thinking of happy thoughts to help me fight off an impending nightmare.

I just fall asleep.

And I know that the simple act of sleeping will never be the same for me again.

THIRTY

Aurora

"**M**ORNING, MATE!"

"Morning," I tell Layla as she follows me into my office. I swear she barely spends any time in hers.

She hates sitting around and always finds things to do outside of the confinements of her four walls. If she's not with me, she's doing rounds in the factory or in the conference room.

I grab the iced coffee she offers and wince as my aching bottom meets the sofa.

The tyrant Jonathan spanked me over breakfast so hard, to the point where I'm sore. Well, more than sore. It really hurts, despite the lotion I applied before going out.

So much for spending our first night together.

I woke up with his cock nudging against my entrance from behind, then he fucked me raw until I screamed the whole room down.

When I asked him why he only fucks me from behind, he told me it's none of my business. When I snapped, he spanked me until tears filled my eyes.

The brute. The arsehole.

Needless to say, I've been in a black mood ever since.

Not even Harris's distasteful snobbishness first thing in the morning could snap me out of this state I'm in.

"What's wrong?" Layla leans over, brow furrowing. She's wearing an oversized long sleeve T-shirt that says, *Black is a Philosophy*.

"Nothing." I take a slurp of the iced coffee, wishing I could somehow pour it on my arse instead.

"Yeah, right. You look like you witnessed the murder of puppies. Come on, spill. Is it because of Johnny's brat son?"

"It's because of the bastard himself."

"What did he do now?" She sighs. "I really hoped not to have to use my karate skills too soon, considering the generous cheque he left for the charity, but I will if I have to."

"Remember when you told me that when I threaten his control, he snaps?"

She nods.

"Well, he did. I challenged his need to stay in his emotional vault and he took it out on me."

She jerks up, rolling up the sleeves of her T-shirt. "I'm going to kick him in the butt."

"Lay…"

"Do you think I was kidding? I meant it when I said he'll have me to answer to. You're family, and no one messes with my family. Ride or die, remember?"

My chest explodes in fireworks at her words, but I say, "Just sit down and help me brainstorm."

"Brainstorm ways to cut off his D? I'm game."

"You're such a dork."

"Okay, all violent plotting aside, you might be onto something."

"What something?"

"He's reacting, isn't he? Which means you're affecting him, BUT if he hurts a hair on your head in any way, I'm serious. I'll sneak into his palace and assassinate him, ninja style."

I chuckle at the way she poses with her hands. "You need help, Lay."

"First of all, suck my D. Second of all, you're the one who needs help. You're so into Jonathan, you're hurt by the way he treated you."

"I am not."

"You are, too. Admit it, you already consider him Daddy."

"Lay, stop it. And he's not my daddy. You're the one who's into those."

"Umm, mate. I only fantasise about them. You, on the other hand, go all the way in. Pun intended."

I hit her shoulder and she laughs, standing to her feet. "Seriously, though. Don't let him get to you and suck your light, or I'll go mama bear all over his butt."

"Thanks, Lay. I honestly don't know what I would've done without you."

"No hugging." She lifts her hands up in the air and runs away before I can do just that.

I touch my watch and shake my head, which fills with a thousand scenarios.

Layla is right about the part where Jonathan is reacting. He didn't like that I somehow coerced him to share the same bed with me, and his knee-jerk reaction was to punish and slam me back in the place he thinks I belong to. I could either back down or push further—which will cost me his wrath.

Unlucky for him, I don't lie down and take people's anger. Especially the unwarranted kind.

My phone vibrates. Unknown Number.

Is this perhaps Ethan? I need to apologise about not being able to take him up on his offer. Though it'd be a nice 'fuck you' to Jonathan if I did.

"Aurora Harper speaking."

"Miss Harper. This is Stephan Wayne."

My muscles tighten and my hand shakes, causing droplets of my iced coffee to spill on the sofa.

Air comes in and out of my lungs, but it's like I don't breathe. Or, rather, *I can't*.

Will I always react this way whenever Dad's presence is brought up?

It's been eleven years, damn it. Eleven fucking years, so how come it always feels as if it happened only yesterday?

Why do I feel trapped in that forest, pedalling down a dirt path but finding no way out?

"I told you not to contact me anymore." I'm about to end the call.

"Miss, please. There's crucial information that I think you should be aware of."

My knuckles tighten around the phone. "What?"

"Are you certain about not being able to participate in the parole hearing? It will be in a few weeks."

"No. If you have nothing else to say —"

"Very well. I understand your choice, Miss Harper. I would like to relay a message from my client. Mr Griffin says that if you don't help him out this time, it'll be like traps and hunting all over again. That will be all. Have a nice day."

My phone clatters from my hand and hits the carpet at my feet.

It'll be like traps and hunting all over again.

A long time ago, when Dad and I went hunting, he used to set traps for the small animals. I asked him why he did so, considering they're put in so much pain for a long time.

Then Dad made me watch him skin a live rabbit and he told me that's what so much pain could actually feel like.

After that, I never questioned Dad about anything he did.

After that, I kind of knew in the deepest recesses of my brain that my father wasn't normal.

His message is clear. If I don't bend to his will, he'll do something worse to make me stop questioning him.

Not that he can do anything from prison.

Right?

That night, I go home late.

It's not actually on purpose since we had a meeting with the factory manager about the production deadline for the newest launch.

If we have a good one, maybe I can buy Jonathan out. Or, at least, the majority of his stocks. I doubt he'd agree considering H&H is merely a drop in the sea compared to his other companies. However, I won't give up on that option.

He called me twice, but I sent him straight to the generic message of 'call me later. I'm in a meeting.'

By the time I get home, the house is quiet. I cross paths with Margot and she merely nods, then continues on her way.

"Margot," I call after her.

She stops and spins around, her expression blank. "May I help you, Miss?"

"Is Jonathan in the dining room?"

"He retreated to his office. Dinner was served an hour ago." She pauses. "I can bring supper to your room, if you like."

"I already ate. There's no need." I sigh. "Am I only imagining it or do you actually hate me, Margot?"

"I do not hate you, Miss." I expect her to turn around and leave, but she adds, "Might I speak freely?"

"Of course."

"You look so much like Alicia, and it feels like having her ghost in the house. But since you don't roam the halls in the middle of the night like she used to, it's a bit confusing, I must admit."

"A-Alicia used to roam the halls in the middle of the night?"

"Yes, she had severe insomnia and it drove her insane with each passing day." Nostalgia covers her features. "I had to protect Levi and Aiden so they didn't see her in that state."

"What state?"

"The talking to herself state. The scribbling on books and every surface state. The crying without a reason state. You name it."

No.

That…that doesn't seem like the Alicia I knew. It sounds like a completely different person altogether. Sure, she suffered from depression, but she had it under control. Margot must be confused, because my sister never talked to herself or scribbled on books or —

The books in her room. She did have those red circles.

"I'm sorry if I overstepped any boundaries," Margot says. "I know she was your sister."

"Did Aiden know about the state she was in?"

"He probably did, but he was too young and has chosen to remember the good parts."

"How about…Jonathan?"

"Of course he did. Who do you think protected the children from her?"

I still don't think my sister was that bad, but I say, "Thank you, Margot."

She smiles a little, and I feel like maybe I managed to break the ice between us.

As soon as she disappears down the hall, I quicken my pace to the third floor and go straight to Alicia's room.

I don't care how disturbing those books are. If they hold any evidence about why my sister kept this facet of her life hidden from me, I need to know what it is.

It's like she lived a double life. One was the soft, sweet Alicia who came to find me and buy me things. And then there was the mentally unwell Alicia whom Margot hated so much, that she ended up automatically hating me just because we look the same.

My hand turns clammy as I sit cross-legged on the floor, my back to the bed, and read from the book.

Six Minutes.

It takes me a while to get past the first chapter, even though it isn't long. Every paragraph, I have to pause, take a deep breath, and stop myself from getting flashbacks of the victims' faces or the members of the public that came to find me, before I continue reading.

After the first chapter of a man burying a body, we're taken back to three months in the past.

That's when I start noticing a pattern.

A few words are underlined in a red pencil crayon. Others are circled.

Emptiness.

Death.

Life.

Need.

Reason.

Strange.

Following the trails of such words distracts me from the flow of the book and I find myself flipping pages just so I can find the rest of the words.

What could this mean?

I touch my watch, trying to put everything I know thus far together.

Alicia's father was abusive. Mum told her to cut all ties with me—which she didn't. She suffered from depression and insomnia, amongst other things.

She read such books and used the red marker to highlight things, which I'm sure means something.

With every new piece of information I learn, the hole that is Alicia's life keeps getting bigger. It's like I know nothing about the real her.

A sound comes from down the hall and I slam the books shut, putting them back how I found them.

I peek out from the door in case Jonathan is there. No one. *Phew.*

Sneaking out, I turn around to close the door as quietly as I possibly can.

"What are you doing?"

I yelp like a girlie girl at the strong voice coming from behind me. Damn Jonathan.

You know what? Enough. It's not like I'm doing something wrong.

Facing him, I cross my arms over my chest. "What does it look like I'm doing? I'm paying you a visit."

"Paying me a visit?" He raises a brow.

"Yeah." I brush past him and head towards his room, which is the last one to the right side of the corridor. I figured that out in one of my earlier snooping sessions.

This is a bit out of the blue, but it's part of my 'pushing the tyrant' plan.

I stand in the middle of his room. It's the same size as mine with a high platform bed and a tall French door that I'm sure leads to the balcony. The walls and sheets and even the carpet are different nuances of grey. Like his eyes. Fitting.

I don't have to wait long for Jonathan to follow after me, but he doesn't close the door. His height fills the entrance, and he appears straight out of a fashion show with his pressed trousers and grey shirt. Only Jonathan would look completely presentable after a long day at work.

"What do you think you're doing, Aurora?"

"You spent the night in my room. It's only fair I spend the night in yours."

"That won't be happening."

"You want payment first? Fine." I throw my bag on the chair, yank off my jacket and shirt, and follow with my trousers so that I'm just in my underwear. Like that first time I came to this house to agree to his deal.

Funny how things come full circle.

Just like back then, he doesn't make a move to touch me. However, his eyes heat with clear lust. "What's gotten into you?"

"Nothing. I simply want to spend the night here."

"And you think that will be possible, why?"

"Because I want to. Isn't that reason enough?"

"Why now? You were completely fine with our sleeping arrangements for two months."

"Well, I changed my mind. People change, Jonathan."

"You don't get to change your mind. You belong to me, not the other way around. You do as I ask and what *I* please, remember?"

"I want my own terms."

"Your own terms were, and I quote, 'what you please.'"

"I can't do this anymore, Jonathan, okay? I can't pretend this whole thing is fine. You have to give me something in return."

He pauses, narrowing his eyes on me for a fraction of a second before snapping back to normal. "No."

"No?" I snap.

"Yes, *no*. And watch the way you fucking speak to me."

"I'm not leaving," I say with a calmness I don't feel. "I'm going to show up in your room every day. So you might as well dish out your punishment and let me stay here."

For a moment, we just stare at each other. I don't back down, even when my skin turns hot and tingly. Even when the look in Jonathan's eyes darkens.

This is one of those times where he's frightening and I should stay away. But that would mean being stomped on, and I won't allow that.

I will not be intimidated. I will not be intimidated.

"Get on your knees." His voice pierces through the silence.

"Does that mean you agree?"

"On your knees, Aurora."

I comply, bending my legs until my knees meet the plush carpet beneath me.

Jonathan moves towards me with purposeful strides, undoing his belt.

By the time he reaches me, my heart almost leaps out of my chest due to both fear and anticipation. No idea how he manages to trigger different emotions in me simultaneously.

"Remember when you said I can't fuck your mouth? This is your punishment."

"Fine," I whisper.

"Open your mouth," he orders.

"I want a deal."

"When I said open your mouth, I didn't mean to talk."

I lift my chin. "Give me what I want and I'll do the same."

"One of these days, I'm going to fuck the defiance out of you, Aurora."

Well, not today, I think, but I manage to stop myself from saying the words out loud. That will only provoke him and that's the last thing I need right now.

"What do you want?" His veiny hands are still on his belt and it takes everything in me not to ogle them. I think I have a stupid obsession with his masculine hands and fingers—or how much pleasure they bring me.

I shake my head internally and speak in my businesslike tone. Being on my knees doesn't mean I'm in a position of weakness. "Every time I want something you usually wouldn't agree on, you can punish me, spank me, fuck my mouth, whatever. But you'll give me what I want."

"Define the 'something I usually wouldn't agree on' part."

Of course Jonathan wouldn't comply just like that. "You have to take it the way it is. In return, I'll take all your punishments without protest."

"And how do I know you won't regret this deal two months from now?"

"I won't. I promise."

"And you expect me to take your word for it?"

"Just do it, Jonathan. I'm giving you the control here."

"While taking some of it away."

My lips part.

"What? You think I haven't figured out your angle, wild one?"

He smiles in that proud way he showed me at the dinner table yesterday. "Well played, though."

"Is that a no?"

"It's a yes until further notice."

Phew.

I know I shouldn't be triumphant yet, but it's a step in the right direction.

"Now, open that mouth. Fucking it is long overdue."

I swallow once before doing as I'm told. I got what I wanted. It doesn't matter that I'm in this position. Jonathan is losing some of his control and I'll thoroughly take advantage of it.

He pulls out his cock and grabs it with a strong hand. My thighs clench at the view. It doesn't matter how much I see it, the size of that thing always sends bursts of both excitement and fear inside me.

Jonathan strokes it once, and my mouth waters at the unapologetic way he handles himself. The man is made for dirty things. After teasing me with the view for a few beats, he runs the crown over my lips. I taste the salt of his precum and heat blossoms between my thighs.

"You think you're at my level, Aurora? I can ruin you if I choose to."

But he doesn't. I'm holding on to that part with both hands and I won't let go.

"This is your punishment for asking for things you shouldn't want." He wraps a firm hand around my nape and thrusts into my mouth. He groans as his length reaches the back of my throat. I can't take all of him in—he's too big. My gag reflex kicks in, but he continues to ease into my mouth. I barely take a breath before he pounds back in again.

As per his promise, he punishes me.

Jonathan fucks my mouth with a ruthlessness that leaves me breathless. He wraps my hair around his fist, using it to keep my head in place, as he rams in and out of my mouth hard and fast.

The power in his rigid shoulders and hands turn me boneless.

My underwear is soaking wet, and tingles cover my spine. I want to stop enjoying this, but I can't find any solution to do so.

"Fuck. Your mouth was made for me, wild one. Only me. You're not allowed to open these lips for anyone else, is that understood?"

Even though tears are forming in my eyes with the lack of air, I hold on to his words, to the lust in his metal eyes, to the way he's losing himself in the moment.

I did that.

I'm the reason he's like this and it's just the beginning.

Jonathan might have brought me to my knees, he might be using my mouth, but his power isn't the only one present in this room.

Mine is here, too, and soon, he'll feel it.

Soon, it'll overpower his.

"I'm going to come down that throat, and you're going to swallow it all."

I nod frantically, my fingers tingling with the need to touch myself and alleviate the ache between my legs or the tightening throb in my nipples.

I don't.

Because that will make this about my pleasure, and it's not. It's his punishment and I'll get paid for it.

Jonathan's groans boom in the calm of the room and strike inside me as he empties deep down my throat. It's too far down that I barely taste anything.

He pulls out. "Finish. Don't waste a drop."

My tongue darts out to lick the smooth skin of his cock. I'm breathing so heavily, my breasts rise and fall with the movement.

He watches me with an unreadable expression, and I can almost feel the influx of power radiating off us both.

After cleaning him all up, I do a show of licking my lips, as we get trapped in each other's gazes. While he thinks he won the battle, the war is far from over.

Without saying a word, I rise to my feet and waltz to his bed. I slide underneath the cover and try to ignore how his woodsy scent entangled with spice surrounds me like a second skin.

It feels so fucking right, yet at the same time, so fucking wrong and taboo and forbidden.

Not that I care right now. I have a goal and I've reached it.

"Whenever you're ready," I say with a confidence I don't feel.

Jonathan remains in place for a while, his cock turning semi-hard by the second.

Oh, God. He might be in his mid-forties, but he has the stamina of a man in his twenties.

He removes his shirt and yanks down his trousers and boxer briefs in one go.

Seeing him naked never gets old. He has a muscular but lean body that's easy on the eyes. Scratch good. It's a feast.

I stop myself from ogling him as he joins me.

His gaze is unreadable as he lies on his back. I expect him to ignore me and go to sleep, but he pulls me atop of him.

Holy…

I gasp as my breasts lie flush against his hard chest and my legs tuck between his parted ones. His erection nuzzles against my stomach, any squirming I do only makes him harder.

The position feels so close, so…intimate.

Something he's never offered.

"I can sleep on the mattress," I offer. Jonathan may be bigger in size, but I'm not that thin. He has, like, sixty-five kilos on top of him.

"You sleep where I want you to sleep."

"But —"

"My bed. My rules."

I purse my lips.

"Or you can leave."

"That won't be happening. You'll just have to pretend I'm an unwanted sleeping buddy. Surely you've had one before."

He closes his eyes and I think he's drifted off to sleep, but then he says, "You're the first person who's shared my bed."

THIRTY-ONE

Aurora

T HE PAST WEEK HAS BEEN…DIFFERENT.

Ever since I came up with that plan that indirectly pushed Jonathan's buttons, he's been shedding some of his façade.

Not all of it. He still punishes so thoroughly for every night I spend in his bed, but it's a start.

Besides, is it really punishment if I get off on it? The jury is still out on that one.

All I know is that with every night I sleep atop of him, I get closer to the man everyone is afraid to talk to, let alone come within his vicinity.

I haven't stopped thinking about the words he told me the other day. The fact that I'm the first person to share his bed.

Surely Alicia used to? But then again, they did have separate rooms. Just like he and I did in those first couple of months.

Maybe Alicia never demanded to enter his room in the first place.

A man like Jonathan doesn't give in without being coerced

into something, or at least being given all the right reasons to go through with it.

That's why I decided to go one step further today. In the morning, he laid me on his thighs and spanked my arse red for what I asked of him. My behind still burns and is marked with his handprint, but it was worth it.

I demanded we eat out. Not in the confinement of the house, where he sits me on his lap.

And I get to choose the place, so no fancy restaurants either. Those are his playground, not mine, and I need all the power I can get tonight.

"Going out for a kebab is your grand plan?" He glares down his nose at the place with that irritating conceit of his.

"Hey! This place is world-famous. Tourists come over here for Layla's parents' kebab. You're lucky I put in a word for us."

"Fascinating."

It's his snobbish 'fascinating'. He can be the most infuriating snob sometimes.

With his black suit and sharp features, he appears like he belongs on a GQ magazine cover, not in a commoners' restaurant.

I'm wearing a simple blue dress that stops a little above my knees. Layla bought it for me without a reason last month, saying it brings out my eye colour, and I haven't had a chance to wear it until today.

My hair falls down my back and I've put on red lipstick. Something that had Jonathan stare at my lips when I descended the stairs earlier.

I consider that a job well done.

I grab him by the sleeve of his jacket and pull him to a corner so we don't block the entrance. "Listen, Layla's family is the only family I have. I will not forgive you if you offend them in any way."

"If you want me to do something, ask nicely."

"*Please.*"

His lips tilt in a small smile. "Good girl."

I try to ignore the flush that covers my skin under the dress and clear my throat. "Is that a yes?"

"I'll consider it."

"Finally!" Layla peeks her head from the entrance, an apron wrapped around her waist. They must be really busy if she's helping out. "Why are you guys lurking in the corner? I had to kick Sam from next door out to protect your table."

"Sorry, Lay." I straighten.

"Black Belt," Jonathan greets blankly.

"Johnny," she mimics his tone.

"A business owner, a karate belt, and now a waitress. Is there anything you can't do?"

"Strangling billionaires. But I'm thinking about adding that to my resume."

I burst out laughing and she does, too. Jonathan merely narrows his eyes as we follow her.

The Hussaini restaurant has gotten a lot of renovations during the years I've known Layla. It's a traditional one that serves North African and Pakistani recipes. Their speciality is the kebab and couscous, which I love to death and always bug Kenza to give me takeouts, even though she says it needs to be 'decorated' right.

There's a homey feel to the restaurant and its cosy decor with Moroccan cushions and traditional colourful Tunisian carpets. Each table is half-obscured from the other with thin curtains. There are spaces fit for sitting on the floor and the others have tables with cushions instead of chairs surrounding them. The soft white lights add a certain type of ambience, a peaceful one.

The word 'Halal' is written in both English and Arabic at the top of the reception area.

I lower my head to avoid getting caught in the curtains, whereas Jonathan simply pushes them out of his way. He's such a tyrant who doesn't appreciate beauty.

"Aurora." We're stopped by the voice of Malik, Layla's lawyer brother and the only other Hussaini sibling currently living in England.

He's a lot taller than his sister, has brown skin like his father, and inherited the striking hazel eye colour of his mother. His body is fit and muscular, and I always thought he was hot as sin.

Only from afar, though. Because he's my best friend's brother and I didn't want to lose her, which I would've if her brother had ever found out how much of a mess I actually am.

So I usually just settle with harmless flirting.

"Malik, how are you doing?" I smile.

"I'm brilliant. How about you?"

"Great. Is it just me or did you gain some muscles?"

"Totes, mate," Layla offers on his behalf. "He's been slaving at the gym."

"Stop talking like a gangster, Layla," he tells her.

She makes a face at him, but he ignores her and focuses back on me. "How have you been, Aurora? You haven't come around in a while."

"I've been kind of busy."

"With what?"

"With me." Jonathan wraps an arm around my waist, pulling me to his side in one firm grip that offers no room for movement. He then offers his hand to Malik. "Jonathan King."

"Malik Hussaini." He shakes Jonathan's hand with the same firmness.

I'm kind of impressed that he didn't cower in front of Jonathan's god-like presence. He must know who he is—everyone in this country does—but he's not intimidated by him. God, I knew there was a reason why I loved Layla and her family.

"Don't be a stranger, Aurora," Malik says as he releases Jonathan's hand and grins at me.

I nod in response.

Layla leads us to a table at the back. One of those with chairs, thank God. I can't imagine Jonathan sitting cross-legged on the floor. He'd probably leave before doing so.

She gives us menus. "I'll come back in a few. Oh, and, Johnny. Mum and Dad say thank you for the donation you made the other day."

He barely nods in her direction, focusing on the menu. His face is blank, completely unreadable.

While that might appear good on the outside, it actually isn't.

Jonathan is the type who becomes eerily quiet when he's either calculating or angry, and both are bad news.

"Remember," I say. "No alcohol or pork. They don't serve those here."

"I have Muslim associates. I know their dietary laws."

"I'm just saying in case you didn't know."

"You seem to be well versed in this restaurant," he's speaking to me, but his attention is still on the menu.

"Yeah, I come here all the time." Hell, before I knew him, all my dinners and weekends were spent here.

His piercing eyes pin me down. "To not be a stranger."

Oh. God. It's about Malik.

Now it's my turn to focus on the menu. "Kind of."

"Do you also wear red lipstick when you come here?"

"Most of the time." *Never.* I only started to wear it regularly since I noticed Jonathan's interest—or rather, obsession—with it.

"You'll stop doing that. Effective immediately."

"Doing what?"

"The red lipstick. Coming here the entire time. Noticing that he grew muscles. *All* of it. Be a stranger."

He's jealous.

Ha. Jonathan King is jealous. That's not something I thought I would ever witness in this lifetime.

I know he's possessive and doesn't hesitate to remind me that he 'owns me', but judging by the distaste in his tone, he's also jealous.

Since this is as rare as a passing unicorn, I need to use it to my favour.

Holding on to my nonchalance, I say, "No."

He narrows one of his eyes. "What do you mean by no? This is part of the deal."

"The deal said no other people. It mentioned nothing about going to my best friend's family restaurant and hanging out with her brothers. The others are coming back soon, you know. I've been waiting for so long to reunite with them again."

"Aurora," he warns. "You should know by now that I'm not the type to be provoked. If you do it, you better be ready to bear the consequences."

"What do you mean?"

"Don't test me or I'll destroy all their careers. Is that the kind of guilt you want to live with for the rest of your life?"

The arsehole. I should've known he'd threaten them.

"Hurt them in any way and all of this is over, Jonathan. I've lost too many people I've called family, and I won't allow you to take this one away from me, too."

"Then do as I said."

"*You* do as *I* say."

"*What?*"

"The deal we talked about the other day works both ways, too. If you want me to do something I wouldn't usually agree on, you'll do something for me."

He releases the menu, letting it fall to the table with disapproval written all over his features. "Let me guess, another night in my bed without the punishment part."

"No. Something before we go back."

He places both hands at his chin, forming a steeple. "Pray tell."

"Not here. I'll tell you when we leave."

"And you'll do as you're told?"

"Let's order."

"Is that a yes, Aurora?"

"It's a yes until further notice."

Jonathan's lips twitch in a smile at the way I repeat his words. Then he mutters, "The fucking attitude."

We order couscous and kebabs after I tell Jonathan it's my favourite. Kenza adds her special type of Tunisian salad on the side. It's too spicy, and my cheeks heat to the point of nearly exploding, but I can't stop eating. Not even when sweat breaks on my temples.

Jonathan shakes his head at me and slides his cola towards me when I finish mine.

When Kenza and her husband, Hamza, come to thank Jonathan for the charity donation, I expect him to be his usual snobbish prick self. To my surprise, he actually compliments their food, saying it's different than any of the high-end restaurants he's visited in North Africa and the Middle East.

Layla and I exchange a stunned look behind their back. She mouths, "Daddy" and I'm tempted to hit her with a spoon.

She runs away first.

The rest of dinner is actually really pleasant. Jonathan and I talk about the food, the culture, and he tells me about his trips to the countries in North Africa and the Middle East.

"You're so lucky." I sip from my water. "I haven't left the UK."

"Not even once?"

"Nope. I went to Scotland, then I came to London. The years in Scotland were a blur, I didn't even get to enjoy it."

"Because you were running away?" He puts his spoon on the table and places his elbows on the surface, his entire attention on me.

"Yeah. I couldn't stop thinking that I'd be found. That's why I never spent long in one place."

"Found by whom? Maxim?"

"No, not exactly him. The victims' families." A shudder goes down my spine. "I was attacked several times by them during the course of the trial, and I always thought they'd come to kill me."

"What is that nonsense?" His voice gains an edge. "You testified against your own father."

"They don't see it like that. Some of them still think I'm an accomplice and…and…some police officers shared their thought process." I shake my head to not let the tears loose and rid myself of the pain I felt as I lay with my blood surrounding me. I don't even know why I'm telling Jonathan all this.

"That's why you dropped out of the Witness Protection Program. You didn't trust them."

"How…how do you know that?"

"I know a lot more about you than you think."

"Really? Like what?"

"I know you're protecting Layla and her family by keeping her in the dark about your past, so even if it does comes back to light, all they would need to say is the truth, which is they didn't know. I also know that Maxim wants you to get him out of prison by revoking your testimony and that his lawyer is bothering you. Which, by the way, will be taken care of. He'll never come within your vicinity again."

My mouth hangs open. God. He's so thorough. Just for helping me keep Stephan away, I murmur, "Thank you."

"Maxim will rot in his cell until the day he dies. I'll make sure of it."

The urge to hug him hits me and it takes everything in me not to act on it. So I smile and thank him again.

A while later, we're out of the restaurant. I tell Jonathan that I want to walk instead of going straight to the car.

He doesn't seem amused by the idea, but he walks beside me as we head to the park.

We stop underneath a tree where there aren't any people. The sky is full of stars, which is so rare to see in the city.

"So beautiful," I breathe out, throwing my head back to enjoy the view.

"Indeed."

My gaze slides back to Jonathan to find his entire attention on me, not the sky. *Me.* My cheeks heat as if I'm a teenager with a crush. Jeez.

"What's your demand?" he asks.

"Demand?"

"You said you'd tell me when we were out of the restaurant."

I trap the corner of my lower lip under my teeth, then release it.

"Any day now, Aurora."

"Hold on, let me think about it."

"If you need to think about it, then maybe you don't really want it."

"Stop putting words in my mouth like a tyrant."

"If you want something, voice it. Otherwise it'll never happen."

"Kiss me."

He pauses, seeming taken aback by the request, but his expression turns back to normal. "Why?"

"There doesn't need to be a why. Do I ask you why when you sit me on your lap or spank me?"

"You like that."

"Doesn't matter. It still counts."

I know why it would seem like a weird request from his point of view, but from mine, I'm taking things a step further. It's the power I paid so much to acquire. This is one more way to stop Jonathan from being distant and aloof.

"Do it already. It's just a kiss —"

Jonathan's hand wraps around my nape and he claims my lips. The softness of my curves moulds to the hard ridges of his body as his mouth takes complete control of mine.

His kiss is dominant and intense, like the rest of him. I'm a rag doll in his hold, my breathing and sanity stolen by his skin, his touch, and sheer power.

By the way his body becomes one with my own and the firm hold of his strong hand around my nape.

I'm a goner.

A complete and utter goner.

He angles my head back and ravishes me with growing intensity and need. Almost like he can't stop. Almost like he'll continue kissing me for eternity.

But he does. Stop, that is.

As he pulls away, he tests my balance; when my unsteady legs fail me, he grabs me by the waist to keep me standing.

His grey eyes clash with mine in a war of hurricanes and storms, and I realise then how fucked I really am over this man.

I was wrong. It wasn't just a kiss.

THIRTY-TWO

Jonathan

I T'S STRANGE HOW CHANGE CAN HAPPEN SO FAST, YET IT FEELS so slow.

Change is one of the things I control with an iron fist. Nothing is allowed to leave my grip, no matter how small or insignificant it is.

That's how I keep my life and my kingdom in order. Some people need to be told what to do so that they stay efficient, and I'm happy to play the role of the whip that snaps them into shape.

Aurora calls me a tyrant. A control freak.

At first, she used to mutter it under her breath, but slowly, she's been saying those things out loud.

I stand over the bed, where she's lying on her side—my bed. She hasn't left it since the day she manipulated her way into it two weeks ago.

Is it considered manipulation if I already knew her plan and still went along with it?

Probably not. But that's how change strikes into your life. At first, it seems unnoticeable, like her toothbrush beside mine or her apple shampoo bottle on the shelf in my bathroom.

It's as little as her scent with my clothes and the fact that I can smell her on me, even while I'm at work. Which is distracting as fuck, considering the blood that rushes to my dick whenever I think about her.

Then when you don't control that change and let it loose, it becomes as serious as looking forward to coming home, to the point of cutting meetings short. It can also become as petty as pulling strings from the background so that an associate of mine would offer that Malik guy a job in a big law firm in the United States, making him scarce from her immediate vicinity.

Black Belt is the only one I begrudgingly approve of.

Even Harris will get a warning to stop joking around or arguing or whatever those two do whenever they're in the same room. I don't like how she finds it easy to get lost in an argument with him but forces her brain into overdrive when it comes to me.

Aurora is always thinking about ways to outsmart me and get what she wants. I indulge her and even let her win sometimes.

I know. I, Jonathan King, who makes sure to crush anyone who goes against him, is letting someone win.

There's a good reason for that. Her expression lights up whenever she gets something from me, thinking she's snatched it away. There's also the way her breathing hitches when she asks me to kiss her or hug her as part of her demands.

The way she sneaks into my bed and mumbles half-asleep that I can punish her for it in the morning.

It's those little things; the smile on her face, the awe in her stormy eyes, and the way she watches me.

The way she pretends I'm bugging her but then begs me to fuck her until she's screaming my name.

The way she says I'm boring yet barges into my office and pushes Harris away so I'll teach her chess.

"It must be a dull game," she said while Harris grumbled in the background before leaving.

"Why would you think that?" I asked.

"Because *you* like it."

"What will you do for me if I change your mind?"

She gulped and then threw her hands in the air, pretending to be engrossed in the board.

I did change her mind and she paid for that one with a rough fuck against the carpet with my hand around her throat.

At times, I say I'll take it easy on her. That today, I won't spank her or roughen her up, but whenever she's in sight, all my resolve scatters into thin air. She brings out the intensity in me and makes me want to take her to unimaginable heights.

It doesn't help that she screams for more, or that her body unravels around me like she was always meant to be mine.

She was.

She *is*.

I stroke a stray strand of her hair off her eyes with a finger. She's hugging the duvet as if it's my chest.

The line of her soft curves has a handprint from when I gripped her last night and fucked her raw. Her arse is completely marked by me and her tits have some hickeys. I like to leave my marks on her skin whenever I can. To see her all mine. To know she chose this willingly.

Her lips part and a soft moan spills free as she leans into my touch.

Fuck me.

This woman has the ability to drive me fucking insane, even when she's sleeping.

I shouldn't feel proud whenever she says I'm unstoppable, or that I'm nothing like anything she's experienced before. But I am.

She didn't tell me that with her own mouth, though. Aurora would never admit to that in front of me.

I overheard her conversation with Black Belt when they were lounging by the swimming pool the other day.

Which reminds me that I shouldn't eavesdrop on conversations not meant for my ears. But when it comes to her, I do it anyway.

Aurora has come into my life like a wrecking ball, and there's no way to stop the change she's bringing on.

I could set her free, give her back the stocks and go back to my balanced life.

But a wild part of me rebels at the thought. Which is ironic, considering I was never a rebel.

My parents were the conservative, refined type. My mother participated in a million associations and my father was a business-man. My older brother and I were brought up to be leaders. Only, we took different routes to achieve that.

James was the rebel—the black sheep who cared more about sports and partying and drugs.

I cared about accomplishments. I lived my entire life aiming for more, but never got enough. It could be because I watched my father hit rock bottom after someone targeted the family business.

It could be because I also watched James spiral out of control after his head injury until he eventually slipped between my fingers.

After witnessing both of their early deaths, I decided I'd never let anything else slip out of my control.

So why the fuck am I letting Aurora sleep in my bed every night?

Her eyes flutter open and she blinks a few times before her focus remains on my face. For a second, she smiles, eyes easing and nose twitching. Just as quickly, she shakes her head as if realising she shouldn't be doing that.

"Jonathan?" she croaks. "What time is it?"

"Late."

"What?"

"You're late. Your alarm went off fifteen minutes ago."

She stares at the clock on the bedside table and groans, sitting up. Her tits are distracting as fuck when she changes position.

"Oh my God." Her eyes widen to that fucking blue. The blue that I want to confiscate and turn into my tailor-made brand.

"Why didn't you wake me up?"

I could've, but then I wouldn't have been able to watch her sleep or witness her current frantic movements.

My head tilts to the side as she abandons the sheets and stands in her full nakedness

That's one of the highlights of my day.

"Jonathan!" she scolds, even though her cheeks tint in red.

"Yes?"

"Did you do it on purpose?"

"What would give you that idea?"

"The way you're watching me." She folds her arms over her chest, narrowing her eyes on me.

"That's kind of useless when you're fully naked, wild one. Or are you perhaps tempting me?"

"Of course not."

"Well, I *am* tempted. After all, you owe me a punishment."

"No, I don't. I paid for spending the night yesterday."

"How?"

"You…know."

"Say the words, Aurora."

A red hue covers her entire body and the nipples peeking from between her fingers harden as she mutters, "You fucked my mouth."

Not really. I actually gave her free reign and she sucked me off like a good girl. Over time, she's been getting used to my pace, making up for her lack of skills with her determination. She's the only one who still manages to stare up at me with defiance even when I'm wrapping her hair around my fist, hitting the back of her throat with my cock, and smudging that red lipstick all over her mouth.

Considering her reservations at the beginning, it's clear she hasn't given much of those before—blowjobs, that is. I have the urge to murder any fucker who put their hands on her before me.

"But you didn't pay for the kiss in my office," I tell her, still taking my fill of her nakedness.

Truth is, I love kissing Aurora. She comes undone when my lips ravage hers. She melts against me and lets me do whatever I please.

There's something euphoric about owning a fireball like her and making her come to me as if that's what she's always needed.

It's one of those bizarre things that are only related to her. Kissing never mattered to me before to the point that I never did it.

But with her, I can't get enough of it.

I don't tell her that to keep her coming back to me for more.

"Later," she mumbles. "I want to have dinner out tonight. A date."

A date. I don't even know how to date, but it usually includes Aurora loosening up and talking about her past. For that reason alone, I take her up on her offers whenever she asks.

"That's two punishments."

"I'm fine with that."

"First one now?"

"No. I'm going to be late."

"Here's how it will go. I'm going to count to three and if you don't go into the bathroom, you might have to call in sick."

Her eyes widen and before I start counting, she jogs to the bathroom. My grin widens as I pick up my phone and leave.

My feet come to a slow halt in front of Alicia's room and my smile vanishes.

I place a hand on the door as I often do.

Alicia is a reminder of when I also lost control. I have to make sure that doesn't happen with Aurora.

She already shares her looks; she won't share her fate.

THIRTY-THREE

Aurora

DAMN JONATHAN.

I curse him under my breath for the whole time I'm stuck in traffic.

The tyrant is bent on getting me out of sorts. He gets off on seeing me helpless, defenceless, and completely at his mercy.

Not that he has any.

He's sadistic to a fault.

And you enjoy every second of it. Hell, you're looking forward to tonight like you've never looked forward to anything before.

I shoo that intrusive voice away and release a breath when I finally arrive at my flat.

Paul called to tell me I had another package. Since I was already late, I texted Layla to carry on with the morning factory meeting without me and fill me in later.

I can't miss any chance to know more about Alicia. I snooped through all the books in her room and even the library. She often

244 | RINA KENT

circled and underlined words in red. Sometimes, she scribbled words like:

I wish you didn't save me.

The worst thing you can do to a life is suffocate it.

A crime is a secret.

Bury them all.

The more I read, the deeper the hole between me and Alicia grows. I'm starting to doubt if I even knew my sister.

It's like an entirely different being possessed her hand and scribbled those words.

Maybe it's like with Dad. I thought I knew him, but…

I shut the door on that thought as I step into my building and smile at Paul, who's watching TV with Shelby. My neighbour doesn't even acknowledge me. It's Paul who strikes up a conversation, asking how I've been.

He reaches behind the counter. "There was a man who came to ask about you the other day."

My muscles tense. It must be the solicitor. "Did he mention his name?"

"No. He left when I told him you don't live here anymore."

Phew.

Shelby raises the volume of the TV and my relieved breath catches. A news anchor appears, his expression serious and it's for a very good reason.

The man who's sitting across from him in a grey room is the main character in my nightmares. The one who digs graves and suffocates people with duct tape.

Maxim Griffin.

The most notorious serial killer in the UK's recent history.

My father.

The news anchor's serious tone drifts from the TV. "Today, we're having an exclusive interview with Maxim Griffin. It's the first time in eleven years that he has willingly chosen to talk. What happens when a killer breaks his silence?"

The camera zooms out to focus on Dad. He's sitting casually on a chair, wearing a black jacket and khaki trousers, appearing serene. His beard is trimmed, but he's still the same—broad, tall. Handsome. Looking like every woman's dream makes him so scary.

It's why they fell at his feet.

When his suave voice sounds, his Yorkshire accent barely there, I almost topple over from the force of it on my nerves. "I chose to be silent, thinking I was protecting my daughter. But now, I realise she needs to be brought to justice, too."

I stumble and nearly fall backwards.

No.

No, no, no.

"Miss Harper?"

I gasp as Paul touches my shoulder. My heart jumps in and out of synch as if it's about to leap out of my throat.

"Are you okay? Do you need to sit down?"

I need to get out of here.

Not just the building, but out. *Out.*

I snatch the package out of Paul's hand and fly out of the place where Maxim's voice rings out, where he's haunting and coming after me. My heart is hammering and my breathing is bursting out.

Tears stream down my cheeks as I feel the world closing in on me with its ghostly hands and meaty fingers.

It's like that time all over again.

A body slams into me and I pause. My lips part when I meet her eyes. Those bright green ones. Sarah. I've never forgotten her name. The way she looks is different now. She's not confused, crying, or begging me to bring back her mother.

She's just like them.

She wants me to pay.

"I knew it was you. Give me my mother back! Give me my life back!" She slaps me across the face so hard, I reel from the shock of it. I don't move, though. I don't even protect myself. If I stay still, if I let them beat me, they'll eventually get it out of their system and leave me alone.

"I'm sorry," I whisper. "I'm so sorry."

"Your apology can't give me back what I lost." *Slap. Scratch. Claw.* "Murderer! Murderer!"

"I'm so sorry. I'm s-so sorry." A sob tears out of my throat as I chant the words over and over again. Not that it will make them stop, but it's the only thing I know to say to them.

My lips burn. I taste the metallic tinge of blood. But I stay in place as she takes out her anger and bitterness on me.

My physical pain is nothing compared to what she and the others have been through.

When Sarah seems spent, she slumps to the ground, bawling, sobbing, and falling apart. I try to clutch her shoulder, pull her up—something to offer a small amount of comfort—but she shoves me away. I fall backwards, my hands and hip taking the sting.

My palms burn and blood seeps from the skin, but it doesn't matter. This type of pain doesn't matter.

I stumble to my feet, ignoring the dirt on my clothes. All I care about is the small box between my fingers.

She glares up at me, her gaze full of tears and her expression haunted, distraught.

Just like back then.

That's what it looks like to steal a little girl's innocence when she's just ten. To steal her only support and the only person she had by no fault of her own.

"I hope you die like Mum did."

I step backwards, my lips trembling. I keep walking like that, not wanting to give her my back. Being hit on the head in the past has taught me to never give them my back.

Being stabbed in the ribs has taught me that, too.

I keep watching my surroundings in case someone else has figured out where I live.

Now, they'll come for me.

Now, they won't leave me alone.

Run.

Run.

By the time I reach my car, I'm a mess. My cheeks and palms and even my neck sting. My lips won't quit bleeding. My heart aches and I feel like breaking apart.

I rummage through my bag and snatch my phone. Jonathan. I have to call Jonathan.

I hate that my first thought is of him, but a sense of safety envelops me like a warm blanket in winter when I think of him.

His phone is off. My fingers tremble as I let it fall to my lap. He's probably in a meeting.

My gaze shifts to the box in my palm and I retrieve the flash drive, jamming it into the car stereo.

Alicia's voice filters in, brittle and shaky. "Claire…I just…I just found out Jonathan wants me dead. He's been poisoning me all this time. He wants to kill me. I…I don't think I can make it. I wanted to take you and Aiden and go, but…I don't think I can. He's after me. Remember when I told you to only call him in emergencies? Don't. Ever. Run, baby sister. Run from all of them."

I gasp as her words creep into my head like doom.

No.

No.

Jonathan didn't…he couldn't…

And yet, he did.

It's just like when Dad told me on that day I was crying when Alicia didn't come to see me.

"You're born alone. You die alone. Why do you keep leaning on other people?"

My mind shuts down. I turn numb as all the events from

today slam back into me. Dad's interview. Sarah's attack. Alicia's warning.

I kick the car into gear and do as she said. As I did eleven years ago.

I run.

I disappear.

TO BE CONTINUED...

Jonathan & Aurora's story concludes in *Rise of a Queen*.

WHAT'S NEXT?

Thank you so much for reading *Reign of a King*! If you liked it, please leave a review.
Your support means the world to me.

If you're thirsty for more discussions with other readers of the series, you can join the Facebook group, Rina's Spoilers Room.

If you're looking to what to read next, jump into *Rise of a Queen*, the epic conclusion of Jonathan & Aurora's story.

ALSO BY RINA KENT

For more books by the author and a reading order, please visit:
www.rinakent.com/books

ABOUT THE AUTHOR

Rina Kent is a *USA Today*, international, and #1 Amazon bestselling author of everything enemies to lovers romance.

She's known to write unapologetic anti-heroes and villains because she often fell in love with men no one roots for. Her books are sprinkled with a touch of darkness, a pinch of angst, and an unhealthy dose of intensity.

She spends her private days in London laughing like an evil mastermind about adding mayhem to her expanding universe. When she's not writing, Rina travels, hikes, and spoils cats in a pure Cat Lady fashion.

If you're in the mood to stalk me:

Website: www.rinakent.com

Newsletter: www.subscribepage.com/rinakent

BookBub: www.bookbub.com/profile/rina-kent

Amazon: www.amazon.com/Rina-Kent/e/B07MM54G22

Goodreads: www.goodreads.com/author/show/18697906.
Rina_Kent

Instagram: www.instagram.com/author_rina

Facebook: www.facebook.com/rinaakent

Reader Group: www.facebook.com/groups/rinakent.club

Pinterest: www.pinterest.co.uk/AuthorRina/boards

Tiktok: www.tiktok.com/@rina.kent

Twitter: twitter.com/AuthorRina